THE
FINAL
CASE

THE FINAL CASE

David Guterson

ALFRED A. KNOPF
New York
2022

Grateful acknowledgment is made to the following for permission
to reprint previously published material:
Shambhala Publications Inc.: Excerpt from *River of Stars: Selected Poems
of Yosano Akiko,* translated by Sam Hamill and Keiko Matsui Gibson.
Copyright © 1997 by Sam Hamill. Reprinted by arrangement with
The Permissions Company, LLC on behalf of Shambhala
Publications Inc., Boulder, Colorado (www.shambhala.com).
Tuttle Publishing: Excerpt from *Japanese Death Poems:
Written by Zen Monks and Haiku Poets on the Verge of Death,*
compiled by Yoel Hoffmann. Copyright © 1986 by Charles E. Tuttling
Publishing Co., Inc. Reprinted by permission of Tuttle Publishing.

Library of Congress Cataloging-in-Publication Data
Names: Guterson, David, author.
Title: The final case / David Guterson.
Description: First Edition. | New York : Alfred A. Knopf, 2021.
Identifiers: LCCN 2021010322 (print) | LCCN 2021010323 (ebook) |
ISBN 9780525521327 (hardcover) | ISBN 9780525521334 (ebook)
Classification: LCC PS3557.U846 F56 2021 (print) |
LCC PS3557.U846 (ebook) | DDC 813/.54—dc23
LC record available at https://lccn.loc.gov/2021010322
LC ebook record available at https://lccn.loc.gov/2021010323

Front-of-jacket photograph © Joe St. Pierre Photography/Stocksy
Jacket design by Janet Hansen

Manufactured in the United States of America
First Edition

For Ruth, Maverick, and Everest—descendants

". . . that things are not so ill with you and me as they might have been, is half owing to the number who lived faithfully a hidden life, and rest in unvisited tombs."

—GEORGE ELIOT, *Middlemarch*

Author's Note

In 2011, a girl adopted by a family in Skagit County, Washington, died of hypothermia. Two years later, her adoptive parents were tried in court in connection with her death.

The adopted girl came to this family from Ethiopia. The adoptive parents were devoutly religious and had strong convictions about child-rearing.

I attended the trial, and conducted research and interviews in both the U.S. and Ethiopia, but—to be clear—this book is a work of fiction. Certainly there are parallels here to what happened in the real world, but they are only parallels, not reality itself.

THE
FINAL
CASE

Prologue

My father was a criminal attorney. In his office, case files filled cabinets on all four walls. A few years ago, those files got transferred into boxes, and the boxes got stacked floor-to-ceiling in the room where I wrote novels. Chronologically arranged, and tagged both with dates and the surnames of clients, they formed a bulwark counterpointed by my windows; outdoor light, then, had to run through tunnels constructed of my father's files before illuminating the pages I was working on.

One morning, sitting in an uncushioned Windsor chair while, outside my recessed windows, wind swiveled leaves so that their hidden sides showed, I opened a file and began to read. It was titled WILTON, THERESA, and the first thing I found there was a letter written on November 6, 1955, by a Mrs. James Lovell to the superintendent of Western State Hospital in Steilacoom, Washington, about her sister, Theresa Wilton, who'd been a mental patient at Western State earlier that year but had since returned to her family. Mrs. Lovell's letter offered background: Theresa had four children; Theresa had left her husband, Frank, many times over the years; Theresa had attempted suicide two years earlier; Theresa had been diagnosed as a paranoid schizophrenic; Theresa currently had two sons at home, Sean and Marcus, ages seven and nine, she was incapable of caring for. At the moment, Mrs. Lovell said, Theresa was in the throes of mental illness, and firm in her belief that Frank planned to kill her and all their children—planned, even, to kill their son Kenneth, who was serving with the army in Korea.

The next day—I found this in a document entitled *State of Washington v. Wilton, Theresa*—Theresa Wilton took a .38-caliber revolver out of Frank's suitcase, waited in a bedroom doorway as he came upstairs after breakfast, and shot him in the back. After stumbling downstairs, Frank died, face-down, on his kitchen floor, while Sean and Marcus looked on.

A judge asked my father to represent Theresa Wilton. There were not yet public defenders in Seattle, which in 1955 had no freeway or skyscrapers. My father was twenty-five at that point, and this was his first case. His initial move was to write to the King County Juvenile Court commissioner to say that Sean and Marcus were in jeopardy now that their father was dead and their mother in jail. They were in the care of an aunt, he explained, but that was temporary. Sean and Marcus had to go somewhere permanently—specifically, to the home of an older brother, Lee, in Fairbanks, Alaska, whom my father had contacted and who was not averse to trying. Could the commissioner sign an order to that effect?

Proceedings were cursory. Theresa Wilton was sent back to

Western State Hospital because she was incapable of stand.
trial. She wouldn't eat while being held, so my father went to
Western State to see what he could do about it. Shortly afterward, Kenneth Wilton, on furlough from Korea, came to see
my father. With the right court order, Kenneth explained, he
could request an allotment from the Armed Services for the
welfare of his younger brothers. My father sought the court
order. Meanwhile, it seemed to him that if Sean and Marcus
were going to Fairbanks, they ought to travel at the winter
school recess, so he wrote again to the Juvenile Court about
them, as well as to a Miss Witzak at the Washington State
Department of Public Assistance.

In April of 1956, Mrs. Lovell wrote my father with two
questions: where should she send Theresa's 1955 tax return,
and why was Theresa's psychiatrist not seeing her more often?
My father asked her to send him the tax forms, and went to
see the psychiatrist. At about the same time, an attorney in
Fairbanks—a Miss Kleeble—wrote my father about a life-
insurance policy in which Frank had named Theresa as beneficiary. Alaska Statute 13.10.130, Miss Kleeble pointed out,
was entitled PERSON CONVICTED OF MURDER OF DECEDENT NOT
TO INHERIT FROM DECEDENT. Since Theresa's trial was pend-
ing, there could be a delay, or contention, about payout. My
father wrote to R. N. Fenstrom, the regional claim-and-service
supervisor for the Lincoln National Life Insurance Company,
and enclosed Frank's death certificate, but Fenstrom wrote
back to say, "A felonious killing by a beneficiary usually dis-
qualifies them from obtaining the proceeds." "To date," my
father reminded Fenstrom, "Mrs. Wilton has been convicted

of nothing and is at Western State Hospital until such time as she is determined to be capable of assisting in her defense." In late April, the Lincoln cut a check.

By May, my father had a trust account set up in a Seattle bank. He had the Lincoln's payout of twelve thousand dollars. He had means of support procured for Sean and Marcus, who then moved to Fairbanks. In June, Mrs. Lovell wrote with a new set of concerns—reimbursement of funeral expenses, Social Security, a monthly allowance for Theresa at Western State, insurance money. The stream of correspondence ran all summer, at the end of which things fell apart for Marcus in Fairbanks and he was sent to the Griffin Home for Boys, near Seattle. My father became his guardian.

Theresa Wilton's psychiatrist now broached the subject of her return to court. In March 1957, she was declared capable of standing trial. A judge found Theresa not guilty on grounds of insanity at the time of the shooting, but since there was a question as to whether this condition might recur, she was recommitted to Western State.

There followed a series of monthly reports on Theresa's mental status, prepared by the director of the hospital's outpatient department and sent to the judge who'd ordered Theresa's recommitment. By mid-September, Theresa was out of the hospital and living with a friend in Portland. By early October, she had a job at a motel. By the end of November, her youngest son, Sean, was back in her custody, and by June 1958, my father was seeing to the paperwork necessary to terminate his guardianship of Theresa and Sean. In November of 1958, three years after the death of Frank Wilton, when my father was twenty-eight, he sent Theresa a check for $5,368.05, which was the remainder of the Lincoln's life-insurance payout once Frank's debts were settled. Interest had accumulated, and that interest was Theresa's, so he sent her a second check, for $36.54. Marcus was still at the Griffin Home for Boys, and my father remained his guardian until Marcus turned eighteen. No one, as far as I could tell, ever paid my father a dime. Case closed.

Pretrial

A while back, I stopped writing fiction. I've been doing it for a long time, I'm not interested anymore, there are other things in life, I'd be repeating myself—I became aware that thoughts like these, uninvited, unexpected, persistent, and gnawing, were proliferating in my head, and outweighed any urge to write fiction, at first by a little, so that I stayed in the habit, but then by a lot, so that I quit.

It was a strange development for me. My situation was unfamiliar. Perplexed at first, I puttered and tinkered. I read books long unread. I took walks that might aptly be described as putting one foot in front of the other while trying not to forget that it was time to change a furnace filter. I swam laps with my wife every Tuesday and Thursday morning in a public pool. About once a week, we went to see a movie; about twice a week, we ate lunch in a café. My life clearly smacked now of bourgeois retirement. Predominantly, I cleaned, organized, repaired, and refurbished, and so the weeks went past without any fiction writing. Some days, I was distressed to learn that it was noon already, but this perturbation, from the start, was mild, a pang at worst, or an ephemeral hollowness. More persistent was a vague intimation that, at the heart of every moment of living, something was wrong. That faded, until I was waking up each morning without giving fiction writing any thought, or missing it. Fiction writing was behind me in full. There were other possibilities now. If that leaves you wondering about this book—wondering if I'm kidding, or playing a game, or if I've wandered into the margins of metafiction or the approximate terrain of autofiction—everything here is real.

One October Sunday afternoon, after I'd headed four rows of raspberry canes that still had leaves but were shedding them as I culled, my father called me. Two things, he said. First, a tree had fallen in his yard. Second, he'd had a minor car accident. The downed tree, while a nuisance, could wait indefinitely. The accident, though, was a problem, because his car was undrivable and he had to be at work in the morning.

"No," he said, "I didn't get hurt. No one got hurt. That's on the bright side. On the downside, I'm at fault. I know that. I can't blame someone else. I plowed into a parked car. I turned a corner and plowed into a car, and I sat there thinking, 'I know what this means. It's the beginning of the end for me.'"

"Your mother," my father went on, "had a series of parking-lot scrapes, and then a serious fender bender, and the result is, for about two years now, she hasn't gotten behind the wheel of a car, which you know, of course, and anyway we only had the one car, and now it's unusable. We're okay, though, in broad terms."

My parents *were* okay—in broad terms. They still lived in

the house where they'd raised me and my sister—a brick salt-
box with brick windowsills and a wrought-iron railing on one
side of the fissured concrete risers outside their front door. It
was full of failed windows with permanently obscured panes,
and hemmed in by bushes irregularly trimmed. It had a half-
basement crammed with objects put aside for a future dispersal
that never came, and a roof that leaked where it met a chimney
penetration. The rooms were low-ceilinged, the interior doorways trimmed by scant casing. Light fell across everything in
a desultory fashion—across the ceramic figurines on the side
tables, across the heaped-up matchbox collection, and across
the sideboard with its display of blue-and-white Delft crock-
ery. My parents, in their eighties, had gravitated toward their
combination kitchen/dining room as the stage on which their
lives would play out. They'd installed a half-sofa and a small
television there, cramping the room with this modest arrangement. It was a bit of a feat to slip around the table where they
took their meals and into the nest they'd made for themselves
beneath a window—a window against which, at the moment,
as my father explained, the whip ends of branches were curled
in the aftermath of tree fall.

I went to their house. It wasn't hard for me to do so. I lived
about fifteen minutes away by car, which you could say sounds
depressing—staying in the approximate neighborhood of your
youth for your whole life. I wasn't down about it, though. In
fact, I liked it. Plus, I would have moved if there'd been a reason for it, like a job, for example, or because my wife wanted
to. My sister had also stayed put. She'd stayed in Seattle, and
had said about that, more than once, "Why move?"

The toppled tree in my parents' backyard was a spruce that

had succumbed to a recent windstorm. About a third of it had cracked off and now lay with its branches either spearing the earth or rising like bristles. Bark, needles, and cones littered the patio, and an acrid scent of resin hung in the air. I went to work with a chain saw until a reasonable neatness had been reintroduced, and then my father and I ducked into the cedar-shingled shed at the rear corner of my parents' lot—ramshackle and dilapidated, with a duff-filled, detached gutter—to look at his car, which was emphatically crumpled on the driver's side at the front, where a headlight dangled sadly. "What happened," he said, "is that by the time I got home—and this accident occurred just two blocks away—all of the water had come out of the radiator. So now it has to sit here until I figure something out."

THE NEXT MORNING, at seven-thirty, when I came to pick him up for work, he was waiting on his porch and crisply dressed. He got into my car looking eager, I thought, with his full-length raincoat clutched in one hand and a plastic grocery bag in the other.

We took off. I smelled Vitalis. My father wore a clip-on tie and suspenders under a single-breasted jacket. For a long time, he'd cut a half-decent figure in that costume or some variant of it, but now he looked like he'd borrowed extra-large clothing. A sticklike codger of his sort can strike people as a buzzard, particularly if his de-facto expression is a frown; in a younger crowd, he can appear to breathe resentment toward life and death both. My father wasn't like that. He lacked the sinister, deoxygenated pall. His eyes were astir, and he smiled when he spoke to you. Mostly what he suggested, to me at least, was high-strung enthusiasm.

Downtown, I pulled into the garage below his office building. "Do you want to come up?" he asked. "Or is it straight to the library?"

I'd assured him the day before that driving him to work was no problem for me because I needed to go to the downtown public library. (Not true, of course.) At the moment, though, it was seven-forty-five, and the library didn't open until ten. I told him this.

We got out. My father, striding along under the garage's stark lights as if late for an appointment, his raincoat over one forearm and his plastic grocery bag slung from the other, pointed at the attendant in the garage's pay booth. The attendant returned a thumbs-up.

We rode two escalators, and then an elevator, to the twenty-seventh floor. My father unlocked the door to his firm's offices, snapped on a long bank of lights, and checked for a memo (apparently his firm still allowed for paper) that might have his name on it behind the reception desk. There were none. The place was silent.

We went to his office. I hadn't been there in a long time. My father dropped his raincoat on a chair and took from the plastic bag he'd been carrying a smaller plastic bag full of bran flakes and a copy of *The Seattle Times*. Next, he opened a desk drawer stocked with paper plates and plastic spoons, removed from it yet a third plastic bag—this one also containing bran flakes—and merged his cereal. "I've got enough here," he said. "Today is a Monday. Monday, Tuesday, Wednesday, Thursday, Friday—positively, I've got enough for five days."

He was in the habit, and had been for years, of buying a pint of milk, a cup of coffee, and a banana around ten, and then eating breakfast at a table in an underground concourse.

For now, though, he shut his breakfast supply drawer, slid his reading glasses from their case, sat down, and started paying bills. He wrote checks, put stamps on envelopes, licked and sealed envelopes shut, returned his pen to its place against his shirt pocket protector, got up, and strode to a cabinet. "I don't want to be in your way," I said. "You have work to do."

"No," said my father. "I don't have work to do. I haven't really had work to do in years. Every once in a while something comes in, but, basically, I just mill around here."

He smiled as if bemused by his geriatric absurdity. There were three windows in his office, two with louvered blinds shut, but through the third I could see that it was getting light outside. "What I do," my father confessed, while standing by his file vaults, "is look at the newspaper or read a book."

He filed his invoices, returned to his desk, and sat down across from me breezily, in his element. "From 1958 until about 1998," he said, "I had anywhere from thirty to forty cases going all the time, but since then, it's tailed off, which is understandable, because I'm almost eighty-four." He shook his head. "In years past," he said, "I never had the kind of time I have now. In years past, I had not just dozens of misdemeanor cases on any given day but also felonies, homicides, rapes, kidnappings—serious matters, life-and-death matters, cases where people could get very long sentences. I don't want it to be like that anymore, I don't want to be as busy as I used to be, but I wish I was a little bit busier than I am right now, because I'd like to have a justification for coming here every day."

My father reclined and put his thumbs through his suspenders. He had long combed his hair straight back so that it lay in regularly spaced rows over the top of his head, but at the moment a single lock, shiny with Vitalis, lay curled incidentally across one temple. "What I'd like," he said, "if it isn't asking too much, is to go on for as long as possible working. I've always said that when the time comes I'd like to drop dead in the middle of a closing speech to a jury, but the odds are against that. It probably won't happen. No, one of these days, my verdict will come in, and then I'll be sentenced to whatever I'm sentenced to."

His phone rang. He had its volume set at piercing. He looked at it, then at me, then at his watch, and said, "Well, well, well. Just a minute."

MY FATHER, after picking up his receiver, swiveled his desk chair toward his windows, the better to speak privately, while I sat looking at a framed photograph on his desk—one I'd given him on his seventy-fifth birthday—of the two of us in Bunker Tower on Mount Cheaha, the highest point in Alabama. We'd gone to Alabama because I'd been invited to read from one of my books in Birmingham and had asked him to come along, and for the most part we'd floated around in a rental car, doing things that tourists do. At the Birmingham Civil Rights Institute, for example, we'd followed a group of children from exhibit to exhibit. It was one thing to learn more about Rosa Parks, *Brown v. Board of Education,* bus boycotts, and lunch-counter sit-ins, another to do it surrounded by seventy fourth-graders. Eventually, the procession of exhibits led to a wide-screen video of Dr. Martin Luther King's "I Have a Dream" speech. Laid out before my father, me, and the tightly bunched children—who'd mostly gone silent—was the deep panorama of the National Mall, with its mass of fervent listeners and long, shimmering pool. "Free at last, free at last, thank God Almighty, we are free at last," pronounced King, and when I turned toward my father he whispered, "In some ways, but not entirely."

My father and I, while in Birmingham, had also attended a soirée at the home of a couple introduced to us, in their foyer, as supporters of the reading series that had brought me to Alabama. I thanked them. We shook hands. Then they told us where the bar was. My father and I got drinks. As soon as we had them, our host clinked his glass with a spoon until the room fell silent, said words of welcome, pointed toward me, called me "our writer of the hour," thanked me and my father for "coming down here all the way from Seattle, Washington," proposed a toast to us—which was undertaken by the gathering—and then that part of things was over and we milled. There were a lot of rooms in the house, all well appointed. This soirée had been cobbled together out of the benefactors and contributors who, like our hosts, made an author reading series possible, and so in attendance there were benefactors, contributors, reading-series committee members, faculty and students from the creative-writing program at the University of Alabama at Birmingham, a university administrator, a municipal arts administrator, a novelist not associated with the university, and a couple who owned a bookstore where, that afternoon, I'd signed stock, as it's said. I was told that some version of this soirée was held three times yearly in rotating homes so that people could meet and greet writers from out of town, told this by a man in a cummerbund and bow tie who cornered my father and me by a fireplace, aided by a woman with a gamine charm—auburn lipstick, lustrous pageboy—both aglow, casual, and jaunty in a way bordering on reckless. They introduced themselves as Loren and Lauren, with Lauren adding that, for thirteen years—the span of their marriage—they'd been explaining to people just met the difference in spelling between "Loren" and "Lauren," and that they were used to amusement about it. "Exactly right," Loren said. Loren and Lauren, he explained, almost always elicited a "What?" or a "Come again?" or a "Maybe one of you should have a nickname." "But we don't use nicknames," he said, "because, as it turns out, 'Loren and Lauren' is a great conversation starter!"

They laughed. My father swirled his whiskey-and-water. One thing about him: for as long as I'd been in a position to notice, I'd noticed that he spurned the body language of male contest, as well as its forms of utterance and expression; he might joust a little, offering up light banter and repartee, but his purpose was always accord. My father was disarming. There were few chinks in his armor of self-effacement. Unassuming, devoid of pretension, he challenged you not to like him; in his bargain-basement suits and clip-on ties, and with his silver hair laid back across his pate in combed striations, he charmed all comers. He put women at ease because—ironically—women made him nervous; in their presence he was assiduously on guard against flirtation; he would do or say nothing that might be construed as interest in the fact that they were female. Men, too, were lulled by someone with so little alpha-desperation. My father didn't seem in the game to win it, though at the same time he didn't exactly want to be on your team; what he'd like to do, if you would let him, is graze without calling attention to the fact. That called for deflection. And so, with a hand in his pocket and a whiskey-and-water, my father carefully orchestrated his badinage with an eye on escaping unfriendly judgment. Maybe he felt he'd been too earnest; that could be balanced with a little measured cynicism. Maybe he'd gone too far at your expense; that could be fixed with self-deprecation. My father's gibes at his interlocutors sounded genial—he meant to say that you and he were of a piece, that he shared and understood your discomfiture, that he invited you to insult so long as it was amiable, that his intimacy extended its embrace in your direction, and that irony and wit have a place in things, though modestly. His barbs weren't poisonous—their purpose was to bring you to the ground uninjured. Too much dignity was as bad as too little, and maybe had less utility.

"The onerous burden of names you describe," my father said now to Loren and Lauren, "that's something I know about, because my parents gave me a strange name, Royal. That's right, Royal. Over and over, I get people saying, 'What? I never heard that name before. How did you get a name like Royal?' Which is a question I asked my parents, too. Did I ever get a decent answer? Not really. They claimed they'd pulled it out of a hat. My mother was a Dust Bowler from North Dakota who got waylaid in Seattle when she ran into my father. My father was an able-bodied seaman, then a short-order cook, then an elevator man, and then he took a course in elevator repair and maintenance and got licensed and went to work for Otis. If you ask me, my parents had aspirations. They wanted me to be a big deal, and my brother, too, because they didn't have much money, so they named me Royal and they named my brother Thorndike, thinking we'd come off upper-class and aristocratic. That's just how it is sometimes, although I guess, if you wanted to, you could legally change your name, in your case from Lauren to Laurie maybe, which would solve the problem, but then you wouldn't have your conversation starter. I've thought of a name change every time some guy says to me, 'Your name's Royal? Royal what? Royal pain in the ass?'"

After he hung up his telephone receiver, my father told me what the call was about. He'd put his name on a list of lawyers willing to take cases free of charge if it developed that all the public defenders were busy, and now someone wanted him. "And here I was just telling you I had no work," he added. "It's serendipity."

The call was from the Public Defender's Office in Skagit County, north of Seattle. That office had been contacted by a woman in the Skagit County Jail who needed an attorney. The afternoon before, she and her husband had been arrested on homicide charges. Her husband had gotten the last public defender the county could find. "I promised I'd go up there right away and have a talk with this lady," my father said. "Which means—and I'll get the gas—could you give me a ride?"

I said, "Sure," rose, and pulled my car keys from my pocket. My father nodded, then opened his cereal drawer and retrieved his bran flakes, a paper bowl, and a plastic spoon. He plucked his raincoat from the seat back he'd thrown it over, and we walked down the hall single file, he in front and I behind.

I DROVE TOWARD Skagit County. The city traffic waned, and we came down onto the Skagit River floodplain. I was familiar with this area, chiefly because I'd lived nearby my whole life, and so, for one reason or another, had been there before. It was quiet country, rural and serene, but it made the news now and then because the Skagit River breached its banks periodically, cutting off roads and rising into houses. Dikes and levees loomed at the edges of fields, and behind these were barns, milking parlors, bunker silos, loafing sheds, tall poplar windbreaks, and homes on elevated foundations. The ground here often looked black and wet, as if freshly exposed by receding water.

When it wasn't flooded, Skagit County felt serene. The most notable event of the past few years was the collapse of the I-5 freeway bridge in 2013. A truck with an oversize load hit a sway strut, the trusses gave way, the support members failed, and the deck and superstructure fell into the river. Otherwise, Skagit County was bucolic, and well known in western Washington for its miles of spring tulip fields.

I left the interstate at Mount Vernon, the county seat, which sits beside a river bend behind a flood wall. It's a bit of bad luck, or a cruel piece of planning, that I-5 was situated here so close to the river that downtown Mount Vernon is squeezed between the two. The freeway also looms like a wall between the town's business core and most of its residential neighborhoods, so that they seem unrelated. Finally, in another example of curious town planning, a railway moves freight through Mount Vernon so regularly that it's common to have to wait downtown for long trains, as my father and I did on Kincaid Street.

The jail was conveniently across from the courthouse, in a building easy to imagine as a jail—impregnable, with the merest of windows. It was windy in Mount Vernon, but not raining at the moment. A density of gray cloud streamed eastward steadily.

We made a plan. My father would talk to his potential client. I would walk around Mount Vernon, return to my car, and wait inside of it until he was ready to go to the nearest grocery store, buy milk and a banana, and eat his cereal. We split up then without ado, and I walked westward aimlessly. The river ran wide, I saw, above the town's flood wall. The pavements were well swept, and the flowers in the municipal planter barrels well tended. Mount Vernon felt, to me, quiet, charmed, and modest. I soon discerned, though, that there was an old town and a new. A diner and a grocery store were remnants of the old. A coffee lounge, more than one bistro, more than one brewpub, and a food co-op with an extensive salad bar were all evidence of change. Over everything rose the three-story courthouse, which I passed on my return to the jail parking lot. Outside of it, a cannon sat mounted between wooden carriage wheels, long barrel facing south. There was no plaque or placard that I could find explaining its provenance or purpose.

I sat in my car, listening to the radio, until my father returned from the jail. "Sad case," he said. "Very sad."

I drove to the Red Apple. This is the grocery store I mentioned earlier as a remnant of an earlier Mount Vernon. My father found a banana there, and a pint of milk, and we bought coffee and sat at a deli table in a corner. My father hunched over his bowl of cereal, wiping his chin now and then with a napkin, and told me about the woman under arrest, whose name was Betsy Harvey, née Huber.

She was forty-one, he said, and had seven children. She was very conservative and a fundamentalist Christian. She'd grown up in Garden Grove, California, which produced—or at least used to—a lot of strawberries. Her parents had come to Garden Grove from West Plains, Missouri, where her father had worked as a sheriff's deputy. Before that he'd been with the U.S. Marshals. In California, he'd worked for the Highway Patrol. Her father's family, Betsy told my father, was originally from Haywood County, Tennessee, but her father had moved to Missouri when he was seventeen to take a job at a meatpacking plant. Her mother's family, on her grandfather's side, was from Yell County, Arkansas, and on her grandmother's side from Oklahoma.

The Hubers moved to Seattle when Betsy was twelve so that her father could work in security for a truck manufacturer. Five months after graduating from high school, she met Delvin Harvey at a church social. They dated for seven months, married, bought a house, and started having children. Eventually, they bought five acres in Skagit County, cleared one, left the other four in brush, and built a house, or, rather, had it built by a contractor, even though, as Betsy assured my father, Delvin was good at a lot of things demanding tools, a millwright who could wire, plumb, frame, pour concrete, and put up drywall. Delvin, added Betsy, had been in the air force. Since discharge, he'd worked at Boeing.

Betsy, my father said, was slight, but her eyes simmered with potent outrage. She reminded him of women he'd seen in

Depression-era photos—hard-bitten, down on their luck. At the same time, though, she was trenchant in speech and volatile in manner. She was wound up, said my father, and couldn't stop talking. Her elaborations tripped over one another, her clarifications demanded clarification, her supplements rushed toward more supplementing, and her magnifications compelled further magnifying, but the net effect of all of this was to highlight her confusion (and his). He didn't know what to make of her. It was alleged, he said, that she and her husband had killed a girl they'd adopted from Ethiopia—that they'd abused the girl until she'd died in their yard.

"They did what?"

"They abused a girl they adopted from Ethiopia until she died from it," said my father. "That's what they're accused of in the charging documents."

In the Red Apple, over cereal, my father sized me up. "What?" he asked.

"Terrible," I answered.

"That woman over there in the jail did terrible things," my father said. "There's no doubt about that. I guess I could tell myself that what she did just fills me with so much abhorrence that I can't represent her. I could say to myself, 'Let some other lawyer defend someone who has without a doubt abused a child and without a doubt been responsible for her death. Let someone else be her voice in the courtroom, let someone else act in court on her behalf. *I'm* not going to be that voice, because I'm at odds with what she did and can't bring myself to represent her. No, let someone else do that—it won't be me, as a matter of principle.' On the other hand," my father continued, "since the homicide-by-abuse statute came on the books in this state, eighty-five people have been charged in accord with it, and every single one of them went to court with a lawyer, even though they'd done things you don't want to know about—things that would sicken you—to children, including infants. Why did those lawyers take those cases? Including me, because I've taken three? And now four, because I'm taking this one, too? Because they thought those defendants were wonderful people? Is that what it takes to deserve a lawyer? Every day, people are charged with heinous crimes because they've done heinous things, and every day, lawyers take their cases so the law can get on with what the law is about. I'll tell you something. Most of the time in my life, I've lost. I've lost a lot more cases than I've won. And, frankly, I've never been surprised when I've lost. I've known from the beginning that I'm going to lose. The evidence is entirely against my client. The evidence is completely and utterly overwhelming. You could say that, this being the way it is, why don't I throw in the towel from the start, enter a guilty plea, and save everyone time and trouble? Not to mention the drain on taxpayers. Why plead innocent when you think someone's guilty? But, look, it doesn't matter if I think my client's guilty. What matters is what jurors think. So let them hear everything and let them decide. Air it all in the light of day. And another thing," said my father. "It's not like in the movies. In the movies, it turns out that A didn't pull the trigger, B did. They had the wrong person all along! The lawyer is a hero because his client was innocent! He revealed the real killer! Someone else did the terrible deed! Do you know how often, in the real world, it's like that? Almost never. Almost always, the person charged is the right person to charge. So what you have to do, you have to figure out exactly what they did—if you can, which is another question—and then compare that to the language of the crime they're charged with. They might have done the most evil things you can imagine, and you can abhor them for it, but if what they did doesn't conform to what they're charged with, then they're innocent. And that's important. If you convict someone because they're abhorrent, and not because they broke the law, you might as well live in a dictatorship. And who wants that? I don't. And another thing. I play my role according to my lights and I'm at peace with myself."

WHEN MY FATHER was finished with his bowl of cereal, he said he had to go to the Superior Court clerk's office and get Betsy Harvey's arrest affidavit.

We went to the clerk's office. There was one person in front of us. We waited until she was done, and then my father stepped up and said to the clerk, "I just came over from the jail across the street for an arrest affidavit pertinent to my client."

The clerk explained how he should get the affidavit. There were computers on the desk behind us where he could log on and enter the case number. There was a sheet of directions taped to the wall behind the computers if he had questions. At the end of his search, he should click on the document he wanted and choose the print icon. At that point, the document would print out behind the counter where she was standing, he would re-approach, she would produce the document, he would pay a fee of five cents per page, she would give him the document and a receipt, and we would be on our way.

My father said, "The lady over there in the jail is named

Betsy Harvey." He spelled "Harvey." "I don't know anything about computers, so, if it isn't asking too much, could we just do it the way where I give you the name in person and you give me the affidavit?"

"Okay," said the clerk. "There's nobody behind you, so let's do that."

While she was gone, we stepped back a little. Leaning toward me, lowering his voice, my father said, "When you're young, you have a big advantage. You're the new kid. Then, in your middle years, there's no getting around it—people think you're a jerk. Then you get along in years like me, and, fortunately, the picture brightens. They all think you're out of it, which is true to some extent, so they're nice again, like in the old days."

The clerk brought the affidavit. My father put on his reading glasses, examined the cover sheet, and took from his pocket a handful of coins. "This is definitely it," he said to the clerk. "Thank you for putting up with me."

We left the courthouse. My father didn't put away his reading glasses. In fact, as we stood on a street corner waiting for the light to change, he slid them on again and perused the affidavit. "Let's go to this place," he said.

He put his forefinger under an address. I read the sentence it was in: "At 0010 hrs, Skagit County deputies responded to a 911 call at 7279 Stone Lane near Sedro-Woolley." My father moved his forefinger to "0010 hrs." "Late," he said. "Ten minutes after midnight."

I drove toward Sedro-Woolley. I knew where it was because on more than one occasion I'd passed through it, or by it, on my way over the Cascade Range. It's a town built on timber, coal mining, rail freight, and a steel-and-ironworks company that once made logging yarders. It has a sodden aspect, and looks forlorn, as if under duress. To me it feels isolated from the rest of Skagit County. It's high above the floodplain, and far from the wide fields of the delta. It sits where large-scale agriculture ends and tall trees close in. During peak tourist season, when, each year, more than a million people tool around nearby to see tulips in bloom, few come there. It's far off the "Tulip Route," and has a name, frankly, averse to appeal. Visitors prefer the farmers' markets on the amiable plain to Sedro-Woolley's Woodfest, with its chain-saw carvings, and to its Loggerodeo, with its logging exhibition. A mental institution, Northern State Hospital, once operated just outside of Sedro-Woolley, on a site selected, in part, for its remoteness; a driver now passing its former campus on Highway 20, following the Skagit River upstream, is headed into dense, lonely mountains. All of this makes Sedro-Woolley feel like the last outpost on the Skagit, which in certain ways it is.

As far off the beaten track as Sedro-Woolley is, though, it still has cell service, so I was able to get directions to Stone Lane. We drove north on Garden of Eden Road, which runs uphill, doglegs over railroad tracks, and ends at a T. On Mosier Road, we came into a landscape of a mud-booted cast—trampled pastures, rotting stumps, wire fences, moss-roofed mobile homes. Cow paths wound through brush. The ferns were laid down by blackberry stickers. We descended, from there, steeply, into woods. The pavement, crumbling on one side, crossed a creek. We were on what felt like a paved-over logging spur, passing modest homes with cropped lawns amid the dishevelment of cut timber—brush, weeds, bramble, thickets—all of it beneath the march of power lines strung in hanging curves from stanchions.

We came to 7279 Stone Lane. The driveway was blocked by wind-flailed yellow tape, because beyond it, now, lay a crime scene. Beside the driveway were some incipient fruit trees that someone had netted against the inroads of birds. Mostly what we saw was bramble. There was no view of the yard where the adopted girl from Ethiopia had died, and no view of the house where the Harveys had lived.

"We can walk down the driveway to the house," said my father. "That wouldn't be out of line for us, as long as we don't touch anything."

We walked down the driveway. My father brought the affidavit. What we saw first was the back of the house, a rambler. A floodlight was posted on a pole in the yard. There was a modest barn, a tool shed, a chicken run, and—strangely—a port-a-potty. I could hear, overhead, the power lines crackling.

We stood on a patio. There was a padlocked chest freezer, a cylinder-style smoker on wheels, a folding aluminum picnic table, a garbage can filled with bats and balls, and a large box that had once held broccoli but now held empty plastic milk jugs. My father turned a page in the affidavit. "This is where she died," he said. "Right here. At the edge of this patio."

He handed me the affidavit. I read the sentence about the 911 call that included the address on Stone Lane. Betsy Harvey had called 911 to report that her daughter had staggered around in the dark, fallen, taken off her clothes, and ended up facedown with mud in her mouth. The dispatcher, on hearing this, had called the sheriff, and deputies had been dispatched.

By midnight, an aid car had been dispatched, too, and by 1:30 a.m., the adopted girl from Ethiopia, called Abigail Harvey by her adoptive parents, was dead on a table at Skagit Valley Hospital.

I DROVE MY FATHER home and followed him inside. My mother, who had a frozen shoulder, glaucoma, swollen feet, and tremors, pecked him on the cheek, and then me as well, and said that while we were gone the tow-truck company had towed the car to Chuck at Safety Service Center. Chuck had called at eleven-thirty. He needed time, he'd said. He had other cars to fix ahead of theirs, a lot of them. He'd take a look, though, and figure out the price. After that there'd been another call, but my mother hadn't gotten to it in time, because she'd been in the basement organizing things—it was an insurance agent, the other person's, the person whose parked car had been damaged, we could listen to the message but it was long and garbled. Other than that, my mother had walked to the senior center for her Spanish Group meeting and, on her way home, gone to the grocery store, since she and my father were out of tea, bread, cheese, tomatoes, and dental floss, all of which she'd stocked up on—especially the floss, because it was on sale—so, in a while, if anyone wanted to, we could eat toasted cheese sandwiches, but she wasn't hungry at the moment. And another thing. She'd been thinking all day about a problem, which was the problem of how her husband was going to get to work the next morning and the next morning and the next morning and the next, and home at night, too, until Chuck got the car fixed, and so, about that, she'd asked around at the senior center, where so many people were helpful, but also where so many people talked so much about things that weren't an answer to the question. Fortunately, there was a desk at the senior center expressly committed to the gathering of information, a place where a coherent, sane, reasonable volunteer sat behind a computer she knew exactly what to do with, and this volunteer, whose name was Linda, had searched around and printed things out and gathered materials, all of which my mother had lugged home and now had sitting in a pile by the sofa, where, later that night, she and my father could go through them together and figure out the solution, and these included bus schedules, car-pool programs, phone numbers for taxi companies, and brochures about senior transportation services.

My mother, on hearing of our day's excursion, made reference to journeys she'd undertaken to see tulips in bloom in Skagit County, but her eyes narrowed, and she pursed her lips, when she heard about the substance of the case there. "That's among the *ugliest* things I've heard," she said with a wince. "Doing things like that to a *child*. It's completely beyond my comprehension as to why our government allows people who believe in that 'spare the rod and spoil the child' hokum— it's beyond my comprehension as to why it's legal for them to adopt."

I stayed and ate a toasted cheese sandwich. We watched a local news show. I noticed on the side table of my parents' sofa a novel called *The Late George Apley,* by John P. Marquand, and picked it up, and then recognized it as a Time Reading Program Special Edition, the Time Reading Program having provided my mother with a book once a month during the middle of her life, each selected by *Time,* and each with an editor's preface. "I'm reading that for the second time," my mother said. "Or at least I *think* it's the second time." She took the book from my hands and turned back its pages. "It says here," she said, "in the preface material, that *The Late George Apley* is a coruscating satire on Boston Brahmin society. And maybe it is. It could well be. But here's the thing: I don't remember reading it. I might have read it, but I can't remember. And I'm not trying to coruscate John P. Marquand with that. I'm trying to point out something about me, not him. Think of the time I spent reading books! As if it was the most important thing in the world! I remember thinking that if I could just find an hour during the course of a day to read, great, perfect, my life had purpose, I was going somewhere—where I couldn't say, but I was reading, and that was progress and self-improvement. Whereas cooking or doing laundry or whatever, all the stuff I did running a household, all that stuff was spinning in place. I'm not complaining. I have no problem with having been a housekeeper and a mother. All the work around here, okay, fine, but what I'm trying to say is, it always seemed like if I got time to read during the day it was salvation, it was like I had a future in front of me where I would be a somebody. And I'm *not* trying to say this was some kind of illusion, because I learned a lot from reading, I deepened myself, I pushed myself. I read all sorts of challenging books, because I wanted to stay with it and be up on what was going on in the world, and I don't have any regrets about that, but, really, did I read this book or not? *The Late George Apley?*"

———

THE NEXT AFTERNOON, while it rained hard, I dropped in on my sister, Danielle.

It's easy to drop in on Danielle because she owns and manages a tea shop called Cajovna—Czech for "teahouse" (we're of Czech descent on my mother's side)—that she's tricked out to simulate Prague. It's in Seattle's Wallingford neighborhood, on Bagley North, around the corner from the Sea Monster Lounge, in a building that used to house a Turkish restaurant. All I have to do to talk to Danielle is walk over there—it takes fifteen minutes—and hang around until she has time for me. On this day, Cajovna was busy, no doubt because of the rain, so I had to wait for a while in the rear alcove, where there is a single long table with a top made from a slab of maple worn to a sheen and battered by heavy use, even gouged in places, but indomitably sturdy: an artifact with endurance. I say all of this about the table because the table reminds me of Danielle.

Danielle, in high school, had been the center on her basketball team. She'd been a bear to contest. Her elbows were always somehow in the way. She once set a record by scoring forty-two points in a play-off game. I was there, and I would say that at least thirty-six of those points were the result of unimpeded, point-blank layups. Most of the girls corralled their hair one way or another, but Danielle just cut hers, with office scissors, to the length of a sandy Beatles mop, and called it good. Her hair is longer now, but she's still tall enough to darken doorways, and looks, by a tea table, woodenly immense. In the rear alcove at Cajovna, she put her hand to her heart, bowed with the restraint of an English butler, and said to me, "Good afternoon."

I asked her to sit. She did, no doubt with her big knees pinched against the table. Danielle has three children—two in college, one in the Peace Corps—and a methodical approach to nearly everything. At Cajovna, she manages five employees and does all of the accounting, payroll, and buying. Her husband, Leonard, owns a company dedicated to pouring concrete. He and his crew work in big, new developments. His back is bad from bending over a screed board and kicking wet concrete around in heavy boots. Danielle started Cajovna after becoming convinced that Leonard was wearing out and that tea had the potential to take off in Seattle the way coffee had. She soon came to accept, though, that in her case it meant half a living if she slaved at it. During summers, Cajovna operated in the red. Once the rain came, things got better.

In her tea shop's rear alcove, Danielle and I traded notes. Like me, she'd been apprised of our father's accident, but, unlike me, she also knew—because our mother had spoken to Danielle on the phone about an hour before I'd walked into Cajovna—that my father was no longer insurable and wouldn't be driving anymore. "Big problem," Danielle said. "Our parents don't drive."

She went for tea. When she came back, carrying a pot and two cups, she said, "Hey, normally when you come here you bring a notebook, am I right?"

She was right. I did normally bring a notebook to Cajovna. I had a place to write at home—my office—but sometimes, just to change things, I'd written at Cajovna. The confines were cozy there on a wintry afternoon, the tapestries were Slovak, and tea was on the house. It was conducive, but those days were over now.

I told Danielle why I didn't have my notebook. "Well," she said, "now you have time for other things, don't you."

We drank tea and nattered. Above us, on a large chalkboard high on the wall, was this, in purple chalk, from Alexander Pushkin:

> 'Twas growing dark; upon the table, shining,
> there hisses the evening samovar,
> warming the Chinese teapot;
> light vapor undulated under it.
> Poured out by Olga's hand,
> into the cups, in a dark stream,
> the fragrant tea already ran,
> and a footboy served the cream.

Danielle told me that, on reading this, one of her employees had commented, "That's beautiful, such a blissful, domestic scene," to which a young socialist, also in her employ, had replied that she couldn't endorse the idea of bliss contingent on the availability of footboys. A third employee, phone in hand, had thrown into this mix, "I put in 'Russian footboy' and the first six entries are all porn," and then laughed at her own commentary. But the socialist wasn't having it. "I'm serious," she'd countered. "Bliss on the backs of other people isn't bliss." There'd ensued a tense discussion. No one backed down. Their shift ended. They all agreed to disagree and left. Bliss on the backs of other people remained in flux. There was no resolution to the controversy over it. "But I've got a new quote up my sleeve," Danielle told me, "from William Cowper. I'm going to erase the controversial footboy later today and . . . Let me get this for you on my phone." She fiddled with her phone and then read:

Now stir the fire, and close the shutters fast,
Let fall the curtains, wheel the sofa round,
And, while the bubbling and loud-hissing urn
Throws up a steamy column, and the cups,
That cheer but not inebriate, wait on each,
So let us welcome peaceful ev'ning in.

Danielle threw up her big basketball mitts. "That should cause less of an uproar," she said. "That oughta be less controversial. Although, in our current climate, everything's controversial. I guess you could say that in those lines from Cowper there's an insufferable bourgeois smug satisfaction, and a privileged cluelessness about who picked the tea leaves."

When we were done, we ducked through the rear alcove's curtain and lingered through goodbyes by the displays of bulk teas Danielle carried. Here, again high on a wall, and again in purple, on a second chalkboard, were lines from Proust:

But when from a long-distant past nothing subsists,
after the people are dead, after the things are broken
and scattered, taste and smell alone, more fragile but
more enduring, more unsubstantial, more persistent,
more faithful, remain poised a long time, like souls.

Danielle saw me reading that and said, "As in Dad's bran flakes—am I right or what?"

THE NEXT TIME I drove my father to Skagit County—at his request, made sheepishly—it was for Delvin and Betsy Harvey's arraignment on charges of homicide by abuse. Almost no one had come to witness this formality—in fact, besides me, there were only three, bunched together in a corner opposite mine.

The arraignment began. Betsy Harvey shuffled through a side door, dressed in a turquoise sweater and orange scrubs, shackled at the ankles and waist, handcuffed and accompanied by two deputies. Her straw-colored eyebrows were sparse, and her shoulders sloped steeply. She was waiflike and bony and, despite her intensity, looked like she might blow away in a wind.

My father and Betsy Harvey approached the bench. It was difficult to hear what anyone was saying. For maybe three minutes, there was murmuring and hobnobbing between my father, the judge, and the prosecutor, while the stenographer sat with a very straight back, keyboarding with a light, silent flutter. Then they were done, and a deputy freed Betsy Harvey of a handcuff so she could sign her bail agreement. Her first order of business with her liberated hand was to curl strands of hair behind one ear and press against her raw nostrils where they flared. Then she signed, the cuff went back on, and, in summary fashion, wedged between deputies, she was trundled through a door that, on thudding shut, echoed. It was at this point, in the lull before Delvin Harvey appeared, that I turned toward the other people in the gallery, and realized that I must be looking at one of the Harvey children, sitting between what had to be his grandparents. His face looked so thoroughly crushed that its features, mottled pink, had retracted.

The side door opened, and Delvin Harvey entered, hand-cuffed to a chain wrapped twice around his waist and dressed in faded red prison togs. Short of stature and broadly built, he had a meaty lower lip, a recessed chin, and a deeply retreating hairline. The thin tuft of hair that remained between his temples had been combed sideways. Delvin Harvey held his chest in an inflated rictus. He looked like someone determined to give pause by puffing up, staying mum, and leaving behind a question mark.

One of his cuffs came off. Left-handed, he signed his bail agreement. The cuff went back on, and he turned toward the gallery. He noted me in my corner, and then the three people in theirs. He nodded at them—or, rather, dropped his chin—before, like Betsy Harvey, he was trundled out a side door.

The proceedings were over. The judge got up and left, followed by the bailiff. The stenographer gathered up her things and left, too. Each of the ostensible grandparents put an arm around the ostensible Harvey boy and escorted him toward the exit. My father, in his raincoat, briefcase in hand, came to my corner. "They wanted to set bail at a quarter-million," he said. "I asked for personal recognizance. In the end, we got hit with a hundred fifty thousand, so now I have to go see a bondsman."

He went to do that. I waited in Barton's, a used-book store with creaky floorboards on Mount Vernon's main street. Barton's has a section on local history, and when my father was done at the bail-bond office, he found me there, reading while perched on a windowsill. "How's your book?" he asked.

I showed him *An Illustrated History of Skagit and Snohomish Counties,* which is a compilation of news articles, county records, anecdotes, miscellany, and photographs assembled in 1906. I told him that its author had begun by assailing the Spanish, Russian, Portuguese, and French explorers who'd sailed off the shores of Skagit County as impeded by shortcomings consistent with their nationalities, before moving on to English explorers, about whom he felt better. I read for my father a pertinent sentence: "Anglo-Saxon energy, thoroughness, and zeal, from James Cook on, would come to characterize operations on the shores of the Pacific Northwest."

My father said, "If I remember correctly, James Cook was killed in Hawaii. Clubbed to death, or something along those lines."

I told my father that, from what I'd read so far, *An Illustrated History of Skagit and Snohomish Counties* was long on murders. Three happened near the Skagit River in the winter of 1869, a time when potatoes were legal tender there. A John Barker, I told my father, had his throat slashed and his store robbed. A mob quickly formed, two "Indians" were hanged, and then someone noticed that Quinby Clark, an Anglo-Saxon, had produced thirty dollars to buy a "squaw" shortly after Barker died. My father took the book and read for himself. "Listen to this," he said. "'Subsequent investigation of the store showed plainly that the robbery and murder had been committed by a white man, for things which Indians would have taken were left, and those which a white man would have taken were gone.'"

He looked at me over the tops of his reading glasses. "Interesting detective work," he said.

I got us onto the freeway. Things went smoothly for a while, but then, a few miles north of Seattle, an accident halted traffic. My father passed the time with documents in his lap, turning pages and underscoring passages with his pen. "How is it," he asked, without looking up, "that you have time to cart me around like this? Don't you have work to do?"

I lied. I said I did have work to do but that, fortunately, the circumstances of my life left time both to do it and to cart him around. "Maybe," said my father, "but, still, I'm an albatross around your neck. Which isn't my point, though. My point is, what about work? I know there are people who say, 'On your deathbed you're not going to wish you'd worked more, you're going to wish you'd gone to Zanzibar to watch the sun set. And loved your loved ones more. Those are the two. Do things, love people more.' Well, I'm not going to argue about Zanzibar, but, as for loving people, that doesn't have to be mutually exclusive with work, does it? Couldn't they happen at the same time?"

WHICH BRINGS ME to Alison, to whom I'm married. I met her twenty-eight years ago at the University of British Columbia's Museum of Anthropology, where I'd gone for its archives, and for its X̱wi7x̱wa Library, in service to the pretense, enacted for myself, that I knew what I was doing as a researcher. At the time, I thought I wanted to assay a fictionalized account of the exploits of Franz Boas, who at twenty-five sailed from Germany to Baffin Island for the purpose of nearly freezing to death in the course of anthropological fieldwork, and then, maybe in need of more duress, pursued an ethnographic project, amid virulent rains, in the Pacific Northwest. As it turned out, the Boas Collections and the Boas Papers were housed at the headquarters of the American Philosophical Society in Philadelphia; however, I was able to ferret out, at this Museum of Anthropology southwest of Vancouver, some copies of letters Boas wrote, which I tracked down with private vindication, and with eager élan, and copied a page at a time against the screen of a loud machine, then stapled and read on a bench in the museum's foyer, occasionally laughing because Boas, at twenty-eight, was the sort of correspondent who wrote, "I hope I shall find another good Tsimshian to replace Mathew, whom I can not curse enough." Alison and I met because I laughed at "Today was my worst day since I have been here. I learned practically nothing as I had to spend the entire day running about in search of new people." "What's so funny?" she asked me—a woman in a raincoat who had just straightened up after holding her hair aside to drink from a low-arcing fountain. The raincoat was rain-beaded. Her hair was wet. I apologized for laughing out loud. Her answer: raised eyebrows. Later, I went to look at bentwood cedar boxes; she came around a corner and stood ten yards from me, nothing, not even glances exchanged, me with my hands behind my back reading about the splitting of boards and the adzing of planks, rigorously keeping my eyes forward. I felt then like a cipher, an apparently aloof guy in a sweater that had dried out in the museum but that still hung rain-limp—a study in detachment, but privately jangled, as if a very loud alarm had gone off.

Certain things are said to happen "without warning"—a tree topples on a windless day, a heart stops, a sinkhole opens between your house and your neighbor's, all things devoid of premonition, of an inkling. Anyway, in the great hall of the museum, the totem poles shuddered. The bentwood boxes moved. I turned. The masks in a nearby glass case changed expressions. A man who had been looking at them looked at me now, with penetrating quizzicality. In fact, the dozen or so people in the museum—we all looked at one another as if among us, somewhere, was the answer to a question not formulated yet but in need of an immediate answer. We were like bobblehead dolls, frozen in place but loose-necked, or like foosball figurines in a game just heating up. I realized then that I had trembling carte blanche to meet the eyes of the "What's so funny?" woman, who had her hands on her head and her arms bent like wings and was looking back at me as if there was no answer not only to the question at hand but to any question worthy of being one. During this limbo of mutual appraisal, the floor began to thrum as if a tank were passing under us. Then it began to pulse and roll. The totem poles seemed in danger of toppling were it not for guy wires that, on second thought, might snap. The cedar baskets lined up in cases leaned like fallen dominoes, a canoe lurched across the floor, a bear reared in my direction, the posts and beams, the concrete and glass, the fifty-foot ceiling, the bowls, cradles, coffins, hats: all of it was seized by a din of threatening seriousness, as if the Strong Man Who Holds Up the World were stomping on the ground with ever greater fury, or the dancer who'd accidentally kicked the drum and thereby gained an earthquake foot were enraged.

Then it stopped, and no one got out a phone and began to text or call, because this was before that.

I turned again toward the "What's so funny?" woman, who still had her hands on her head in the manner sometimes seen in grainy military prisoner-taking footage but that in her case suggested humor. She looked toward the ceiling. She looked at me again. "I think we should leave," she said, pointing overhead at totem-pole guy wires that were twanging as if electrified.

We fled. It had stopped raining, and the sort of light you might associate with magnanimous divinity filtered through the clouds. With no earthquake, I would have felt like a liaison was in progress, but with one, there was room for ambiguity. I lagged a half step behind the "What's so funny?" woman in deference to that as we put a gap between us and the museum, which looked, from where we turned for a summation, undeniably sturdy. I had a car, but it was subterranean, where I had paid to lodge it in what had become, while we were in the museum, a no-go zone, as announced by a line of orange plastic cones and a ticket-booth cashier sitting on a curb by a newly opened concrete crack. Alison's car was down there, too.

Behind the museum was a reflecting pool. Its water looked suspiciously mobile, shimmeringly suggestive of aftershocks so subtle they registered only as liquid impressions—although, at that point, everything, the merest footfall, suggested aftershocks, which as tactile mirages or felt hallucinations are equal in force to shocks that nudge the Richter Scale. We stood listening with our feet. Now that we were here, and there was nothing to be done, Alison sank in for me. And what I noticed was that, in peering across the pool, over the crest of a rise, she went up on her toes and didn't come down or waver for an impressive duration, which made me wonder, was she now, or had she been, a dancer, as this looked *en pointe,* or close to it anyway, in a relaxed sense, so relaxed that she had her hands in her raincoat pockets, although one did emerge briefly when she needed it to push aside some dangling, still-damp chestnut-brown tendrils of hair obstructing her view, and let's face it, does it take more than that? She said, "So what do you do?" I answered that I was "between jobs," but that not long ago—this was true, given a generous construing of "not long ago"—I'd worked for a company that poured concrete creatively: counters, sink tops, hearths, stairs, terraces; meanwhile, I'd become interested in Franz Boas and was thinking of writing a book about him, or, rather, doing research for one. Before Alison could respond to this, there was an actual aftershock, no doubt about it, aggressively roiling the reflecting pool and, like a *frisson,* producing, in me at least, giddy pleasure, since it was mild, I was outside, there was nothing tall nearby, and the world, as it shook, was alive like I was, though at the time I formulated no simile relating the dawning lover to the world, or to an earthquake, those were, or are, posterior formulations on the part of an author who at the moment has nowhere to hide. And when it was over, though the pool hadn't settled yet, Alison said, "That was a good one." Then we went for a walk along Tower Beach, in the hope that, when we returned, the orange cones would no longer be lined up in front of the parking-garage gate, and where spume, or froth, sparkling and billowing, had been thrown out of the Georgia Strait onto low tide's sloping shingle, along with the wreckage of polished red madrones lofted against cobbled groynes meant to thwart the work of an ocean threatening to undermine, undercut, and finally end the work of the University of British Columbia on the cliff above, where Alison had studied Global Resource Systems. An hour later, the cones were still there, so we walked across Marine Drive to a pub Alison knew about and, with other survivors—actually no one died in that quake—ate poutine.

Early this morning—I had my nose against her neck, my arm across her belly, and the edge of my hand against the small of her waist—Alison twitched as she slept. First her shoulder leapt, then her thigh, then her hip, and then, as it seemed to me, she ran softly in place, all of which made me feel like a voyeur, but also lonely, because Alison was warm and her throat moist and she smelled of coconut oil in the solitude of night's end, and I was already thinking that before long she would get up and go off to her current job as the assistant director of an international campaign devoted to the preservation of boreal forests, and thinking also that Alison's current wander through disassociated images, fragments of event and encounter, fluid and morphing exchange, surfeits of emotion, fleeting confabulations of voice, character, and place, paranormal hauntings, and other irreducible perplexities of mind were all unavailable to me and always would be, so that I wanted to wake her and urge her toward me in the hope that a companionable convergence marked by mingled respiration, poignant and freighted by mortality as it might be, would nevertheless help us outrun the sun, which wanted to rise again, as always, and also, selfishly, I hoped our coupling, if it were to happen, might blot out my singularity, which I have always found burdensome, but such is the vanity of the one who lies awake feeling desire mingling with the reluctant recognition that, in the cold, he must first and foremost be humbled by his body, rise, and stand over the toilet. And as for the poutine, I had to tell Alison that I had never tried it before, because the idea of French fries and cheese curds in gravy had always seemed offensive to me, but why not; our recent seismic event had opened a poutine door, and so we stuck our forks into the contents of a heaped plate and I gave her my honest opinion, which was that, however you looked at it, the best thing about poutine was that its curds squeaked.

I'm a little ashamed of the fact that all of this fooling around with words means that Alison ceases to exist and is replaced, as far as posterity is concerned, if there is to be a posterity (we have no children); a time is coming when no one living will have lived when Alison lived; she will, for a generation to a generation and a half, be sporadically reconstituted via photos, letters, potentially some hard drives, whatever remnants of her are retrievable from clouds, and for who knows how long by references to her in this book and maybe others to come, so that what remains is inference, distortion, short shrift, and other forms of once removal, forever incommensurate and insufficient, a false record, a substitute, a life lost not to silence but to reinvention, to selection and omission, a disguise instead of gross anonymity but equaling the same: utter loss, nothing, the woman I kissed for the first time with poutine breath rendered invisible by writerly choice, by a scribbler choosing traits and events, deciding which tics, proclivities, etc , will have relative endurance in the public record and by that means ensuring that no one will know, for example, that Alison has a drawer so full of old sweaters that the wool rises in relief when she works it open; that, as a schoolgirl in saddle shoes arriving home at 3:40 p.m. with a three-ring binder clutched to her chest, she sometimes spied a cigar stub on a ledge by her front door and knew because of it that her grandfather was leaning on his cane inside; that she'd seen a moose charge a clothesline hung with bath towels in Saskatchewan; that, when disconsolate, she sometimes stands with her head down, drawing with a pencil;

that her husband is enamored of the winter coats she wears, or has worn, and says so on those occasions when she dons, for the first time, a replacement for a beloved predecessor (something that happens at intervals of years); that she makes envelopes out of advertising circulars while talking on the phone; that her right foot turns out more than the left by a slight degree when she descends a slope; that frequently in autumn she goes about with bits of leaf in her hair; that when she emerges from her scalding showers the skin beneath her clavicles is rouge, or ruby; that on many mornings her first words are "What time is it?"; that she listens to a solar-powered wind-up radio while weeding; that her shoe soles wear out mid-foot and on their outside edges; and that she prefers glass to plastic for refrigerator storage. That these things might appear here distorted and employed essentially for artistic effect I'm not going to call a tragedy, but it's close.

The day after the arraignment of Betsy and Delvin Harvey, Alison and I took a pruning class. We have a tree in our yard called *Acer* × *freemanii* that our guesswork and ignorance had stressed to the point where we vacillated over keeping it; goaded by naturally occurring steroids, it kept thrusting up double and triple leaders and shooting out laterals as if the sun threatened to flame out tomorrow. A master of rabid, overnight fecundity, it so summarily defeated our efforts to beat it back that we'd begun to wonder if it felt animosity toward us. We also had a Camperdown elm that was supposed to grow in the shape of an umbrella but that looked like a man's beard, and some Himalayan birches that had nearly succumbed to bronze birch borer and were in need of triage. Problem after problem, but the pruning workshop we'd signed up for was led by a horticulturalist who more than knew the ropes when it came to the trees at hand. It was held on a day of odd, rare, and even punishing fall sunshine in an atrium of the University of Washington's horticulture building, so, when it was over, Alison and I walked on campus. We wanted to see a Camperdown elm our pruning instructor had referred to as nicely shaped. We found it in a side yard near the Art Building. It had a lofty and symmetrical umbrella, and it resembled topiary. Nearby, we sat on a bench for a while. The campus was landscaped to a veritable T. Everything imperfect had either been removed or bore signs of active, well-considered renovation. The parklike setting, anodyne to a fault, featured flowering cherries and London plane trees. Alison and I watched students pass—people of an age our children might have been if we'd had children, so that we felt them as a vaguely wistful absence—and then we walked to Wallingford, where we noticed a theater marquee advertising a movie we hadn't meant to see but weren't averse to. It seemed worth a try, so we went in, bought tickets, and sat down.

At four on a Saturday in a neighborhood theater, you find, at our age, people like yourselves—slow, with time on their hands, deferential, not asking much from life, and collectively aspiring toward the faint traces of courtships that had played out, years before, in run-down, stuffy, and unhygienic movie houses featuring esoteric European movies and surrealism. Alison and I sat loose-limbed, an island to ourselves, canoodlers sharing a huge tub of popcorn, ensconced in the general celluloid blue darkness with plenty of seats between us and other moviegoers. The film was a Canadian festival favorite starring James Cromwell and Geneviève Bujold as rural holdouts who, though weathered and worn, love each other with indelible chemistry. He's become craggy; she's become fragile. They must face facts, many of which are bureaucratic—in a way reminiscent of a politicized youth—others morbid. They suffer well. Sex is implied, wrinkles and all.

Ahead of our viewing, the theater manager had opined before all that this film, *Still Mine,* initially called *Still,* had been poorly retitled by the distributors who'd swooped in on it at the Toronto Film Festival, because *Still Mine* sounded maudlin, and one thing this film wasn't was maudlin. That wasn't true. It *was* maudlin. Alison said as much afterward, as we were walking away—that it was maudlin, and also that, when the time came—or if it came—it was okay with her if our lives felt maudlin, but not too much, and as for maudlin, what did it mean anyway?

We went home. I sat down to read a book. From across the hall, Alison yelled, "Listen to this! A Genèvieve bio! 'In 1977 Bujold met her current partner, carpenter Dennis Hastings, while he was building her house in Malibu'! 'They are still living in California together today'!"

"No wonder she did *Still Mine*!"

"*Still*!"

Soon, from across the hall, I heard Bobby Darin singing "If I Were a Carpenter." A little while later, Alison shouted, "Can't find a picture of Dennis Hastings. . . . Here's Genèvieve with Jean-Paul Belmondo . . . Genèvieve with Michael Douglas . . . Genèvieve 1966 . . . Not sure anyone was ever better looking than Genèvieve. . . . Here she's kissing Yves Montand. . . . Here she's in *Obsession* with Cliff Robertson! So what happened to Cliff Robertson? Let me see. . . . Oh, he died!"

In bed, I told Alison what my father had said while I was driving him home from Mount Vernon the day before: that love and work aren't mutually exclusive. "Couched as formal logic," she replied, "which doesn't make it any less true."

"He's going to need a lot of rides."

"Do it," said Alison.

The next morning, she got up before I did and started pruning the Camperdown. On her side of our bed—proximate to which I regularly wonder how she cooks up so much heat—or, rather, on the floor next to it, sat eleven books, a box of Kleenex, her reading glasses, a bobby pin, a hair clip, a small bottle of aloe vera skin cleanser, a receipt for a library overdue payment, a wooden back-scratcher, and three pencils. I opened our curtains onto a breadth of morning sun. The silk tree outside our window had no pink flowers on it at that moment, but its pods were pierced by light such that its shrouded beans wore nimbi; meanwhile, the lost blossoms were a brown morass gathering toward a fall. I got up, looked for my nail clippers, and found them, at last, in the room where I used to scribble fictions. It hadn't taken very long for the smell of dust and emptiness to seep into everything there. My desk and shelves, my sideboard and file cabinets, had quickly metamorphosed into a figureless diorama, had become inert, had taken on the pallor of a stage set; all that was needed was a velvet rope hung across the door frame to complete the portrait of a historical phenomenon, in this case one with no interest to anyone but myself, although, at bottom, I wasn't interested in anything there other than fetching the nail clippers and looking out the window, and then in noting that the ivy growing vigorously up the house imperiled the gutters, which weren't sagging but threatened to. It's a shame to view things this way. Everywhere I turned on our plat, I now saw maintenance. It had come to seem that the life of a homeowner—or at least of this homeowner—was a series of staying actions against ruin. I'd noticed, and it was streamable, a show about ruin, a series devoted to imagining places once humans stopped doting on them, and I'd binge-watched it against the odds. In one episode, while a narrator sounded a basso profundo of ominous notes, feral hogs rooted in a desolate and weedy Buckingham Palace. In another, Seattle appeared as a salt marsh over which the Space Needle made a last, contorted stand while a torrent of Biblical proportions fell out of a toxic sky.

THE AFTERNOON AFTER *Still Mine,* or *Still,* my father called. "If this was the old days," he said, "I'd drive out to the Boeing plant in Everett and talk to people there about Delvin Harvey, since it might be him and not Betsy Harvey who's at fault here, but the old days are gone now, so I can't do it."

I didn't answer. "Actually, I *could* do it," my father said. "I could go by cab and try to work my way in. But I think your status as a writer helps, because you can just call them up and say you're writing a novel and have to get your details right and have to do some research and you'd like to get permission to go inside the plant and see what millwrights do and talk to millwrights, and of course, in the course of that, you can ask these millwrights about Delvin Harvey and see what kind of guy he was, was he a jerk to everybody or something else entirely, did he say anything pertinent, did he do anything telling. You get the idea. Be me."

I CALLED the Boeing plant in Everett. Whoever picked up thought I should talk to someone in Chicago. The person in Chicago said that the Everett plant was open to the public and that if I looked on the Boeing website I could sign up for a tour. No, I explained. It's not a tour I have in mind. It's more that, for purposes of a book I'm writing, I'd like to hang around some Boeing millwrights. "A book," she said, which made me realize that my request must trouble her because Boeing had been blamed for plane crashes, accused of war profiteering, and widely characterized as an unscrupulous lobbier incestuously coupled to the Department of Defense, so that my disclosure— that I was writing a book—must raise for her a red flag. "It's just fiction," I said. "A novel."

I was to call Jim Little. I could also call Leslie Schmad. She would call them both first and give them my name and tell them what I wanted to do, and they would put me through the vetting process and get me the forms to fill out and—music to my ears—it shouldn't be a problem. All because—I think— fiction isn't true, so you don't have to worry about it.

I GOT THROUGH the hoops and over the hurdles. In Boeing's lobby, where large, shiny models of airplanes were displayed in glass cases, Leslie Schmad gave me a preprinted name badge. Then she and I got into an open-air but canopied electric vehicle driven by Jim Little. We moved as if weightless, and our vehicle was nearly silent. It was 2:00 p.m., and the Boeing Everett premises seemed languid. A placid sterility prevailed. Everything seemed bland, muffled, clean. We turned a corner and came to a lurching halt. Jim hopped off and pushed buttons on a keypad. A large door rolled open, and we entered what I suppose you would call the Boeing Everett main production facility, or maybe the assembly building, and as we rolled onto the factory floor, following more striping and maintaining a careful speed limit, Leslie Schmad leaned toward me and said, "I'm going to give you a factoid that you might want to jot down. This is the largest building in the world. It covers almost a hundred acres. Its volume is four hundred seventy-five million cubic feet. It's a mindblower, a mindblower. Every time I come in here, and I don't come very much, but every time I come in here, it's: Wow."

There were airplanes, of course, in progressive stages of production—some skeletal, with skins off, others bright with rivets. I saw a fuselage in cutaway view, as if a side had been peeled away. I also heard the pop of pneumatic riveters. People were scrambling over wings and ducking in and out of tailpieces. I couldn't understand anything. It was too complicated. And it made sitting in a room by yourself making up stories seem ridiculous. While I was thinking this way, Jim Little got us to the warren, or corner, or sector, or whatever you want to call it, where the millwrights were quartered, and I was delivered into the hands of Brian Kleist, who had agreed to shepherd me, or babysit me, and who murmured with Jim and Leslie before they disappeared in their personnel carrier. Then, with Brian, who had shaved his head until it gleamed as if burnished, and who looked like the actor Woody Harrelson— heavy brow, Roman nose—I went into what he called "the pod room," where about a dozen millwrights, all male, were sitting around, mostly in slouches of varying degree, at a long, scarred, dinged, and dented table. It was the beginning of "second shift," meaning 2:00 to 10:00 p.m. The millwrights were drinking coffee, eating potato chips, reading newspapers, and mousing away at desktop computers. On their table were some fat, old-school Thermoses, scattered plastic safety glasses, toothpicks, and salt and pepper shakers. There was a strong smell of burned coffee. My presence was explained but not commented on. I felt that everyone in the room was attempting to appear unflappable, and also pondering whether or not to say something about me. All opted not to. I sat there with my notepad. At two-thirty, Brian Kleist passed out work orders, and the millwrights exited. I followed Brian. Outside the pod room, he said, "Hey, come here," and two guys did, and then three others turned around and appeared to think about it for a moment, whether this directive meant them, too, and from among those three, two decided it did, so that in the end we were a group of six—Brian, me, Ralph Gibson, Wade Lantz, Jeremy Barrett, Ron Richardson—and Brian said, "Okay, this guy is a writer, like I said, and he needs to follow people around today, so, Ralph, Wade, Jer, Ron, he follows you around, and just whatever it is or whatever happens, and you just answer his questions or whatever." Brian turned toward me. "So hang around with these guys," he said.

Ralph, Wade, Jeremy, and Ron had a work order that called for building a crib. (A crib is an enclosure, in this case one that would contain wiring harnesses.) It was supposed to include a four-foot sliding window with a shelf and a four-foot sliding gate. There was another work order calling for the construction of pallet racks. The shelves were supposed to be ten to sixteen feet high to accommodate storage of fuselage rails. I tagged along while Ralph, Wade, Jeremy, and Ron got the right tools and the right materials for these projects, and as this was going on, I singled out Jeremy as my most likely conduit to information about Delvin Harvey, and focused on him in what you would have to call an ingratiating way, thinking simultaneously of something the journalist Janet Malcolm had written in a book about a murder trial: that every journalist (my circumstances were essentially journalistic) who is not too stupid or too full of himself to notice what is going on knows that what journalists do is morally indefensible. That didn't stop me, though. After about forty-five minutes of working Jeremy (not without shame), I said to him—in hearing of the others—"I heard about a millwright here who was arrested for murder."

Jeremy sported long gray hair in a kind of mane. He also had a mustache. And very heavy eyebrows that were not gray yet and that included little up-sweeping points that made him look devilish. He wore a chambray shirt with a couple of its buttons unbuttoned, and in the long V formed by that grew a dense coiling forest of salt-and-pepper hair. He also featured what I called patrol boots in grade school. His gut pooched. He was creaky. His shoulders were narrow. His mane was well coiffed. He wore plastic safety glasses held to his head by a tight elastic band that bit into his hair. "Murder?" he said, but not incredulously.

They talked about it for a while, Jeremy, Wade, Ralph, and Ron, going back in time—many years, in fact—figuratively scratching their heads in unison as they built the crib meant for wiring harnesses, doing so amid an astounding density of pneumatic tool noise and moving machinery, until, finally, someone hit on Delvin Harvey, and then they were telling me about him with profuse insistence and texting millwrights in far corners of the facility who could "fill me in on the guy." And here I will ratify the maxim I mentioned earlier (the one about journalists knowing perfectly well that what they do is morally indefensible) by acknowledging my exploitation of the will to participate. Most people, properly primed, will speak to a writer, even if in principle they're prepared to refuse. You can study that in a journalism school. Or more broadly in a course on sales. By lunch—6:00 p.m. on second shift—I was recording guiltlessly.

FIRST MILLWRIGHT: "Harvey was an interesting guy who kept to himself but would say unexpected things out of left field. I remember, a few times, he talked about the Civil War. He was a history buff when it came to the Civil War. Like, at the Battle of Chattanooga, if only General Confederate had gone left instead of right and put the artillery on his flank and— What is this guy talking about? Mainly, though, you didn't toy with Harvey. There was no back and forth. He wasn't, you know, loose about stuff. He had twelve kids or sixteen kids or fifty kids or something. 'Cuz he was Christian, I guess. Personally, I don't have a problem with Christians, and I don't have a problem with anybody, really. My thing is, live and let be. Not Harvey, because when he got on Christian it was: I'm right and there's no two ways about it. But I never had a problem with him. It's okay with me. No biggie. Either way. Here's the thing, though. You can't say Harvey was like this or like that, because I knew him twenty years, and that's, like, I don't know, age twenty-eight to age forty-eight, and people change. Like I can remember Harvey, he actually talked quite a bit about his kids, like you would be out there on the floor with him and he would tell you how over the weekend his kids, whatever, and he would go on to where it was like he was a chatterbox. So that was different. Some of these guys won't remember this, but for a long time Harvey was flat-out hillbilly. What does that mean? It means big-ass beard. You guys remember that. Some guys called him Smith Brother, 'cuz he looked like the guys on the Smith Brothers Cough Drops. 'So where's Smith Brother?'—stuff like that. Big fuzzy beard. Lunch break, for a while there, Harvey played a flute. Feature that. Or guys called it a flute. Personally, I don't know what it was. It sounded like a flute. Anyway, he played that. So, going back a while, guy with a Smith Bro beard playing a flute in the corner, what's that all about? I would say he looked sorta like an Amish dude at that point. Pretty weird.

"What did he play? Hell if I know. Little songs, I guess. 'Johnny Comes Marching Home'?"

SECOND MILLWRIGHT: "That thing was called an ocarina. Reason he had it, it was smaller than a flute. Type of thing you can put in your pocket. Smith Bro played that through his hillbilly beard. His monster muff. Whatever you call it. One time, Smith Bro told me he was making little wooden stuff to give his kids for Christmas instead of going to Kmart. I told him I make wooden stuff. Because I do. Quick stuff. Blocks, toys. Del was making these wooden guns look like BB guns, and these little cowboy corrals. And he whittled. Do I remember he had trouble with anyone? Yeah, he had trouble with people, but the people he had trouble with were troublemakers anyway. He didn't look for it. He left for a while to do something other in the plant—like he was inspecting crane cables, servicing elevators—but then he came back, and I remember, when the eight-seven plane was coming out, we had this job, Del and me, we had to pull all the rubber out of the tracks for the hangar doors, and he was in a shoot-the-shit mood, and he was on religion a lot, like 'God has a plan for you,' and I thought that was flaky. When I was a kid, my parents, they made me go to Bible camp, and when they picked me up after three weeks, I told them I wasn't gonna go again next year, because they try to scare the shit out of you there, but I didn't say this to Del, because he was such a hard-core church guy you couldn't say that to him. Massive hard-core church guy. He was in Planned Jobs, remember? So he had something to say. He had control for a while there, and there were guys didn't like how he handled that. They thought he turned down jobs. Underestimated them. Didn't trust. Made you feel small. Not everyone. But there were guys felt like that. Didn't understand him. Always took overtime, though. One time, Del and me, we worked twenty-four straight, because the seven-seven line was down, they had these hoists for the wing frames out of whack, and so we did that. There's also this thing called the 'body section turn fixture,' which you oughta see while you're here, because this thing, it rolls the body sections around for inspection, and it always needs maintenance, so we did that, which was a drag. What else? You wanna know what else we did? What Harvey and me did? We worked on the crawlers.

We put in jib booms. One summer, me and Del, we were down in an elevator pit all summer, where they put in the landing gear, and we were working on the portals and messing around with the jackscrews, and Del, he hardly said two words for three straight months, which was fine with me, 'cuz I'm the kind of person wants to concentrate on his job, get outa there, and go water skiing."

THIRD MILLWRIGHT: "I don't know what kind of book you're writing. You're looking for anecdotes, I guess. With me, out of nowhere, Harvey started talking about political crap. One of these people thinks the Rothschilds are the tip of the iceberg. There's these people, these families, they control everything, they meet in secret, they control the banks, whatever happens, it happens because they make it happen, the rest of us are pawns. I didn't say nothing in response to that. Let it fade away. He got the message. But then it was like I missed the boat. Like I was just another pawn. He'd poke at it a little. Like, did I know they wanted to reduce the world's population to five hundred million? Which, actually, I don't think is a bad idea. He said it meant there would be no more Christians. They want to do away with cash, too. Like, wait and see, that's how they control things. No rise out of me. Didn't take the bait. He let some time pass, then it's 'You know what their strategy is? Divide and conquer.' They got the world carved up. They control the IMF, the Fed, the Chinese, the North Koreans. What is this? I don't get it. Any of you guys hear Smith Bro on this? I turned my ears off, let him talk. But at a certain point, I had to say, Look man, I wanna be polite about it, but I don't go that way. Let's talk about something else. Sorta flat after that. There was a cool thing he did. He put together solid steel casters. We used them to roll pallet racks around with a forklift. One time, we had to move this carpet-cutter machine. Smith Bro rigged our dolly. Fifty-five building, they wanted a new overhead crane, new sectional doors. Harvey and me, we did the sectionals. The crane rails were like twenty-four-inch and weighed nine hundred pounds. There were seven to a side. Like I said, I give him credit. We used to tear apart old boxcars. We'd make 'em taller, shorter, whatever, for shipping. Took apart a lot of boxcars with Smith Bro. He and I welded up a shitload of guardrails. We made Jersey barriers—like, hundreds of 'em. For some reason, they thought we had to move our shop from the fifty-six building to the twenty-three. Grumble, grumble. 'Cuz we were being marginalized. They wanted contract union millwrights, 'cuz it was cheaper than us. We're down to humiliating jobs only. Harvey was no grumbler. He didn't want to shoot the shit on that, just George Soros and the Rothschilds, the Bitcoin. I don't even know what currency manipulation is. And I don't care. Life's too short. And there's nothing you can do about it. So shut up and look on the bright side."

THE LAST MILLWRIGHT I recorded summed it up, or maybe I stopped there because it felt like he did: "I kinda got the vibe that something was causing Harvey to talk religion. Like something eating at him. The in-laws do that. Chips are down, they pray harder—that's their way. And lecture people—God this and God that—'cuz they're stressed out, and they gotta convince themselves. But I'm no psychologist. Man, you could see something on Harvey's mind. My mother used to say, 'What's your brow knit up about, boy?' Harvey's, his was knit up like that. And on his phone at lunch. Talking to his wife. Phone rang at lunch, he paced off to talk. Could see his hands moving. Funny how people do that. Walkin' down the street with earbuds, talking away, moving their hands around like the person on the other end can see—it cracks me up. Delvin's on with his wife. It's gotta be his wife. I ask him what's up, he says, 'Girl we adopted has got hepatitis, and my wife sorta likes everything just so,' by which I took him to mean she's one of those types paranoid about things being sterile, which is a problem my wife has, too, like hand sanitizer, like that's going to do anything, but, oh well, let her sanitize her hands if it gives her peace of mind, stuff's cheap. Harvey—it just so happened I was working with him a lot before he got arrested, and, like I say, he was tearin' his hair out. What I sorta thought, he was headed toward divorce, 'cuz I've seen guys split up and the signs were there, divorce. I was wrong. It wasn't divorce. It was this other stuff. But everyone was like 'What?' when he got arrested. I mean, our jaws hit the floor. Not a guy would whale on a child. You couldn't see Harvey whaling on a kid for nothing. I never even heard him raise his voice. Just blew me away. It would be totally out of the ordinary for him. What they said he did, it wasn't his MO. Anyway, I was there when they arrested him. Surprised the hell out of me. Out in the parking lot. It was like he knew it was coming, too. Didn't argue or nothing, just took the cuffs. I'm, like, flabbergasted. What the hell? None of us knew what was going on. You see these stories all the time, someone blows up a subway or stabs people in a mall, afterward his neighbor says, 'Never woulda thought it, guy seemed like everyone else.' I used to crack up at this Adam Sandler song. There's this guy, he buys the school candy bars, he's got the jumper cables, he takes your mail on vacation, and the chorus? His hobby is *moyda*. So what I mean is, you can't pin Harvey down. Maybe he whaled on his kids, who knows. I look at the Nazis in the Nazi pictures, they look normal, so maybe, when Harvey got home, he's evil. He's got a stick or a whip and he's a child beater, mean as hell. Then he puts on his coat and he comes to work, and when he gets here, you'd never know. Plus, I got another theory. To him, he's the same guy both places."

AFTER THEIR ARRAIGNMENT, the Harveys were released on bail. One stipulation of their freedom was that they couldn't communicate with each other or their children—who now lived in foster homes—so Delvin Harvey returned to Stone Lane, and Betsy Harvey went to live with her parents outside of Everson, near the Canadian border. I drove my father there in December. It was a long journey in gusting winds. Betsy Harvey's parents lived in a double-wide mobile home land-scaped with plastic flowers. Beyond it lay flooded alder for-est. Beside it was a van, bronze, with stripes. When I pulled up next to it, my father asked me to come inside to "make a recording of what transpires." I said I would try.

We went to the porch. Betsy Harvey opened the door. She wore an oversize hoodie, an ankle-length denim skirt with big pockets, moccasin slippers, and no makeup. Her front teeth met the way two playing cards do when stood on end and propped against each other. She gaped at me, brought a hand to her mouth, and said, "Who's this?"

"This?" said my father, nudging my arm. "This is my son."

"Why'd you bring him?"

"To make a recording."

Betsy Harvey assessed me further through the screen. "Wait here," she said.

She shut the door. All the way. *Click.* We stood in the wind, which smelled dank and felt frigid. "Betsy," said my father, "is untrusting of people. And something else. Hygiene is important to her. I say that so you won't try to shake her hand. Because she won't do it. She won't shake your hand. It's two-fold. One, germs. Two, suspiciousness. She doesn't know what to make of you. She takes one look and figures you're a liberal. And then she thinks that if you're a liberal you support this apparatus that's against her. And if you support the apparatus that's against her, then you're part of the conspiracy that got her arrested. The world divides into two kinds of people for her, and she's in the category that's persecuted."

Betsy Harvey opened the door—using, in fact, a tissue. "Wipe your feet," she said.

We went in. The house smelled like rug cleaner. We followed Betsy Harvey into a living room, where her parents, Henrietta and Carl Huber, sat in chairs with the television on but the sound muted. They'd been watching a drama, I saw, at least in part about romantically entwined police officers. On Mr. Huber's lap was a miniature poodle, and next to Mrs. Huber's chair a dog of indeterminate breed, its breathing obstructed, lay asleep in a fleece bed. Beside it was a rubber bone. I looked closely; it seemed to be part schnauzer. I also understood, though it took a while, that Mrs. Huber was sitting in a wheelchair, one with so much padding that in her living room it looked like part of the furniture. She was dressed in an auburn pantsuit and wore her hair in a truncated version of Margaret Thatcher's Iron Lady 'do. That style contributed to her masculine mien and abetted her aura of indomitability. In short, she looked intimidating.

Mrs. Huber toggled the joystick on her armrest. Her chair pivoted. Her eyes met mine. "My daughter told me one," she said, pointing at me with a television remote.

My father pointed at me, too. "This is my son," he said. "He writes books, and because of that he does interviews, and because he does interviews he knows how to use his phone to make recordings, and so today he's doing that. He's making a recording. He'll make a recording, and then we'll leave. We'll go back to my office and get a transcript made, and that transcript will help me prepare my case so I can represent Betsy. I hope that makes sense to you."

Mr. Huber tilted upright. For a moment I thought he was going to say something, but as it turned out, no. He'd decided not to lounge in our presence, maybe. Anyway, he kept a straight face, and a hand on his poodle, then coughed. "He writes books," Mrs. Huber said. "What kind of books?"

"Novels," said my father.

"What *kind?*"

"General," my father said. "I don't know what else to call them."

Mr. Huber stirred again. Light from a window caught his impassive face, and I noticed that the lenses of his glasses were tinted yellow. His sandy hair, or what remained of it, was uncombed. He piped up hoarsely, and with difficulty. "My uncle Lester knew Louis L'Amour when they were in the 3622 Quartermaster Truck Company together," he said.

"Quiet," Mrs. Huber said.

There were no more preliminaries. My father, briefcase in hand, asked the Hubers if either of them would be willing to take the stand. At this, Mr. Huber put a forefinger up and said, "When it comes to public speaking, I'm no good at it, whereas the missus there can speak with the best of them, and so can my daughter—she's a good public speaker. Both of these gals can hold their own, but me, I'm not sharp when it comes to that; fact, I tend to stutter if you put me on the spot, so I try to work things where I stay in the background. You all know that," he said to his wife and daughter.

Mrs. Huber acted as if he hadn't spoken. Instead, she pointed at a sofa with her television remote and said, "You two sit there and we'll hear about this."

My father and I sat. He set his briefcase down. "What I want to do," he said, "is simulate the kind of questioning you could get under cross-examination, Mrs. Huber, before we decide anything. Are you okay with that?"

A bare smile—one with a hint of relish—creased Mrs. Huber's face. "You want to see what happens when someone tries taking me apart," she said.

"I don't know if I'd look at it exactly that way," said my father.

"They're always trying to make a fool out of people."

"Who?"

"Lawyers."

"I'm a lawyer."

"Do your lawyering, then. Get it done."

I DIDN'T FEEL comfortable asking Mrs. Huber to hold my phone close to her mouth and speak into its microphone. Instead, from my perch on the sofa, I aimed my phone in her direction as discreetly as possible. My father said, "All right, then, here we go. Mrs. Huber—can I call you Mrs. Huber?"

"You're not grammatical. You mean *may* you call me Mrs. Huber."

"Mrs. Huber," said my father, "did you provide your son-in-law and your daughter with a length of plumbing line to use for disciplining their children?"

Mrs. Huber: "I did not."

My father: "Did you provide them with anything to use for disciplining their children at any time?"

Mrs. Huber: "I did not."

My father: "Did you ever see Abigail physically disciplined with any sort of a belt, or a plumbing line, or a glue stick, or any other instrument?"

Mrs. Huber: "I did not."

My father: "With a hand?"

Mrs. Huber: "No."

My father: "Did you ever see anyone in the family spank Abigail?"

Mrs. Huber: "I just answered that."

My father: "Were you aware that a port-a-potty was brought in for Abigail's use only?"

Mrs. Huber: "They had that port-a-potty out there for all the children, so none of them came in from playing and got the floor dirty with their shoes every time they needed to use the lavatory."

My father: "Did you ever see Abigail being separated from the rest of the family for Christmas dinner or Easter dinner or any holiday dinner?"

Mrs. Huber: "I never saw that. She got treated like all the other children."

My father: "At any time, did you see Abigail being served food that was different from what the other children were served?"

Mrs. Huber: "I remember one time she got a turkey sandwich instead of a peanut-butter sandwich because peanuts were causing a problem with a fungus she had."

My father: "Do you recall Abigail being served frozen food on any occasion?"

Mrs. Huber: "The only thing I recall is, she ate plenty, and she ate seconds and thirds if she wanted it."

My father: "Was Abigail in any way treated differently than the other children?"

Mrs. Huber: "I already told you. She got the same as them. Nothing different."

My father: "Were you ever present when Abigail was sent outside as a disciplinary measure?"

Mrs. Huber: "Sure. And I sent my own children out, too. Your son—you never sent him out?"

My father: "Mrs. Huber. It's not helpful to be combative during cross-examination."

Mrs. Huber: "You never sent him out?"

My father: "I can't put you on the stand if you're combative."

Mrs. Huber: "You know what? You're from Seattle. In Seattle, they elect communists to sit on their city council. They call it socialist, but it's the same—communist. Seattle got the wool pulled over their eyes. By the people make the commercials on television. You realize that? People at the companies saying to themselves, Where's the profit at? And the profit's in putting Blacks in the ads, and putting gays in the ads, and putting women in the ads—and all this women crap. 'Cuz they want to sell stuff. They want to sell, that's all. So they go on television and use their ads to change things. To make the wrong things normal. These companies are selling us downriver, you know. They don't care what happens to us, long as they make their money on it. That's what freedom's all about for them. All this Black music in the ads. You can't even call it music. What's music about it? It's terrible music. And they got the kids hypnotized with it. All the ads, people gyrating around and making fools of themselves so they can sell you a cell phone. Little speakers in your house listening in so they can spy and figure out more ways to get your money. Things are deteriorating. All these people talking about 'woke.' Not even grammatical, way they use it. Stupid idea anyway. Like they're awake and the rest of us asleep. When actually they're the ones swallowed the Kool-Aid. Calling people woke. What does that mean? Woke to getting brainwashed? They're all brainwashed. Kids going around acting like Black people and using Black-people language. And even then they get bashed. Just for being white. It's to where being white's the worst thing you can be. Whites at the bottom of everything now. Call us names, put us down, tell us we're the problem, then they say we ought to be allies. I heard that word 'ally,' 'white ally,' and I just laughed. Ally. You know what an ally is? Temporary. Like Russia and us, World War II. Not friends. Nothing like friends. Black people just using white people to get to the top. Every company now, they got to hire as many Black people as they can find, doesn't matter if they're good enough to do the job, long as they hire Black people they can say they hired Black people, and then everyone loves them and buys their product. Oh yeah. I see the stuff that comes out of Seattle. They think they can commit crimes and break the law and then, when the police come in to do their job, it's the police get spit on and treated like criminals. The police! The police got a thankless, thankless task. Black does something against the law, police officer says one word about it, everyone takes videos and tells the officer he's scum. Where'd we be without police officers? All you have to do is show some common sense and some basic respect and just put your hands up and do what you're asked and everything's fine, but, no, they have to argue and show disrespect and threaten, and then, when they end up on the ground getting handcuffed, they blame the police officer for doing his job, and it's stupid and it makes me mad. So does this women crap. 'Empowered.' If I hear that word one more time I'm going to strangle somebody. You remember, World War II D-Day, they open up those landing-craft rear ends, all those boys jump out and get killed? Where were the women then? They out there getting killed? Next war, it'll be the same, men out there dying, women glad they got men. Real glad again. Glad for real men. Not these little weenies you see in the ads. Men in the ads now aren't even men. Put a real man in an ad, he's there to be made fun of. Toxic masculinity. I hear them say that, too. Huh. Wait till the next war comes. You have a war, they'll be showing respect for men again, 'cuz it'll be men keeping them from rape and pillage. Wonder Woman. You see about that? Every movie now, women out there karate-kicking men or blowing up tanks, that's not reality. Reality is, you watch football, where's the women? Women are weaker. We're not as strong and we're not as fast. It's obvious. You don't even have to talk about it. So what's this Wonder Woman crap about? Same thing. They're pulling the wool over your eyes. And I know it's not popular to say, but a lot of them are Jews. They're the ones pushing this stuff, and it's because of the money. They put the money first. They know how to make money. Right now, it's women. They want to make James Bond a woman. James Bond a woman? That's about the stupidest thing I ever heard. Or they want to make him a Black. James Bond a Black? If it makes money, they'll do it. They don't care. Let society fall apart. Let Christian values fall apart. They don't care if we lose our values. They don't care if it all falls apart and we can't protect ourselves because we're too busy turning our hair pink and being lesbians and gays, or not even being that, just being someone who won't say they're male or female 'cuz they think it's in their head. Another thing beyond stupid. We can't even say anymore, Look, you got born with two x-es or an x and a y, period, story over—you can't say that anymore. And they want to make laws about it. They want to say you can go into any bathroom you want depending on how you're feeling that day, man or woman, whatever you decide in your head, and that's so stupid it's beyond stupid. How'd we come to this? We came to it because we got too fat and happy, everything easy, no war to fight or hard times, everything good, so stupid white people decide, Hey, we got plenty, let's give some away, and they turned the key and opened the door, and once it was open, naturally, the Blacks came through, and now they got their hands on our throat. What they want, they want to take over. They want everything. They smell blood. Guess what? When it's just them alone, they laugh at how stupid we are. They call our men white boys, or they call us crackers, and no one says a word. Not wrong for them to do that, but if we call them anything we get fired over it. How'd that happen? And bringing people in from other countries. Bringing in Blacks and browns. That's a big part of their plan. Bring them in and give them welfare checks and free health care, which the rest of us don't got, just so's they'll vote against white people. You know what? They want to be the majority. They want to outvote white people. We live in an insane world now. You know why? It has to do with colleges. The colleges is where it starts. The colleges decided all the professors have to be Blacks and minorities and gays and lesbians, and now the kids who go to college learn the craziest stuff. They get propaganda. In every class. Everywhere they go. Propaganda. They tell those college kids, If you're white you oughta feel terrible, and the right thing to do is give all your money to Black people and, oh yeah, Indians. They actually have this con job in Seattle where, if you're white, you write a rent check once a month to this Indian tribe that used to be here. These Indians, they're richer than we are. They got their own special laws where they don't pay taxes and they got their casinos. What's that about? Paying rent to Indians? They're crazy in Seattle. You know what? My daughter and my son-in-law are victims of this stuff. You want me to pretend I'm in court answering questions? All right. You know what I'd say? If they gave me the chance? If they give a stupid hick like me one chance? I'd say I've had it with this trial of yours. I've had it with this game you're playing. That girl had mental illness. She came here from Africa with mental illness. That girl had problems. Number one, she was disrespectful. She didn't know how to behave in a household. Number two, she wouldn't respond to discipline. She went down the wrong road, and she paid for it and died. That's all. She wouldn't come in the house. She's dead because she wouldn't come in the house. My daughter tried everything to get her to come in. But she wouldn't come in. Simple as that. She went outside, she wouldn't come in, she got cold, she froze to death. There isn't any more to it than that. Unless you just want to take some Christians and crucify 'em for being Christian. And white. That's what I'd say if you put me on the stand. That they hate us 'cuz we're Christian and white."

WE GOT IN the car. "I can't put Betsy's mother on the stand," my father said, before his door was even shut. "Contempt of court would come into play."

We left the Huber home behind. Everywhere, the fields were flooded and the forests leafless. The fretwork of meadows under reclamation by thorny brush and interlacing, bare vines rose out of dark, spreading pools. It should have been a pleasure to pass through this area—a country where water had its way in fall and winter—but, for me, a pall lay over these inundated, cold pastures in the wake of Mrs. Huber's tirade. My father couldn't enjoy our drive, either. He shook his head and rubbed his temples. He'd been working long hours for the past three months, getting up in the dark, packing his briefcase, pulling on his overcoat, and walking to a bus stop, and he was now eighty-three years old, which I think he handled by giving in to the delusion that he could deny age the victory it won over others—namely, by slowing them to the point where their accustomed endeavors felt wearisome. He wouldn't allow it. He was going to keep going. "Beyond whatever else was wrong about what Betsy's mother said," he said now, "I'm her daughter's lawyer. I'm trying to do whatever I can to make sure facts see the light of day. Is she against that? Is she against a determination of guilt or innocence made on the basis of the facts of the case? She could have been helpful to her daughter on the stand. She could have told the jurors a lot about Betsy, so they could come to understand her better. But no. She's full of anger instead. The world's a terrible place in her head, filled with terrible, horrible people who are one hundred percent wrong about absolutely everything. That's her whole point when I come to her and say, 'Can you help me put facts in front of the jurors?' Anger instead of anything else. Plus, she was surly to you, and you're my son, so that sort of got to me, too."

It was raining slantwise now—a syncopated tattooing against our windshield. The car rocked leftward in the gusts, and the wipers beat at full throttle. Between that and Mrs. Huber's verbal harshness, I felt agitated behind the wheel. My father, though, fell asleep with his hands in his lap. His right hand rested on top of his left, and they were both ravaged by years. His knees were pulled up, which made his long legs look more spindly than usual. The ribbing on his stockings showed, as did maybe two inches of his chafed shins. His head was down, so that I could see into his scalp through the striae of gray hair he wore swept back over his pate, where there were knobby protuberances, rough patches, liver spots, scars, gouges, and crevices. That's right, sleep, I thought. You need more sleep.

Just before I dropped him off that day, my father dug into his pants pocket, pulled something out, and showed it to me. "What do you call this item?" he asked.

"A thumb drive."

"This thumb drive," he said, "came in the mail from the adoption agency that sent Abigail to the Harveys, and apparently their file is inside of it."

"I see."

"Is it hard to deal with?"

"No."

"It's easy to get the file out?"

"Yes."

"In that case," said my father, "can you do whatever has to be done so I can look at what's inside this thing? I don't want to use up all of your time, so just tell me, if you want, to take a hike."

"It'll take one minute."

"I'm a burden to you," said my father. "I'm an albatross around your neck. Like when I got vertigo in the middle of the night and your mother made you come over."

I knew what he was referring to. He was referring to a phone call I'd gotten from my mother about a year before the events I'm now describing. She called to tell me that, while watching late-night television, she'd heard a thump from the bedroom. After rushing in there (which for her meant limp-ing, because of corns and swollen feet), she'd found that my father had fallen onto the shag-carpeted floor between his bed and a wall. There he was, down in that cavity, grimacing and gesticulating—"thrashing," she said, "through another fit of vertigo." The situation, said my mother, was impossible, as there was no room for her to take the steps needed—which were anyway steps she wasn't capable of anymore, she knew that—no space for her to work her way in there and haul him up onto the mattress, which, again, was something she couldn't do even if such space existed, she didn't have the strength, but nevertheless the circumstances were such that few choices were available, and so she had sought to help him up and in so doing had stepped on her husband "a little" before giving up in the face of it all and calling me instead of continuing to fail, but not before opening the cedar chest at the foot of the bed, tak-ing from it an ancient quilt, draping this over him (probably in a billow of dust, I thought), and then, from the mattress, in a prone position, with no small difficulty, wedging a pillow under his head, thereafter resting a little before picking up the receiver of the turquoise Princess phone on her nightstand—with its forever tangled rat's nest of coiled wire—and calling me while my father, from the floor, still flailing, admonished her with "Don't bother him! It's the middle of the night!" I heard him say this at my end clearly, and after hanging up told Alison that the call was about vertigo and that I had to go to my parents' house, prompting her to ask, "Should I come with you?," the sort of question you ask in response to the premoni-tion that a death is at hand. I understood that, but of course

I said what people always say: "There's no reason, you don't have to come, I'll be right back, it shouldn't take long."

Then I went, on a night in October when, even with the ambient light of a large city compromising things, it was nevertheless possible to make out stars, a night when everything was sparklingly frigid. I drove over the speed limit in the battered little four-cylinder truck Alison and I used as a workhorse in service to domestic projects, but only after girding ourselves, because the traffic in Seattle is horrendous and we're exasperated by the throngs of vehicles now filling up even the snaking back avenues of our onetime circumventings. (Alison and I are confounded by all the changes in the city even while telling ourselves, and each other, that such is life, who are we to complain, there is always someone behind you in history who wishes you never came, there is never a point at which you have an intrinsic right to draw a line and demand that the unceasing, disconcerting, and inevitable fact of change must come to a halt at the doorstep you've come to think of as your own, no, it doesn't work like that, we're all just passing through.)

When I got to my parents' house, there was frost on their lawn, and the lamp on its post by the steps was out, a circumstance I understood was in my hands to improve. Inside, my mother had turned the heat up on the order of a steam bath, and had maneuvered warm socks onto my father's feet, and my father's pallor, where he lay on the floor, was gray, or at least what I could see of him was gray, because for the most part he was swaddled in a quilt of thick batting with a yellowing pattern to the effect of rosebuds, I think, hoary and smelling of mothballs. "His teeth were knocking," my mother told me.

From somewhere in the well beside his bed came my father's voice, in a muffled rasp, saying, "My teeth weren't knocking."

I peeled back the quilt to find my father in his boxer shorts and nothing else, curled on his right side, with his arms wrapped around his shoulders and three curves of rib visible beneath jaundiced-looking skin. I got into the little aisle he lay in by forcing the issue and, back against the wall, picked up my father the way grooms of yore did to carry brides across thresholds, or the way firefighters in advertisements carry limp children from burning houses, and set him down slantwise on his bed before sliding his legs around until he seemed approximately parallel to the bed's edges, and then, in a series of short full-body jumps, maneuvered him by degrees toward the bed's center, where the chances of a second fall were minimized, and where he looked even smaller than he had on the floor, and in doing all of this I grasped, frankly with despair, that he was lukewarm to the touch in the manner of a carton of milk left on a kitchen counter for an hour, but anyway, with two blankets and a quilt over him he came to look like a long dimple beneath a smooth, cottony weight, and seemed "stabilized," as my mother put it, standing alongside with her hands on her hips, redoubtable as always but riven by circumstance, while I, on my side, once things seemed calm, drove home in the dark wondering about my father's lukewarm skin.

Alison, who was awake when I returned—in bed with a lamp on, reading *River of Stars: Selected Poems of Yosano Akiko*—listened to my summary rendition of events, then said, "I'm glad he's all right and it was just his vertigo. Your mom sure stays up late watching television. So they're okay, you think?"

"They're okay, I guess. How's your book?"

"'Concentrated so completely on each other,'" Alison read then, "'I can't tell us apart: you, the white bush clover, from me, the soft white lily.' That's the entire poem right there. The whole thing. Just that."

ON THE NIGHT I returned home from the Hubers' double-wide, I went upstairs to my abandoned garret and opened the thumb drive while sitting in darkness. The files included video footage under the heading "Available Children" that began with two sisters in an orphanage in Ethiopia. They were seated on a threadbare sofa, each with her left leg over her right, each with her hand covering her chin, both smiling when asked to smile, and as they sat this way—nervously—someone, from behind the camera, celebrated their characteristics in English. Next came a girl who'd been there for two weeks—"a nice girl, with no siblings, in the fourth grade, ready to go to fifth"—followed by a girl "who gets good grades at school," by a boy "who is awfully shy and hasn't wanted to say very much," by two siblings new to the orphanage ("such cute girls that we will probably have a family in place for them quickly"), and then by Abigail, her hair tightly braided. "This is Abeba," said whoever was talking. "Abeba is attending sixth grade and seems like a very bright girl, very quick to answer all our questions and learning English quickly. She's got no siblings. Both her parents are deceased, and no relatives have been able to take her, so they brought her here."

Abeba looked self-deprecating in a beaten-down way. The composure in her posture might have been exhaustion. Her humility might have really been defeat. She was thin through the face and, though bedraggled, trying hard not to be, in a jacket with a white fringe collar. Twice she looked down—once, near the beginning of her advertisement, like someone adjusting to the reality of these circumstances wherein her merits and biographical data are selling points; and once, a bit later, when her brightness was extolled. Later, she glanced to her right, where you could infer from her reaction—an eye crease of acknowledgment—that someone off-camera was goading her to smile. Finally, just before the camera shut off—at the conclusion of her advertisement, the formal inter-lude done—Abeba looked relieved. There were dark crescents of sleeplessness under her eyes—eyes conspicuously wide, not in the metaphorical sense of credulity, but literally.

I clicked on another file and opened its first document. A man was identified there as "Solomon Addisu, nearest kin." It was Solomon Addisu who'd brought Abeba to this orphanage. A social worker there had recorded in her intake notes that, according to Solomon Addisu, Abeba was ten and had no sib-lings. Her mother had died when she was one and a half. Her father—his brother, Temesgen Addisu—had been dead for three years. During that time, Abeba had lived with Solomon, whose wife was dead, too, and with Solomon's two daughters and two sons. They lived outside of the town of Sebeta, where Solomon had no work and suffered, at intervals of greater and lesser severity, from tuberculosis. Despite his ill health he grew papayas, teff, and lemons, kept chickens, and sold eggs. His sons and daughters could only find work that was intermittent and paid a subsistence wage, to the point that the family was in arrears and buried in debt to Solomon's sister, who owned the home they lived in. Solomon's sister had told him about a year before that her generosity had to end because of health problems that demanded expensive medicines, but that she knew of an office where a person could find work: a company that hired women to serve as domestics in the Middle East. At that point, Solomon's older daughter, Fasika, went to this company's office. The people there got her a passport and sent her to Kuwait.

They'd thought they had their financial problems solved, Solomon told the social worker. But then Fasika wrote to say that she worked sixteen hours a day for three families in adjacent flats and was passed between them on a rotating basis, after having been told that she would work eight to ten hours a day for just one family; also, her pay wasn't what had been promised. One of the Kuwaitis told her that her wages were less than expected because the Ethiopian middleman who collected them was a thief. This middleman, when Solomon went to talk to him about it, said that the Kuwaitis weren't paying what they were supposed to be paying; that was how things stood, and he was working on it.

The answer to the problem of Fasika's paltry paycheck, Solomon told the social worker, was for his other daughter, Tigist, to also take a job in Kuwait. There, she slept in her employer's maintenance closet. She got strep throat and couldn't work for a while, so they didn't pay her. She got conjunctivitis, too, and her feet developed fungus. Her back itched. Something small bit or stung her at night, leaving welts. Tigist got back on her feet, though, and started working again, but her employer caught her dozing when she was supposed to be working and punished her by putting a blindfold over her eyes and spanking her with a flat length of wood. In sum, Solomon told the social worker, they had little despite his daughters' sacrifices.

Abeba was an orphan, Solomon said, and therefore eligible to live in an orphanage. He'd done what was required to establish that she was an orphan by filling out the right forms and procuring the right signatures and getting seals affixed to everything by the chair of the justice committee in his administrative district, who'd written an official letter, which Solomon was now handing over to the orphanage, a letter stating that the committee had confirmed that Abeba was an orphan. On top of that was a second letter, from the manager of social affairs in the town of Sebeta, and a third letter, stamped by an official of the Alemgena District, stating that here was a letter of proof as to the orphaned status of the girl in question, as required by the Federal Ministry of Women's and Children's Affairs.

Abeba's height, weight, and head circumference were recorded. Her nutritional status was noted as adequate and her developmental status as satisfactory. Abeba had an asymptomatic hepatitis B infection but was HIV-negative. She had not been circumcised. She was calm on intake, with no signs of anxiety. She was conversant in a logical fashion. She didn't put up a wall against the social worker. She was willing and able to talk about how she felt. She said that she didn't want to live in an orphanage but accepted it. She said that she had all manner of dreams about her future. She wanted to be a doctor, but then, no, she didn't. She wanted to be a journalist or a diplomat. She'd gone to school off and on for three years, and liked to read when she had the chance. She had done well in math without enjoying it. She had friends she hoped to see again if circumstances changed and she was able to return home, which is what she preferred and the outcome she hoped for: a return to the life she had lived in Sebeta. Her uncle was kind, but he was sick a lot, and his sons, in her opinion, were shiftless and unmotivated, and didn't take care of the chickens as they should, and didn't try hard enough in general at what they undertook, if they undertook anything. Which made no sense to Abeba, because she believed in the importance of making efforts. She believed in doing what needed to be done. She was an Orthodox Christian, she told the social worker, who kept feast days and fast days and paid respects to all the saints but in particular to Saint Gabriel and Saint George, praying consistently for their intercessions on her behalf, but even with that she believed in taking initiative on every front, no matter what, always, in a determined way, and despite obstacles.

The file I was looking at included a copy of the photo ID page from Abeba's Ethiopian passport; a copy of the birth certificate she was issued by the City Government of Addis Ababa on the cusp of her adoption (whereon her name appears as Abigail Delvin Harvey); and a copy of a judicial decision rendered by a judge in the Federal First Court asserting that he was "convinced of the benefits the aforementioned child would enjoy if raised under the care and protection of adoptive parents rather than in said orphanage," and "convinced that the Ministry of Women's and Children's Affairs has ascertained and confirmed the personal, social, and economic status of the adoptive parents as reliable to raise a child in a good manner," and adding that, as "nearest kin has been summoned to court and agrees to such adoption," he was now issuing an order pursuant to the matter, approving the contract between the petitioners. There was also a letter in the file from the minister-in-chief of the Ministry of Women's and Children's Affairs, notifying the agency that, "based on website information recently developed, we are aware that the child Abigail Delvin Harvey (named by adoptive parents) was found dead, and we hereby urge you to provide information concerning conditions, along with medical results, police investigation reports, as well as other essential information with tangible evidences." This was followed by another letter, sent three days later by the same minister, stating that the agency was "urgently required to submit a death report with medical and police evidence," and by a third letter, sent another three days later—this one from the director of children's rights and safety—reminding the adoption agency that "a detailed report over the death of the child Abeba Temesgen was recently requested," and that "accordingly it was found that a concerned staff member of our office shall, along with you, personally investigate the death of the child." This was followed by a letter from the chief criminal deputy prosecutor of Skagit County to the adoption agency's head office in Seattle, reading, in part, "Concerning the request for information regarding the circumstances of Abigail Harvey's death, please be advised, and please relay to the appropriate Ethiopian authorities, that an investigation is currently ongoing, and as is the case with any other law enforcement agency and prosecutor's office in this country, we will not reveal, or in any way discuss, facts, circumstances, suppositions, or anything else regarding the investigation until the investigation is complete."

I opened another file. There was a letter in it from the director of the Children's Rights and Safety Office in Addis

Ababa to the director of the orphanage, informing her that he was sending a representative to "undertake an investigation regarding the death of Abeba Temesgen, who was held in your care prior to release for adoption and subsequent death, the purpose being to determine if there exists relevant information on the premises to incorporate." Like all of the administrative documents in every file, it had been translated into English by a private service that fell short, and stood behind a copy in Amharic.

I COULD INFER some things. One of the social workers on the premises of the orphanage, Elsabet Tesfaye, had been trained both to fulfill an administrative function and to interact with institutionalized children. It was her job not only to process the paperwork generated in volume by international adoptions, and to see to it that every requisite document found its way to the appropriate repositories, cabinets, ministries, offices, and authorities, but also to mill about in the orphanage's play areas and in its dormitories and cafeteria, where she engaged children in conversation, invited them to her office for consultation, or sat with them in private corners for informal dialogue.

The representative of the Ethiopian government's Children's Rights and Safety Office tasked with discovering if there was information on the premises pertinent to the death of Abeba Temesgen found his way to Elsabet Tesfaye and demanded a written report containing all relevant information. Tesfaye then duly reported that, as far as she knew "from consultation and social work with the deceased child," Abeba Temesgen had been born in the province of Bale in 1998 to a mother who died eighteen months subsequent to her birth, leaving her in the care of her father, Temesgen Addisu. Temesgen Addisu had passed the bulk of his life in Addis Ababa but had fled to Bale after three of his sons were killed under circumstances that threatened to include him, too, if he didn't leave. He'd gone to Bale because he thought he had a half brother there—a half brother who, it turned out, was dead—and eventually acquired, after years of making bricks in a factory and transporting, erecting, and dismantling construction scaffolding, a seven-room hotel that, in Abeba's memory of it, was a slatternly hovel, and baked in the sun at an arid crossroads when it wasn't inundated by floodwaters. Her father had added to this dilapidated hotel a dirt-floored terrace, shaded by lengths of corrugated tin, where guests and travelers were served tea, coffee, bread, bottled soft drinks, bottled beer, popcorn, and nuts, and where a television was always on.

Abeba's father hired a woman crooked toward the earth and canted to one side—a woman who'd run away from a husband in the countryside—who acted as cook and maid in the hotel, and with whom Abeba slept nightly. That woman moved on, and another one came, and then another and another, all of whom Abeba loitered with in the kitchen and followed about and assisted until harsh events, still vivid in her memory during her time at the orphanage, began to unfold. Shortly after the last of the hotel maids ran away, she told Elsabet Tesfaye, and near the start of the dry season, she began to hear gunfire sporadically in the distance, sometimes in staccato, isolated bursts, other times through interludes of hours—muffled reports or blasts echoing off the mountains or the noise of a cascading and then crescendoing fusillade. Over the course of weeks, this din drew closer, and a stream of people, including children, began to straggle past on foot, some of them blank-faced, some with their heads down and carrying loads so that Abeba couldn't see their faces, some driving goats, some perched or slumped on the backs of trucks, some in carts drawn by donkeys, even a man pulling behind him a camel through whose lip a ring was threaded, the better to coerce the beast forward by the tensioning of a lead rope run through the ring at one end and, at the other, clutched in his fist. All who stopped outside the hotel's gate were let in and allowed to sit on the shaded terrace, and given water at no charge, and *injera* and *shiro* as long as they could pay for it, and invited to rest before traveling on, but none were allowed to stay overnight who couldn't pay the rate (anyway, the rooms were taken), and before dark they all had to move along, because, as Abeba's father repeatedly told the people on the terrace, he would be overwhelmed otherwise and go out of business; there was no way around this, and it had to be understood. When night fell, he forced the last hopeless stragglers out under threat and locked the gate and the door to the hotel, and watched from a window suspiciously for hours. Maybe it was this locking of the gate, Abeba suggested to Elsabet Tesfaye, that angered people in the town two kilometers to the west and in the hamlet a kilometer and a half to the east, or it could have been other things, any number of things she would never understand, but at any rate, an anger toward her father developed with the coming of the refugees, and with it a current of threat that broke into open conflict, all this while the battles in the mountains went on, which meant her father had to stay up at night to confront enemies throwing rocks and shards of concrete, and yelling at him in the dark, and banging sticks against the walls of the hotel while Abeba lay awake in her bed.

Days passed. News emitted from the television on the terrace until the television lost its signal and the gunfire was so close that Abeba slept, thereafter, under her bed and behind sandbags her father arranged in tiers, which turned out to be useless when men without uniforms arrived in a convoy of jeeps and trucks and appropriated the hotel simply by walking in with automatic weapons, either in their hands or on their backs, and with machetes and scythes, and telling Abeba and her father to leave, an eventuality or inevitability her father had prepared for by concealing his cash in intimate locations—some in his shoe, some sewn into his trousers, some sewn into his shirt, some in a suitcase tied shut with hemp twine. As they were leaving, Abeba tried to herd away their goats, but the goats were appropriated almost immediately by a man who kicked her in the small of the back so violently that, in falling, she struck the shardlike stub of what had once been a power stanchion, gashing her forehead open and instigating a headache that caused swimming vision in her left eye.

Abeba was eight at this point. She scuttled away with a hand to her forehead while her father hauled the suitcase onto his shoulder. They made their way to the nearest town with the idea of catching a bus, it didn't matter which one; the main thing now was to leave this area, her father said, before things got worse. As it turned out, places to stand or sit on buses were available, suddenly, only to those who could pay the most for them, which meant that Abeba's father had to give up a lot of money; this happened again three hours later, in a larger town—an exorbitant price was demanded for a bus ride—but as they were farther from the trouble now, Abeba's father elected to hold his cash in reserve and walk once more, which they did, at first through this town Abeba had never seen before, where the schools were still open, and the government offices and the police station, and where her father bought biscuits, which they ate in an alley against an embankment before turning northward, out of winding streets, into a dry waste of weeds and strewn garbage. Here Abeba saw the carcass of a goat with meager, gray strings of meat still on its bones. Wherever there was meat were massed green flies.

Abeba's head wound oozed as they traveled. She doused it when she could. They walked in the sun and rested in snatches. Four men surrounded them as they approached a hamlet, demanding payment of a toll, and scoffing at Abeba's father when he claimed to have no money before throwing him to the ground and prying off his shoes, wherein they found the segment of his cash supply he'd concealed there and stole it, although one of the men took pity on them by dropping to the ground a flurry of small notes—enough, maybe, to buy some canned or packaged goods later.

When they were gone, Abeba's father rose from the dust with some of it coating his hair and one side of his face, where pebbles were embedded. He cradled his left wrist in his right hand, and said he thought that his arm had been broken when he'd been thrashed to the ground, and indeed, it appeared so, as if his wrist were held to his arm only by slack cords, and as if his hand no longer worked in cooperation or coordination with the rest of him and was instead a disjointed appendage. Abeba's father splinted his fracture along two lengths of stiff plastic he found discarded on the road verge that might have once been chair parts, cutting free some of the twine that held the suitcase shut so that he had a length of it with which to bind these staves from his palm to his elbow, top and bottom both, and needing help from Abeba for this one-handed maneuver, during which he also used his teeth and a foot. Triaged sufficiently, he nevertheless could no longer raise the suitcase to his shoulder without Abeba's help, or lower it to the ground again. He was anyway a man of fifty, with ropy cords in his neck, ears that stuck out of his skull, and joints swollen by a generalized arthritis and by fallout from youthful rickets. He weighed fifty kilos, spread out over a stiltlike frame of about a meter and three quarters. With one arm broken, and carrying the suitcase over his shoulder in humidity and heat, he was forced to rest often in shade with his bones against the earth, and in silence except for his breathing, and in stillness except for the rising and falling of his chest, while Abeba picked at grass, watched ants, scratched her mosquito bites, rubbed her gashed forehead, and, on one occasion, unknotted the cord that kept shut the suitcase and opened it on its corroded hinges. Inside, among the items of clothing, lay an envelope stiffened by water-bottle plastic cut and flattened to protect seven photographs. She examined these. They were photographs of her father's family from when he lived in the capital. All of the people in them were gone now, he'd told her more than once. His wife, Amsala, had died of kidney disease. His youngest child, Mulumebet, had died from fever. Beyene, who worked on the Dire Dawa–Djibouti train, was killed when it derailed. Beruke, Fikru, and Itzak had been shot in the street. Abeba put the photos away and helped her father to stand. That night, a trio of robbers accosted them where they lay in a depression off the road and took the suitcase, inside of which, besides the seven photographs, was another portion of their money.

Thereafter, Abeba's father took little initiative beyond putting one foot in front of the other until, after three days of walking with little food, they neared a city whose name Abeba remembered while telling Elsabet Tesfaye her story, a name, Shashamene, that stuck in her head because, she said, it was pretty. On the verge of Shashamene, then, they rested beneath a tree by a cistern while on the road before them donkeys bore water in both directions, slapped on their hind ends by boys with sticks, one of whom stopped and gave them water when Abeba called to him pleading for it, and stayed with them while his donkey took the shade as well, and removed from his pants a wad of khat and poked it in his mouth and spit for a while, and then asked if they were hungry, following this by producing a pouch of boiled pasta alongside chunks of goat meat going bad, and giving them half of it and eating the other half before continuing on his way. This was proof, Abeba had told Elsabet Tesfaye, that not everyone is bad.

She and her father took a room in Shashamene, where mosquitoes had their way with them, and where the electricity was jittery and intermittent, and where the cockroaches hardly skittered away when the lights came on. In the morning, they spent almost half of their remaining money for seats on a bus going north to Ziway, where they got off and, as luck would have it, almost immediately found a ride in the bed of a truck, sunk low under a heaped load, to which they clung alongside other riders. This load was composed of a powder of some kind that had been pressed into sacks so efficiently and tightly that the sacks would not deform when sat on. They emitted a caustic odor as the truck made its way over potholes underneath a sun that, as the hours wore on, drew from the powder, Abeba said, an odor that made her sick to her stomach. She and her father climbed off when the truck turned south, toward Butajira, and began to walk again, northward.

They ran out of money. Her father became unsure of their location or direction, and suffered from dizziness and swollen lymph nodes. But at last, after walking for three days, they came into a fallow field of dry furrows where a man with a chicken under his arm said they'd indeed found their way to the vicinity of Sebeta, and coaxed them up and led them to a police station, where Abeba's father inquired regarding the location of his brother, Solomon Addisu, who after a few hours came for them in a cart pulled by a donkey, bringing along a water jug and a bag filled with bananas, mangoes, eggs, biscuits, and a box of toasted corn.

ABEBA'S FATHER DIED a half year later, after a period of lassitude and dry heaves. She'd noticed that he sat a lot, tired and short of breath, and got sick to his stomach easily, and then, during the rainy season, he'd complained of headaches, and woke one morning and couldn't see straight anymore, and then he lost all feeling in his left hand—the one made useless when robbers broke his wrist—and went to bed in daylight. The next evening he curled on his left side, facing the wall, and died.

Abeba told Elsabet Tesfaye that, for the next two years, her life was stable. In the compound where she lived with her uncle's family, she chased after chickens and held pullets in her arms, or wrapped them in her shirt so that only their heads showed, or hung around the tap to help her cousins launder, or hung around the garden pulling weeds, or hung around the wood shop or the granary or the kitchen, which was out of doors, beneath a thatched roof. Sometimes she played with a neighbor boy named Tensaye. They knelt by the tap, rolling clay balls and lobbing them over a wattle fence. They visited neighbors, built dams across rivulets, kicked mud, raised dust, thrashed in brush, and booted a half-deflated soccer ball. They were bound by one rule—don't cross the stream. They crossed it anyway, when the water was low enough, and wandered in hills where juniper, olive, and yellowwood trees stood in scattered groves, and where red acanthus and wild figs grew. Sometimes they tracked bushbucks through thick bands of acacia, mainly to hear them snort or watch them browse.

For school, Abeba had to have a uniform, a book bag, exercise books, a box of pencils, and money to rent texts, all of which her uncle provided so she could attend Gethsemane Primary Academy, which lay on the north side of the road to Jimma and was owned and operated by an order of nuns. Each morning, Abeba walked to Gethsemane with her neighbor Tensaye. They stood in the bare earth yard outside a run of low classrooms, the classes lined up behind marks on the ground, while the national anthem played over a loudspeaker and the flag of Ethiopia was raised alongside the flag of Oromia. A teacher next read news aloud. Then they went inside, and classes started. There were seven classes of forty-five minutes each—English, Amharic, science, math, sports, art, and music—taught by nuns who wore the garb nuns wear and were often strict, as nuns can be, and lived in a nunnery uphill from the school, which the children never visited, and showed up each morning wearing sandals and socks along with their tunics, scapulars, and cowls.

Abeba sometimes had homework, sometimes not, but the main thing was, she told Elsabet Tesfaye, that in school her ability to read improved, so that, when she arrived home, her interest, now, was in reading what was close at hand—newspapers, the Bible, and books she borrowed from neighbors. She preferred reading to playing outside, and began to keep a record of her reactions to what she read, and a record, too, of her daily activities. Not having a bound diary in which to write, she scrawled on sheets of exercise-book paper, tore them out, and put them in a box.

Abeba had a strong memory of something. One night, just down the road, between where Uncle Solomon's house stood and the hills of scattered acacia began, a pack of hyenas moved in to consume, in a riot of noise, the flesh, blood, offal, and bones of a calf they'd killed. Uncle Solomon went to look and returned to report that the beasts were too absorbed in their meal to pose a threat, upon which news the whole family ventured out. A lot of people were already on the scene. They formed a ring and made an arena, at the center of which a savage scene unfolded that held everybody with a kind of magnetism. The throng of spectators went four or five deep, so that children like Abeba couldn't see what was going on. Uncle Solomon lifted her onto his shoulders. People were yelling and jumping in place, waving torches, and brandishing knives. The calf had toppled onto its side with its hind legs askew, and the hyenas were snarling over it with bloody fangs. After a while, Abeba pulled her uncle's hair and said she wanted him to put her down. He settled her on his arm for a moment, and she told him that, in her opinion, everyone should look away while the hyenas ate the calf. Elsabet Tesfaye stopped Abeba in the midst of her recounting of this event to ask why that was so. It was so, said Abeba, because the spectacle of the hyenas and the calf bespoke evil. Why did people want to look at this, what were they so excited about, when, inside *her,* the spectacle of the hyenas and the calf elicited sadness? She'd had the sinking feeling, hurrying home, leaving everybody else behind, running, finally, with tears blurring her vision, that something was wrong with people. You would think, she told Elsabet Tesfaye, that people were better than that.

ABEBA HAD "strong maternal instincts," Elsabet Tesfaye recorded in her notes. She gravitated, on the playground, in the direction of toddlers. She held their hands, wiped their noses, consoled them when they cried, pushed them on the swings, met them at the bottom of the slide, and poised herself to catch them should they fall from the play equipment. She pulled up their pants and tucked in their shirts. She read to them, pointing at pictures. She perched them on her shoulders, swung them in her arms, braided their hair, and brushed the dust from their legs and arms. She let them chase her, and she let herself be caught. She sang to them, and played a game with them called "corkies." You stacked up bottle caps, Abeba explained to Elsabet, and if they toppled, you had to stand against a wall while kids threw soccer balls at you.

Abeba was a calm presence, Elsabet Tesfaye wrote, calm

in the sense of mature and reasonable, not given to emotional extremes in front of other children, not acting out or in need of discipline, known to others as a prodigious reader, someone who refused invitations to games in favor of a book, someone who bowed out of games in favor of reading, someone who read on her bed and in the cafeteria and on the playground. She didn't engage in squabbles or conflicts. She saw feuds and arguments as dead ends in which the consequences of resolving a problem by such means were more damaging than the problem itself. Math was her weakest subject, because her heart wasn't in it; she excelled, though, in civics and English. She was an adequate soccer player. She was a moderately good jump roper. She was interested in the foreigners who came to the orphanage on missions she was curious about—people who volunteered or donated or were there in a professional or charitable capacity. She watched them come and go mostly, but sometimes sought to speak with them, making use of what English she had when it turned out a visitor spoke English, otherwise surrendering to circumstances and receding into observation of their mannerisms, voices, gestures, and clothing, their gaits or the way they climbed stairs, their bags, purses, backpacks, and phones, the clips or bands they wore in their hair, their vials of hand wash, sunscreen, and insect repellent, their sunglasses and umbrellas, their bracelets, necklaces, tattoos, and makeup, their shoes, their laptop computers, their expressions, their gesticulations, their laughter at times. She followed them about on tours and listened, from a distance, to what their guide said—that children slept generally eleven to a room with a nanny present overnight, and that their sheets and clothing were washed once a week, and that they showered regularly and ate healthy breakfasts, and that each had been issued not only two sheets, a towel, a pillow, and a bedspread, but also a donated stuffed animal. The tour guide introduced the visitors to children by stating a child's name, age, and former place of residence, as in "This is Meron, age nine, from Gondar," and "This is Marta, age eleven, from Harar." When the time was right, the foreigners broke for liquid refreshment in the cafeteria, where the tour guide always spoke at length, explaining, for example, that the orphanage had once sought to save money by buying cows, slaughtering them, and freezing their meat for use in the kitchen, but that this had turned out to be a bad practice, because power outages were frequent, and gas for the generator was at intervals in short supply, so the meat would thaw and go rancid before they could use it, which meant that they needed larger reserve fuel tanks and a more efficient generator than they had, since the current one balked regularly and was old. When the visitors were finished in the cafeteria, the tour moved upstairs, to a room where chairs were arranged in a semicircle, and where the visitors were each handed a baby and given a bottle to feed it from, and where babies lay in cribs along the walls and toddlers sat in plastic potty chairs, and where the tour guide illuminated certain stellar cases—for example, in this very room, she said, there was once a child so tiny he literally fit in the palm of my hand and was supposed to die and had no chance, but then a Dutch woman appeared who wanted to volunteer at our orphanage and was determined that this boy would live and believed that she could make this happen by tucking him against her chest and keeping him there, which she did, said the tour guide, so that the boy survived, and he is more than a year old now, and in fact sitting in the lap of the woman three chairs to the right of me at this very moment. Then all traveled down the hall to the special-needs room, where there were children in donated wheelchairs.

Elsabet Tesfaye noted that among the volunteers at the orphanage there'd been a French woman adept at knitting. Abeba had sat with her frequently, watching. They had no language by which to communicate, but the French woman was good at demonstrating, and eventually put needles in Abeba's hands and stood behind her, guiding the movements of those needles, and let Abeba knit, which she enjoyed, and it was too bad, Elsabet Tesfaye wrote—though it also made sense—that Abeba couldn't have needles of her own, or yarn, even though both were offered as gifts by the French woman, because advantages of that sort caused trouble in the orphanage, where no child was allowed to have more than the next.

WHAT IS IT like in America? was a question strongly on Abeba's mind once the processes of her adoption were set in motion. Elsabet Tesfaye had to say she didn't know, but that, since it was a country larger than Ethiopia, it had to have variety in its cultures and regions, there had to be different realities there, just as there were different realities here—people with enough or more than enough, people with close to little or even nothing, people who liked what their government did and people who didn't and people in between, in all those ways, it had to be like Ethiopia, though, on the other hand, it had to be different. Regarding those differences, Elsabet couldn't be helpful—all she knew was what she saw on the news or read

about in newspapers—and as for the videos Abeba had seen
in the cafeteria alongside other children, she shouldn't assume
that they depicted life as it was lived by Americans. Elsabet
was sure that those videos were false and that there was nothing to be learned from what was in them, that those shows
had to be like all the other shows—illusions, entertainments—
and said nothing real about America. Elsabet *could* say that
she had met Americans in the course of performing her duties
in the orphanage and found them no different from Austra-
lians or Canadians, or from British people, or from German
or Dutch people, really from any of the Westerners who visited, not any better dressed or any louder or quieter, not more
polite or more rude, not any more ignorant or enlightened
about things, not standing out in some particular way—except
for one thing. A higher percentage of Americans, she noticed,
were Christians, not Christians in the way that Ethiopians were
Christians but Christians nonetheless, which they made clear
to her by referring to God and Jesus when they spoke, references Elsabet generally did not hear made by visitors who
came from elsewhere. In sum, it might be the case that Abeba
was going to a particularly religious country. Beyond that,
Elsabet didn't want to speculate. Still, though, it was okay for
Abeba to dream. Okay to hope for a good country and a good
life, as long as you didn't take your hope so far that reality,
when it came, was ruined by expectation. That was something
you could do to yourself. You could leave with dreams and
expectations that by their nature were counter to your own
best interest. Better to go with an open mind and take what
comes and see what you can make of it. That was what Elsabet
told Abeba. And it was tempered advice, essentially optimis-

tic. But in me, reading it, and reading it again, eight thousand miles away in my garret—on a December night lit, outside my window, by holiday bulbs and yard lamps on posts—the irony of it provoked sadness.

ABEBA KNEW PEOPLE in the orphanage it was difficult to say goodbye to. There was a girl named Kassech she thought of as her best friend, who had no family and therefore no visitors on Sundays, when the families of other children came to visit; a girl named Kalkidan who slept in the next bed; a girl named Emebet who also liked to read; and a girl named Samwarit who was also from Sebeta and who had also gone to the Gethsemane school. They all slept in the same dormitory. They had all seen other children leave, and been to their goodbye parties, and watched the vans pull out bearing them away. There was a nanny Abeba was fond of, too, and a teacher who'd loaned her books to read, and a woman who hung laundry in the courtyard who also liked to read and had suggested to Abeba a novel called *Fikr Eske Mekabr* by Haddis Alemayehu, claiming that it was very famous and should be read by everyone and that it was so beautiful that it would make her cry. It was about young people who fall in love, the young man a tutor and a poet, the young woman possessed of great intelligence and beauty, the two warding off parental disapproval and an onslaught of social condemnation. The laundress had given *Fikr Eske Mekabr* to Abeba, handing it to her with the warning that it had been written for adults and was sad. With these caveats in mind, Abeba hadn't opened it, but brought it instead to Elsabet Tesfaye to ask her opinion—should she read this book or not? Elsabet had answered, By all means, yes, because if it's beyond you in terms of what you can understand, so what, you'll still take something from it, and if it's sad, so what, too, you already know about sadness, there can't be anything in the book sadder than what you already know.

THE LAST THING WAS to say goodbye to Uncle Solomon. On the day she was to leave for the airport, he came to Elsabet Tesfaye's office, took off his hat, and sat down beside Abeba. With the two of them in front of her, Elsabet could see plainly that they were relatives: both had conspicuously wide-set eyes, tapering fingers, and narrow shoulders, and both had calm, reserved demeanors and spoke with the same quiet clarity. Solomon had brought Abeba a necklace, a pair of earrings, and an envelope with photographs in it of her father, himself, his sons, his daughters, the neighbor boy named Tensaye she used to play with, the exterior of the home she'd lived in with Solomon and his family, and, finally, a photo of Abeba herself, squatting by the water tap inside their compound, wearing plastic zoris. If I had better pictures I would give them to you, he said, but these are what I have. Then he turned each of the photographs over and showed Abeba the dates he had written there, and the names and ages of people he'd inscribed, before sliding all of it back into the envelope and handing it to her.

Uncle Solomon held Abeba's hand. He said that he knew the story of her life from the beginning, having heard the missing parts from her father, and that he remembered seeing her for the first time in the police station when he'd come for them after their sojourn from Bale, and that on first impression it had seemed to him a good sign that Abeba was in a strong condition after so much travail, not as beaten down as she might have been after what she'd been through. He remembered that she picked at a large scab on her forehead and ate bananas in the donkey cart as they made their way to his house, and that she drank a lot of water at first and slept a lot and ate all they put in front of her, but within two days seemed recovered enough to play outside and look around the garden and poke her nose into things. Anyway, said Uncle Solomon, we all loved you right away. How could we not? As far as I'm concerned, you're my daughter every bit as much as my other daughters; I feel the same about you as I do about them, not one bit different, exactly the same. I've watched you go to school in your uniform. I've watched you feed our chickens and gather their eggs and water our garden. I've been ill a lot, and you've shown me gentleness. But the main thing I want to say is that if things were different and better for me, I would never have sent you here, to this orphanage. I would have kept you at home, because I love you like a daughter, but also, selfishly, because you help our family. Keeping you at home might have been better for me in the long run, and I thought about that a lot and prayed about it, because, really, there was no right answer, there were only these bad circumstances in which it seemed to me that the time would come when you would have to go do what your cousins have to do in Kuwait, and live like that, and be treated like that, and be spit on and beaten, and when I thought about that, and understood you had an option, that there was something possible for you not possible for them, then I came to accept that I could not be selfish, and that if I loved you I had to lead you toward a better life, and that's the reason I brought you here, Abeba, not because I didn't love you. I don't want you to go away with the thought in your head that I didn't love you, or that I abandoned you, that somehow you were the last thing on my mind and the easiest burden to drop, that I brought you here because it was convenient for me, an easy way to lessen a problem, a means of making my own life easier, when the fact is, bringing you here has made me feel like your betrayer. I've second-guessed myself about it. I've wondered if I did the right thing. Is it better for you to have what you have now, this opportunity in another country, or is it better for you to be with the people who will always love you no matter what?

Uncle Solomon's eyes welled. I made a choice, he said, on your behalf. I love you, Abeba. May you be blessed.

He was quiet then, and tearful. It was Abeba's turn to speak. Uncle Solomon, she said, I'm going away, but only for a while. I'm going to live with Americans, but I'm never going to forget about you. Is that what you think? Well, it isn't true. I'm coming back to Ethiopia one day. We're going to see each other again. Wait and see, Abeba said. I'm going to return and take care of you.

Trial

The Harvey trial unfolded in a bland summer heat wave that shimmered across the fields of the Skagit Delta. In the courtroom, the hum of air conditioning was heard daily. The louvered blinds were always closed. The fluorescent lights were always on, and the wood surfaces always shone. Each morning, the stenographer entered carrying her stenograph, while behind her a clerk wheeled a cartful of documents. The gallery filled, the lawyers entered, and the accused were brought forth, grimly, by deputies. The bailiff, curtly, told us all to rise, and at last the judge emerged from her chambers. Perched high on her bench at the epicenter of symmetries, she banged her gavel underneath the pronouncement FIAT JUSTITIA emblazoned below the ceiling trim.

Each morning of that trial, I roused myself at five, collected my father, and sped him in the course of seventy-five minutes to the front doors of the Skagit County Courthouse in Mount Vernon, where that cannon sat mounted between wooden carriage wheels with no plaque or placard explaining its provenance. I passed through the courthouse metal detector and sat, with others, in the courtroom gallery. Many of them were veterans of a sort. They were there because murder trials constitute a spectacle. Things that are nakedly true about humans, however ugly, were real and on the table. It was reality television without the television. Other people, though, were there for other reasons. For example, women who were, like Abeba Temesgen, Ethiopian in origin, all of them dressed in white, gauzy garb, all of them sitting shoulder to shoulder, and all of them making clear by their presence that this set of circumstances was so wrong and untenable that if justice wasn't done in response to it, it would have to mean and could only mean that right and wrong are so upended in the United States as to have no useful or realistic meaning. This band of women, in shawls so thin that light passed through their interstices, were counterbalanced by a cadre of white evangelical Christians, who looked equally firm in a faithful conviction—namely, that Delvin and Betsy Harvey were victims of liberal progressive ideology and, in their pain and suffering, martyrs.

On the one hand, the State, a disembodied monolith, abstract but present with intimidating gravity; on the other, two people who in their flesh and blood stood accused of terrible and unacceptable transgressions. It made for drama of an age-old cast, and we, in the gallery, whatever our sentiments, participated in it by bearing witness. The defendants, their attorneys, and the prosecutor for the State—all of them were literally turned away from us. We saw only their backs; they saw us not at all. I sometimes thought things should be reconfigured, so that somehow everyone could see everyone else—that we should look into the faces of the accused, and at their lawyers' faces, and at the prosecutor's, and that they, in turn, should look into ours. But that was not to be. We bore witness without it. But surely, I thought, they still felt us there, immediately at their backs, close, bearing down, like a Greek chorus or a communal tribunal.

It was otherwise when it came to the judge and jurors. From a kind of summit, and from a far remove, the judge had no choice but to look down on us, and we had no choice but to look up at her, and to wonder who she was, what she thought, what she felt, her convictions, her doubts, her sense of the law, her moral vision and its inevitable ambiguities— inevitable because, beneath her robes, she was, like us, human. Her name was Mary Ann Rasmussen. She was only visible from the shoulders up as she presided from the bench. She looked small there, an effect I knew was magnified by the black judicial gown hanging from her shoulders. Judge Rasmussen often studied documents while people spoke. When she did raise her head, it was to say something terse. At those moments, her face came into view. It was an open face, intelligent and homespun. But, as I said, for the most part she kept her head down, maintaining a cogitator's undistracted privacy. It seemed to me that, the more challenging a legal question, the more interested she was in it. A truly problematic legal hairsplitting elicited from her a long, suspenseful silence during which it was possible to infer that she was working through shades of meaning at speed. Judge Rasmussen was in the habit of looking at people over the rims of reading glasses. She was also in the habit of tapping her pen against the bench while dressing down attorneys. For the most part, she manifested a deep well of patience. On the other hand, she had her limits.

Most judges know perfectly well that attorneys are going to waste their time with meaningless motions and niggling objections, but there's a point at which even the most patient judge has had enough, and when an attorney hit it in Judge Rasmussen's courtroom, she abruptly swung off her reading glasses and launched a caustic fusillade of barbs.

But back to us, bearing witness from the gallery. Mary Ann Rasmussen had to take note of our presence. In principle, we had nothing to say; in reality, we had only to show up to speak. There was a moment when the evidence became so horrifying that, from the women of Ethiopian descent, weeping could be heard. At this, Judge Rasmussen, gavel in hand, issued the requisite reprimand: "You are not participants in these proceedings. You are observers. And if you can't keep your opinions to yourself, you'll have to leave." But did she feel that way? Was the weeping in the gallery nothing to her? Did she quash weeping in the gallery with no remorse about it? Was she placating, or mollifying, the two defense attorneys? Was her motive to ensure that, in the trial transcript, she would appear to have acted with such rigorous exactitude that nothing she'd done laid the grounds for appeal? Was she doing what she had to do to avoid a mistrial? Was she, while issuing her reprimand, a sterner person than she knew herself to be, in the name of demonstrating impartiality? Did she wish, via harshness, to engender regret, specifically in Delvin Harvey's attorney, who'd goaded her to this act of frank admonishment? Was her point in being forbidding and severe to indicate emphatically that none could accuse her of manifesting a political bent, that none could appropriately or rightly say, "Judge Rasmussen, you're a politically correct ideologue who looks down on fundamentalists and shows favoritism to people who came here from Ethiopia"? "No," Judge Rasmussen's warning about weeping maybe said, "here is proof to the contrary; fair is fair and will always be fair; no one weeps in my courtroom, period; it doesn't matter who they are or where they're from; this is America, and we live by these ideals, and if you don't get it, what I'm doing, then you have some learning to do." Is that what it was?

The jurors sat at a right angle to us, so that mainly we saw the left sides of their faces. How rapidly they embraced their roles, and became ciphers, and gathered to themselves a silent magnitude, and seemed, at least, to ignore our presence feet away, and distanced themselves by refusing to acknowledge us—so willingly did they engage the law's purposes for them that they receded and appeared like actors. But still we were there, in the corners of their eyes at least, bearing witness.

I didn't miss any of the trial, not even jury selection. I watched and listened to every witness. I sat there guessing what the jurors were thinking. I tried to read the mind of the judge, who, high on her bench, appeared removed from the proceedings. She was a mystery to me. So were the jurors. The prosecutor, on the other hand, was transparent, as was Delvin Harvey's attorney. So was my father, but differently, because I knew him. The parties to the battle were overt and explicit, whereas the judge and jury were sealed off and expressionless. It felt, to me, the way it does when two magnets, charges aligned, refuse to be joined in wavering, occult fashion. On the one hand, effusiveness, drama, assertion; on the other, the silence of an enforced neutrality. The seven days of that trial were dark and procedural, with the pace of something that refused to unfold, with the sense of something outside of living, and with a quality of interminable, idiotic sadness. A desert onto which blood had been spilled. An interregnum outside of time wherein things felt despoiled, blank.

TO BEGIN at the beginning, 180 citizens lined up for jury selection. They filled the folding chairs in Hearing Room A, where there was a flag in the corner, twin speakers on stands, a rolling whiteboard, and a portable projector screen. Their winnowing began. By the end of the first day, the field had been cut in half. By the end of the second, fifty-eight remained. On the third day, God and religion were broached, at which point someone asserted that if selected she would be "used by God in an appropriate way." This was followed by alternative avowals. "As an atheist, I have a negative reaction to religion." "I believe God wants me to follow the rules."

One man said that photos of a dead child would make him feel vengeful. Another said he'd been beaten as a boy—head-slammed, locked in a cellar, and deprived of food by an alcoholic father. A woman, in a cloud of outrage, gathering her things, said she didn't believe in spanking children, and that she was "pretty emotional and couldn't presume them innocent." By the noon recess on the third day, there were thirty people left. "They spanked me at school, so I'm used to it," one of them revealed. Another admitted he knew perfectly well that when he denied his kids dinner they were going "to hit the fridge at night." A woman confessed that, after losing track of her daughter in a Walmart, she'd "felt like putting a leash on her." A man told the court about a boy he knew who'd been locked in a room regularly because otherwise he poured honey and ketchup on the floor; he was "straightened out" now, a paramedic in the navy.

Fifteen jurors were announced at the end of the third day. Three of them, the judge said, would have no part in the verdict, though she couldn't say which yet; before deliberating, they would draw straws to find out. One juror was retired from both the military and an oil company. Another was in construction. A third worked for Diebold, and a fourth was a program analyst for an educational service district. A fifth was a high-school math teacher, a sixth an electrician, a seventh an online bookseller, an eighth a homemaker, formerly a legal secretary, who now sold art on the side. The other seven were an employee of a poultry company, a logger, a bookkeeper at an oil refinery, a diesel mechanic, a data engineer, a lab technician, and a trucking consolidator. Eight were women and seven were men. All of them were white, as were the judge, the prosecutor, the two defense attorneys, and the two defendants.

DAY FOUR. The prosecutor rose. He was a Democrat with a long jaw named Lincoln Stevens. No doubt he'd been asked a thousand times about his name, since it sounded so illustrious and historically pregnant. You couldn't blame someone for believing they'd heard it before, maybe in the context of the American Civil War—wasn't there somebody named Lincoln Stevens who'd done something or other in that bleak era? The answer was no. I was present once for a conversation my father had with Lincoln Stevens, during which the latter drily hypothesized that a majority of Skagit County voters had marked the box beside his name because they thought they were familiar with it. He also said that he'd gone to high school in Gaithersburg, Maryland, with a Roosevelt Washington, and that he and Roosevelt Washington had played football together, with Stevens at quarterback and Washington at wide receiver, and that they'd been "in synch" a lot. Stevens had gone on to Lehigh, where he'd also played football, though not at quarterback. "Actually," he said, "they kept me around as a backup punter." From there, he'd gone on to Fordham's law school.

Lincoln Stevens was, you might say, aware of fashion. He wore custom dress shirts and, sometimes, a denim blazer. He had appeal in a way that might make other men resentful. If you were with Lincoln Stevens, say, at a party, you would note that gazes turned toward him, not you. His brand of attractiveness could be a disadvantage in court, which he clearly knew, and which he sought to address by conducting himself politely. The word for all of that is "charisma."

Lincoln Stevens now said, "I am the prosecutor in this county, elected by the People—the People with a capital 'P'—to represent us when we have cause to suspect that individuals among us have committed crimes. Well, let me tell you, we have cause in this case, not just for suspicion but for guilty verdicts, as the facts will show. They will show that the defendants adopted a girl from Ethiopia and proceeded to brutally beat her, not only with their hands but with a variety of cruel and vicious instruments, and to strike her on the head, the feet, the arms, the legs, and the torso, and to do all of that not in a manner in accord with what most of us would think of as a relatively benign spanking or a within-the-bounds-of-normal form of corporal punishment—which they would have you believe—but, no, much, much worse than that. But guess what? This beating of a child was just the beginning. Just the tip of the iceberg, the start. You're going to hear that the defendants also locked their adopted daughter up for long hours, at first in a little shower room, where she was made to sleep alone in a bathtub; later in a closet literally shorter than a coffin, if you can believe that, and with the light switch on the outside, meaning there was no way out of a terrible darkness and a claustrophobia and a suffocation. She was not allowed to use the bathrooms in the house and had instead for her use an outdoor toilet behind a barn, located next to a chicken coop, the sort of thing you might see on a construction site, a porta-potty that wasn't regularly cleaned. But this was not the end or the extent of her mistreatment. Far from it. You're going to hear that this poor girl was not allowed to take an indoor shower, and that the defendants instead made her wash under a garden hose out of doors, and you're going to hear that they cut off almost all of her hair on more than one occasion as a form of punishment, and that they took her clothing away and made her walk around with a bath towel knotted at her waist, and that she was regularly banned from the dinner table and made to eat cold food out of doors—scraps, leftovers, even food taken directly from the freezer and dropped like ice cubes onto her plate—and denied food until she lost a lot of weight, and that the defendants didn't celebrate her birthday, and gave her nothing for Christmas or on other holidays. The punishments, the punishments she endured, were just plain evil. She stood three inches to the left of the spot one of these defendants wanted her to stand on, whap, she got hit; she spelled a word incorrectly on one of her homeschooling assignments, whap, she got hit; she didn't respond in a timely way to some command or order they gave, whap, she got hit; she mowed the lawn grass an inch too short, whap, she got hit. There were times she had to march in a rectangular pattern, for hours on end, around a concrete pad in the defendants' yard, and there were times when she had to move rocks from point A to point B and then back to point A, and there were times when she was struck not just by her parents but by the older male children in the home, victims themselves, who were authorized and commanded by their parents to be their henchmen. You're going to hear how these defendants concocted, together, a scheme of child-rearing that constituted nothing less than torture, and how they both participated in it, and you are going to hear about the tragic night on which Abigail Harvey died, just outside the back door of the defendants' house, with her face in the mud and no clothes on, while members of the family looked on through a window."

Delvin Harvey's attorney, Pam Burris, went next. Burris had only recently passed the bar, but confidence still exuded from her gestures and diction. She didn't rise to speak. Nor did she become animated. Her chin was set, her shoulders square. With her elbows on her table, fingers laced at chin level, she spoke in a voice that never rose but was evenly insistent in its toneless rhythm. She was patiently propelled, and propped up by fortitude. It was as though she were conducting a congressional hearing. Unlike Stevens, she had no interest in fashion. "Now you've heard from the prosecutor," she said. "He's pretty convincing. He sounds pretty good. But let's look at the facts here. Let's live in the real world. My client, Delvin Harvey, is charged with homicide by abuse. Before he was arrested, he was a millwright at Boeing. He worked the swing shift there, at the Everett plant, which meant a very long commute. Five days a week, he left home at noon and didn't return until approximately midnight. That's twelve hours, Monday through Friday, when he wasn't present in his home and didn't participate in child-rearing. That's not to say that he didn't participate when he had time and opportunity. Delvin liked to make breakfast for his family. He took his children on weekend outings. He was a family man first and foremost. When Delvin was a child, his parents were, for a time, missionaries in Jamaica. There he'd been the only white student in his class, and there he'd learned to appreciate other cultures. So, for those of you who think racism plays a role in this case, that Delvin mistreated his adopted daughter because of the color of her skin—that just isn't true of Delvin Harvey, because he doesn't have that bone in his body. He never has and he never will, because Delvin is a good and decent person. You should know that Delvin served in the air force. He served his country and was honorably discharged. He met Betsy at church, and they married and settled down. They lived in Kent at first, and then they lived in Arlington, and then they built their dream house near Sedro Woolley. Throughout it all, Delvin was the breadwinner. He had children to feed and clothe, so he worked overtime whenever he could. It was a hard life but a good one, and he had no complaints. He and Betsy got along well—that is, until they adopted Abigail. Betsy stayed home and did the housekeeping and the homeschooling. Betsy raised the children while Delvin was at work. And, as it turned out, they loved having children. Eventually, they had seven, but were eager to have more. Then something happened they hadn't expected. Betsy experienced a difficult pregnancy that didn't end well, and was counseled by a doctor to stop bearing children. So it was that they were inquisitive and drawn when they came across another family that had adopted a child from Ethiopia. From there it was only a hop, skip, and jump for Delvin and Betsy to move toward an adoption of their own. And what joy they felt. How eager they were to share their love with a girl who needed them so. But then it emerged that this girl was troubled and had come to them from a traumatic background. Delvin could see that she wasn't bonding with Betsy, and that Betsy, in turn, wasn't bonding with her. Betsy had always been particular about hygiene and dedicated to cleanliness in her home, so it was hard for her to bear the lice and fungus Abigail had brought with her, and, even worse, the hepatitis B. Betsy just scolded Abigail at first when she broke family rules, but then Betsy began to punish Abigail sternly, and then her punishments turned brutal. What could Delvin do about it? Betsy grew angry when he spoke against it and refused to listen to his point of view. She reminded him that he was gone all day, and that the business of running the home was hers—that she was the one who had to deal with day-to-day realities. Delvin, she said, was always working and didn't know what went on at home. And you know what? That was true. She was right about that. Delvin didn't know that his wife was deceiving him about the depth, cruelty, and extent of her punishments. He didn't know about the things she'd been doing. Only after his arrest did he learn that Abigail had been locked in a closet for long hours. Only after his arrest did he learn how Abigail had been treated while he was gone. And consider this. On the day Abigail died, Delvin left, as usual, for work at noon. He'd seen her that morning at the breakfast table, eating what everybody else was eating, and dressed in warm, dry clothes, as usual. He'd gone to work, and when he returned, Abigail wasn't breathing. At a loss, stricken, he tried to revive her—he did all he could to save Abigail's life—and when he couldn't, he fell into a grief so deep you can see it in his face to this day. Think about that. This man next to me is charged with homicide. But this is the same man I just described to you who wasn't even home when Abigail died and did everything he could to save her. I don't even know what this case is about when it comes to the behavior and actions of my client. I don't know why he's sitting here, charged, when nothing points to his guilt or complicity, and everything points, instead, to his innocence. The state is just arguing that Delvin is guilty by virtue of being married to Betsy, and that's it, that's all they've got."

It was my father's turn now. He stood like Stevens, but crooked because of his years, and looked a little comic because he didn't fit inside his clothes. "Well," he said, "I guess I could say that my client, Betsy Harvey, is a wonderful person who never did anyone any harm. I guess I could reverse course on what you just heard from the other defense attorney and toss her husband under the bus. I could say that, on returning home from work each night, Delvin Harvey brutalized his adopted daughter while my client, Betsy, tried to stop him. I could say that Betsy was a victim, like Abigail, of the abusive, violent Delvin Harvey. I could say she cowered while he did the dirty work. I could point out that, in Delvin's view of things, the man is always master of the house and the woman always plays second fiddle. I could assert that, due to his self-avowed and self-professed theology of male authority, Delvin has nowhere to hide and can't pretend he's not responsible. I could tell this Delvin-is-the-culprit story, but even if I do, the lawyer for Delvin will still stand up and, as you've heard, present a lot of evidence that Delvin is a fine, upstanding person whose wife went down the wrong track while he was away at work all the time, leaving her responsible for the home and the children. And of course the prosecutor over there is going to say that Betsy and Delvin are equally guilty. So be it. Story on story. Story after story. Not just two stories, in this case, but three, because these two defendants are being tried jointly. These two defendants are codefendants. The judge has joined together two trials, because the charges involve a merged set of facts. Because the circumstances cannot be separated. Not because they compose one story, but because three stories should be told side by side: the story of one defendant, the story of the other, and the story in which they are joined, by the prosecutor, as mutually guilty, as guilty in tandem. I thought of objecting at the outset to this. I thought of asking for a separate trial for my client. But, actually, I think the judge is right. These three stories should be told side by side. So—cutting to the chase—let me tell you what my story is. My story is that my client, Betsy Harvey, is guilty. Yes, I'm her lawyer, but I'm saying she's guilty. Guilty in a way that deserves not just censure, not just retribution, and not just punishment, but, more than all of those, guilty in a way that compels her to make amends, to put things as near to right as they can be, which, as we know, can't be done, because a girl is dead and never coming back. Do you hear me? The girl who died, Abeba Temesgen, is never coming back. The transgression committed cannot be uncommitted. I'm telling you my client is guilty. Guilty of an outrage against humanity and of a moral wrong. Guilty of mistreating and abusing a child. Guilty of bringing Abeba Temesgen here from Ethiopia and treating her with utter contempt. Guilty of letting her die of hypothermia. Guilty of hatred, anger, enmity, rancor, pride, selfishness, heedlessness. Guilty of self-seeking self-regard, of self-serving self-centeredness, of self-absorbed certitude, of maniacal self-confidence, and of an inexcusable abuse of parental powers. Guilty, guilty, guilty, guilty, my client is guilty of multiple horrors, this is undeniable and can't be argued with. Look," said my father, "you should condemn somebody if they're patently evil, and condemn them thoroughly, without compunction or adulteration. But—and here's what I'm getting at—you shouldn't condemn them in a court of law, because there's no law against being patently evil, there's no such charge as 'patently evil,' there's only whatever charge is at hand—in the case of my client, homicide by abuse. Homicide by abuse. Homicide by abuse. There's a cause-and-effect relationship in that charge. It speaks to a death that's caused by abuse. The one thing has to cause the other. There can't just be abuse and death; there has to be abuse that *causes* death. Which can be proven in some cases but not in this one, where there's abuse and death but not a causal connection. Now, you can say that I'm playing a trick on you with this. That if I say, 'Well, Abigail Harvey was abused, horribly abused, but that's not what she died from, that's not what caused it,' you can say to yourself that I'm just another lawyer who doesn't care about right and wrong and just wants to get his client off the hook by any means and no matter what. No. That's not right. I don't want my client off the hook at all. I want my client to suffer and pay. I want her to be punished and condemned. It's just that we're going to have to find a way to do that without finding her guilty of homicide by abuse. Why? Because if we say what she did is close enough, or 'sort of,' if we say she was evil and jail her for that, the law gets bent a little to one side, and when it gets bent like that, we begin to have trouble. The law gets bent, a maniac comes along—a dictator or a tyrant who wants to crush people—and the maniac puts that bent law beneath his fist. He presses down, he presses again, he keeps on pressing until the law is flattened, and then we have a country without laws."

My father swiped at his nose with a forefinger. "This is a tough one," he said. "We want to do the right thing. We don't want to insult the memory of Abeba Temesgen. We don't want to say that the life of Abeba Temesgen meant nothing and can be taken with impunity—no, we don't want that. *I* don't want that. That's the last thing I want. What I want is justice. I want it understood that my client did terrible things, awful things, things that cannot be excused in any fashion, and I want her to make amends for that for the rest of her life, and to do nothing else. I want her life to be about amends, I want my client to do nothing but make amends, tangible, real, explicit amends with the work of her hands and by the sweat of her brow, but I don't want to mow down the law to get it done, and in the end I'm going to have to argue that, while Betsy Harvey is guilty of evil deeds, and of crimes, she isn't guilty of homicide by abuse.

"I mentioned crimes," said my father. "Yes, my client is guilty of crimes. She is guilty of child abuse. She is guilty of first-degree assault. She is certainly guilty of first-degree manslaughter. All of those charges have been made in this case, alongside the charge of homicide by abuse. I don't contest those charges in the least. If those were the only charges in this case, we wouldn't even be in this courtroom together. I would have pleaded guilty on behalf of my client—given that she'd let me—and, outside of court, worked for the right sentence. It's homicide by abuse that's the problem here. It's homicide by abuse that I don't believe happened. Anyway, the state is going to have to prove that the actions of my client are in accord with the language of the homicide-by-abuse statute, and that what she did fits the definition of that crime in no uncertain terms, and I don't believe the state can do that. My client is guilty of a lot of things, but not of homicide by abuse."

I MENTIONED EARLIER that, each morning of the trial, I collected my father at his home in Seattle. That isn't true: it didn't happen on all seven days. On the morning after his opening statement I didn't do it because we'd checked in the night before to a motel called Pipler's, between Mount Vernon and Burlington. We stayed there because, after his statement, my father went to the jail with Betsy Harvey to speak with her about her defense, and this meeting between them was longer than expected—in fact, it went on for more than two hours—and after that it didn't make sense, to me at least, to drive home. I'd waited for my father behind the courthouse on a cobblestone promenade, or a municipal plaza, or something having elements of both—anyway, a place with shade trees and benches. The afternoon heat there was beginning to fade. In storefront windowpanes, late sunlight shimmered. I

sat with my elbows on my knees, watching pigeons and turning over in my head, among other things, something Lincoln
Stevens had said—that the closet in which Abeba had been
locked was shorter than a coffin, and that the light switch was
outside. This kept coming back to me, accompanied by a seeth-
ing I tried fending off. I couldn't do it, though, and eventually
got up and moved to a bench in the lee of a cold-storage facility
with a view of people fishing and of fields beyond the river,
and then I walked some more and finally went to wait for my
father in the front seat of my car, with the door open to let out
the interior heat, and while I was there I remembered how
Abeba had told Elsabet Tesfaye that the boy near Shashamene
herding a donkey with a stick, the one who'd given her and
her father water and chunks of goat meat, was proof that not
everyone is bad.

Our motel room was thin-walled, shag-rugged, and
popcorn-ceilinged. Its air conditioner condensed noisily and
wept, and its windows rattled when a truck blew past on the
nearby freeway. Its twin beds were separated by no more than
eighteen inches. We sat on them, eating chow mein from a grocery store. I said, during dinner, "What do you think?," and my
father answered, "Well, first, the main thing is how completely
sad it is. But even so, you have to go forward. The prosecutor,
Stevens, he's no slouch. Meanwhile, Burris, the attorney for
Betsy's husband, she has in mind innumerable motions. I told
her that if she wanted to do that I wouldn't say no, I wouldn't
whine or cry, I wouldn't sit there in the courtroom shaking my
head. I told her she should do whatever she thought she should
do, and she said, 'I'm going to do that anyway.'" My father ran

his plastic fork through his chow mein. "You don't play games with Pam Burris," he told me, dead earnest about this cautionary dictum. "If you play games with Pam, you lose."

We turned off the lights a little after ten. Five minutes later, my father said, "Are you awake?"

"Yes."

"I had a case once for a guy who killed four people at a Christmas party," he said. "He was a used-car salesman. He went by 'Buster.' One of the first things I did when I took the case was interview his wife, who was nineteen or twenty. She had a boy with her, about three. She was pregnant. I remember she told me that Buster, the week before, had run over the family's puppy without meaning to, cried like a baby, and then buried it in their backyard. Is this okay? Me talking like this?"

"Sure."

"When Buster was seventeen," my father said, "he accidentally shot and killed his younger brother. After that, he dropped out of school, enlisted in the army, and got sent to Germany, where he drank like a fish until they booted him. He went home and ended up living on the streets for a while, and then he stole a car and served jail time. One way or another, though, he pulled himself together enough to get the used-car job, get married, and father a child. But then he started drinking again and looking for fistfights. The holiday season came, and that got Buster and his wife at odds, because Buster hated the holiday season. Still, he agreed to go with his wife to this party. It was a neighborhood party, right across the street. People were drinking and dancing in a basement. Buster got drunk and acted like a jerk, to the point that his wife went home and went to bed. Eventually, a fellow at the party felt provoked to say to Buster, 'Take your hands off my wife and don't ever touch her again.'"

"I see."

"Anyway, this guy and Buster went at it. Then a whole slew of guys took Buster out onto a patio and beat him up. So what does Buster do? He goes home, loads a rifle and a pistol, and comes back, bare from the waist up. Then he goes down into the basement, and with his rifle in his right hand and his pistol in his left, he fires into the dancers. And he kills two. And he wounds two more. Then he strolls away down the middle of the street and knocks on someone's door and yells, from their porch, 'This is Santa Claus, trick or treat, let me in.' That kind of stuff."

My father paused for emphasis. "I ended up claiming Buster was insane," he said. "I said that at the time of the shootings he was laboring under a defect of reason deriving from a disease of the mind. I said that, due to this, Buster didn't know what he was doing when he shot four people, and didn't know that it was wrong. I argued that he was too insane to even form an intention to kill people. I argued that the charges should be dismissed and that Buster should go to a mental institution. The prosecutor wasn't having any of it. He wanted the death penalty. He said, 'How can there not be intention in this case? The defendant got angry during a neighborhood Christmas party, went home, got firearms out of his closet, loaded each, returned to the festivities, took aim, and killed people. He wasn't crazy. He was angry with people and wanted to kill them.'

"I called psychiatrists to the stand," said my father. "One said that while Buster was in the service he came unhinged because he couldn't take the regimen. Another said Buster's parents had been absent from his life and that this plus guilt over killing his brother had made him self-destructive. Well, that just led the prosecutor to call his own psychiatrists, who all said it was obvious that the defendant was just a drunk who'd gotten angry and shot people. So two stories. Mine—Buster got dealt a bad hand in life and went crazy. The prosecutor's—simple, plain, cold-blooded murder.

"Anyway," said my father, "let's face it. Nine out of ten times, the person charged with the crime actually did what they're accused of. Like I told you a long time ago, it's not like on television, where the lawyer pulls a rabbit out of a hat to prove who the killer was. Mine is a profession where winning ten percent of the time is a good track record. Sometimes—most of the time—the facts are against you. You don't have a case. But of course, if clients think there's any chance at all, even the slightest, they want to go to trial, and they want you, as their attorney, to pull out all the stops. So you end up doing the best you can while knowing, from experience, that it's useless, it's hopeless, and that if you're going to take any satisfaction from your work, it's going to have to come with losing. Anyway, the jury found Buster guilty on every count. The judge gave him four life sentences. The good thing is, he didn't get the rope, which I was afraid of—that they'd execute Buster. The whole thing was sad. To tell you the truth, a lot of things in my work are sad. It's sort of a sad world to have to move around in."

• DAY FIVE. Lincoln Stevens put witnesses on the stand. It emerged from their testimony that Delvin and Betsy Harvey had, over time, pieced together their own religious program. Dissatisfied with every church they'd tried, they'd come to identify with no denomination. They'd practiced, instead, a personal religion cobbled together from books they'd ordered, videotapes, and audiocassette sermons. They were apocalyptic, meaning they believed that the world will end soon in a bloodbath, and that afterward all those who haven't taken Jesus as their savior will go to hell. They believed that the fires of hell burn as real flames, and that heaven is a physical place—that both heaven and hell take up space in the universe. They believed that males are ordained by God as heads of households and females as their "helpmeets." They believed they shouldn't spare the rod, and in their home kept a manual devoted to stern child-rearing. It called for swatting children as young as six months with wooden spoons; it called for swatting them if they tried to crawl off a blanket on the floor; it called for striking children with rulers, paddles, lengths of plumbing line, and tree branches; it called for cold-water baths, outdoor sequester, and the withholding of meals; it called for pursuing punishment until a child was "without breath to complain"; and it cited Scripture as the basis for all of this.

One state witness was a young woman named Annelise Kolb who wore a tightly braided pigtail over her right shoulder and a large pair of bottle-bottom eyeglasses. Annelise Kolb said that when she met Betsy Harvey, Betsy was no more than twenty-five years old. She was talkative, Kolb said, and had a voice heard easily across a room. Kolb was twelve at the time. She'd gone with her mother to a baby shower hosted by a woman named Sarah Tolt. Sarah Tolt's father was a pastor in Mexico. Both of her parents were missionaries, and all nine of her siblings were missionaries, too, in Mexico, Honduras, and Nicaragua. Sarah Tolt, Annelise Kolb said, was charismatic. She hosted events regularly in her living room, and her events were well attended. She was older than most of the women by fifteen years or more, and had eight children who were well behaved. Soon, said Kolb, "my mother, Betsy Harvey, and a number of other women who went to these things started dressing like Sarah Tolt, in what they called modest clothing. Like skirts or dresses to their ankles. Jumpers. Tunics. Long-sleeved tops. Stuff I had to wear until I got away from all of that."

Sarah Tolt gave talks, said Kolb, "about having a lot of children and homeschooling and being a stay-at-home mom, and also about the right techniques for child-rearing. She said that there was no point in discussing things with little ones, because they're too young to understand. They understood actions, not words. They understood training, not explanations. Sarah Tolt said people were good at training their dogs to sit or fetch but terrible at training their children to do what was asked of them. She said children want to know where the boundaries are and how to make their parents happy. Sarah's method for getting a family to function smoothly was, you trained kids hard. You put something where a kid could reach it, and when they reached for it you told them not to touch it, and if they defied you instead and went ahead and touched it, you rapped them on the hand. Sarah said this was known as conditioning. She said suppose you're nursing and the baby bites you. Simple. As soon as the baby bites you, pinch its arm or leg hard. Every time the baby bites you, pinch right away, so the baby feels pain. The message is 'If I bite, I'll feel pain.' That's something the baby can understand. It isn't going to understand anything else. Sarah thought that, as the baby got older and becomes a toddler, that toddler is going to test the limits. So that was when people like my mother and Betsy Harvey and all these other women who were listening to Sarah Tolt had to hold the line and persevere. They had to be strong and not give in to their feelings. Sarah was like, 'Your children are going to rebel against your authority, and it's your job, if you love them, to make sure you win. Because they're sinners. Through the fault of original sin. They'll yell and scream to get what they want because of original sin. They'll be selfish and self-centered, and it's up to you to take control of their development and bring them to God.' Sarah thought the critical age for that was twelve. She said twelve was the age where God drew the line. She said at twelve a child was responsible for his actions. At twelve, God wouldn't cut you any slack. You could go to hell for what you did at twelve. Because of that, parents had to do this conditioning. Unless you condition kids, they're going to sin after twelve and go to hell. She made it sound like that. She scared people.

"Sarah Tolt was really good at pushing everyone into a lot of whippings and beatings," Kolb said. And it was, like, the Bible says women should be helpmeets and do whatever men say, and stay home and don't use birth control and whale on your kids, and that was the situation, the culture I grew up in, those were my circumstances. And, really, the thing with Sarah Tolt and my mother and Betsy and these others was a cult where they talked about disciplining out of love, when I know from my own experience that in fact you were being whaled on. I mean really whaled on. And after a while, I guess some of the women questioned it, but they were living in fear now, because, like I said, it was a cult, and you couldn't go against what Sarah Tolt and my mother and Betsy Harvey were saying or you ran the risk of being kicked out of the inner circle and scorned and ostracized. But then this one woman spoke up, and a second one—they were having misgivings, like, it can't really be love if you're whaling on a child, can it? And Sarah Tolt and Betsy and my mother, they were like, no, here's more literature, we're going to pray for you, stuff like that, and then those two women, they dropped out, because they just couldn't take it anymore, this beating their own children, and then Sarah and Betsy and my mother, they started worrying about the Child Protective Service, they were always talking about the Child Protective Service, and they thought that these other women, the ones who quit, that they were going to exaggerate stuff and bring the Child Protective Service down on their heads, and then the Child Protective Service would take away their children. Because they all had this tendency, Sarah and Betsy and my mother, to do conspiracy thinking, and they figured the government is out to get you and take away your kids. Especially Betsy, who was over the top. And after a while, Betsy was going even further than Sarah Tolt, and they had a falling out, and there was a lot of drama, and Betsy started acting like she was in charge now and got bossy and controlling. We started going over there, where the Harveys lived, instead of to Sarah's, because my mother was like Betsy's second in command, so I saw a lot of what went on in that home, I saw a lot of how they lived. I remember Mr. and Mrs. Harvey always evangelizing and trying to get people to do what they did, and they were both just so into it. Because I guess it's just really rewarding or something when it works, and kids hop to, and the next thing you know, you ask a child to pick up a toy, he does it no-questions-asked immediately. Also, Betsy had this big obsession with personal hygiene, like keeping things antiseptic and sterile, and organizing everything in plastic bins, like the kids all had these little bins with their names on them for their toothbrushes and whatnot. Stuff like that. And I saw, I saw for myself, many times, how she and Mr. Harvey were swatting their kids a lot, right in front of me, and it wasn't any little smack on the butt or the hand—it hurt. They had all these kids, and every ten or fifteen minutes, out came these little whips they used, these little plumbing lines, like twelve inches long, except their infants got hit with a hand instead, because they weren't ready for the plumbing line yet, according to their child-raising theory. But when these infants got to be over six months—just six months—okay, they don't come when you call, or they don't pick up their toys and stuff like that, okay, out comes the whip, you know, right below the bottom, like where your thighs meet your bottom. I know because I got whipped that way a lot, and it hurts and it leaves these red marks.

"Later, it got even weirder," Kolb said. "Betsy started holding these seminars in her home under the title 'Crowning Joy,' which she lifted from the Bible, where it says that a wife should be a crowning joy to her husband or something—that kind of language. And she stood up in front of these other women acting like she knew what she was talking about, and they believed what she said because her kids were so well trained and so obedient, and I had to go with my mother to these things, and I remember how Betsy revealed to us, smiling, that she kept her tools for disciplining her children tucked into her bra so they'd be handy there, and one was a piece of plumbing line and the other was a fat, long length of glue stick like you'd use in a hot glue gun, which she told us was her mother's idea, that her mother had given her a whole box of glue sticks. I also remember when she changed her seminar title from 'Crowning Joy' to 'Sin No More,' 'sin no more' being something she was finding all over the place in the Bible suddenly, like her eyes had just been opened to some secret code in there, 'sin no more' meaning that sinless perfection is possible in life, or something like that, something about being perfect in God, whatever that means. It's heretical, actually, when you think about it, to say that people can be sin-free and perfect. It's kind of like the obsession Betsy had with cleanliness—push all the dirt away, wash your hands a million times. In her 'Sin No More' lectures, she kept implying she was perfect and that she felt called by God at this point in her life—this was just a year before Abigail came—she felt called to proclaim a new Christian doctrine of personal perfection and freedom from sin. And every time, at every meeting, at the end of her lecture, she made everyone stand up and say a prayer together, which went like this: 'We proclaim Him, admonishing and teaching everyone with all wisdom, so that we may present everyone perfect in Christ. To this end I labor, struggling with all His energy, which so powerfully works in me. Amen.' As if the rest of us were there to hail her perfection."

Annelise Kolb shook her head in disgust. "This was not that long ago," she said. "This was right before the Harveys adopted Abigail. This is where their heads were at when Abigail came into their home."

————

A WOMAN NAMED Cheryl Hodge took the stand and said that she was Delvin Harvey's sister and that their parents, who were missionaries, had divorced when she was twelve, but that the family had lived in Texas for a while, and in Portland, Oregon, and in Woodland, Washington, and in Colville, Washington, where "we lived a little hand-to-mouth, because my father's job died out." Cheryl was six years younger than Delvin, "so growing up I don't remember him being around a lot. I have another brother, Bruce, who is closer to Delvin in age, eighteen months older, and Bruce knew how to push Delvin's buttons, and he could make Delvin blow a fuse. Which wasn't hard, really. He blew a fuse easy. Bruce was popular at school, whereas Delvin—Delvin wasn't. He didn't care at all. The in-crowd at school, you know, wore bell-bottoms, but Delvin didn't care, he could be who he wanted to be, he didn't care what people thought. He took, I guess, like, a moral stance. People got into drugs—like, Bruce did a little, but Delvin stayed on the straight and narrow. And his personality was such that if he thought something was right, then it was right, and that was the end of it. He was, kind of, everything is black and white and there aren't any gray areas, there's a line, and either you're across it or you're not. Can't be in the middle. So, if he thought something was right and you thought different, there was judgment. Like, later in life, when he started having children and I hadn't had any children yet, he told me I shouldn't be using birth control because it was killing life, and it was a serious offense to kill an unborn child. Another thing: I'm a teacher in a middle school, and I teach science there, and

Delvin let me know I shouldn't do that, because I was teaching evolution and that God didn't create the earth, and when I told him I didn't agree with him, he started giving me books to read, anti-evolution books, and he was always just letting me know that I wasn't living up to proper spiritual living and that I wasn't living life right, and it's just that kind of religiosity that can be so judgmental. Not that it was always like that with him. This kind of thinking got more intense when he married Betsy. Pretty soon, they sounded the same. There was a way they communicated. It's, you gotta read this book, or you gotta see this article, or you have to hear this sermon, or your version of a Bible quote is wrong and you need to use this other version. Or, there's people in this country getting control of things who want to make us, like, a socialist/communist/fascist dictatorship, and once I made the stupid mistake of arguing with them about that by saying, 'You're mixing things together that don't go together—communist/fascist, that's a contradiction in terms'—but they weren't having any part of it; as usual, I was wrong and they were right, and the problem was that I hadn't read the correct books and wasn't listening to the correct people. I should have known better than to argue, because I lived with them a long time ago. Delvin was in the military for two years, and I didn't really see him, and then he got married and was living in Kent, a half hour from Seattle, and I wanted to go to the University of Washington to get my teaching certificate, and I didn't have very much money, so I asked if I could stay at their house. So I stayed there, but I didn't stay there for very long, not even for a month—or it could have been a month, I don't remember now. But as soon as I could find a job, I moved out, because Betsy was so controlling. For example, as soon as

I was out of the shower, she'd be in the bathroom, checking to see if I'd pulled the curtain so it wouldn't get moldy, and if I ran the dishwasher when it wasn't all the way full, that was a problem, or if I left the cap off the toothpaste or used too much laundry soap or didn't close the bread bag tight, and I just had to move to get away from all of that. Betsy's grandmother, we found out, had germophobia, and Betsy's mother had it, and then Betsy had it, and when Betsy was little, if she went to someone's house—like, to play or something—then, before she could come in, her mother would spray her down with a hose. So that's her background. I mean, Betsy scrubbed out the corners of her rooms with a toothbrush. This one time, I had these leftover petri dishes that the school district was just going to throw away, and I didn't know what to do with them, so I gave them to Delvin, thinking, you know, for homeschooling. And these dishes had nutrient agar in them so you could just do a little swab and see the bacteria, and I went over there and showed them, Hey, you can open these up and use the swab or even use your hand, just put your hand on it and then close it, and you'll see the bacteria that was on your hand. Then, later, I had some more of these petri dishes, so I asked Delvin, Do you want these ones, too? And he said no, because the last ones had sent Betsy through the roof. She'd washed her hands a zillion times after touching a petri dish, and then she made Delvin put the dishes in a plastic bag and put that bag inside another bag and twist-tie it shut and put the whole thing outside over-night and then get rid of it the next day.

"There was this one time after Abigail came, I saw Delvin at the Costco in Burlington, and we talked, and it was 'How's your family?' and stuff like that, and he said that he and

Betsy were having these problems with Abigail. So, naturally, I asked him what kind of problem, and he said Abigail was rebellious and it had become a war, to the point where if they told Abigail to stand right here she would stand two inches to the left on purpose, or if they said, Put down your book right here, she would put it over to the left two inches, and now they were having to punish her a lot, with spankings and time-outs and missed meals and eating by herself, and I was just looking at him and going in my head, 'Delvin, have you gone nuts?' And, finally, I couldn't take it anymore, so I said, 'Delvin, are you nuts? You kidding me? What's happened to you? You've become just like Betsy. Betsy—she owns you.' And Delvin did what Delvin does. He says, 'Go read your Bible. Go and make a close study of your Bible.' And then he gives me quotes from the Bible. One goes something like, 'The head of the woman is the man.' And another goes, 'Wives, submit yourselves to your own husbands as unto the Lord.' Delvin laid out that Scripture for me. And, frankly, it was hugely embarrassing. We're standing in the aisle at Costco, and it's busy, and Delvin is raising his hands like a preacher and giving me one of his sermons."

ON THE SIXTH DAY of the trial, a Child Protective Services investigator testified. On the night Abigail died, she said, someone from the Skagit Valley Hospital left her a phone message to the effect that a girl had been transported to the emergency unit and had died en route, and that she'd been notably thin and had succumbed to hypothermia near the house she lived in with seven minor siblings. By nine the next morning, the investigator had a report in hand from the sheriff's office indicating that the deceased's head had been shaved, that there were marks and abrasions at multiple sites on her body, and that she'd died with no clothes on a few feet from her back door. This all implied, the investigator testified, a site visit to ensure the safety of the seven surviving children.

As soon as she parked by the house on Stone Lane, a boy came out to confront her. He looked to be sixteen or seventeen years old, but was, in manner, militant and brusque, and demanded immediately that the investigator, who had only just stepped away from her car, identify herself and her purpose. As soon as she'd done what he'd asked her to do, he put up his hands to communicate blocked passage, told her to wait where she was, and went inside.

A moment later, two other boys emerged alongside the first, two boys who looked a little younger than he did and were, in their manner, equally unwelcoming. All three wore their hair in crew cuts. All three wore white short-sleeved cotton shirts tucked into belted, pleated khaki pants. All three conducted themselves with a presumption of authority. Together, they formed a trio of blunt defenders, doorkeepers, watchers at the gate—a detail of security guards, the investigator thought, instead of adolescent boys. One announced that he knew what the law said, and the law said they didn't have to answer her questions, and another said the investigator was trespassing and should turn her car around and leave. The three of them were so conspicuously suspicious that she decided then and there that something needed getting to the bottom of—that something was amiss behind their obstructionism, their assumption of command over her, and their bullish effort to block her in her mission. Their behavior seemed blindly ironic to her, too, because these strong-arm tactics and assertive remonstrations actually ran counter to their efforts to make her leave, which seemed to her like something they should know: how much better off they would be, in achieving what they wanted to achieve, if they were instead inviting and gracious. But no. The more they insisted that she leave, the more she knew she had reasons to stay. "I'm not going anywhere," she told them. "Go in and get an adult to come out here."

One went. When he came out again, it was behind Betsy and Delvin Harvey. There were now five members of the Harvey family confronting her in the driveway. Delvin Harvey was dressed the way his sons were dressed, in a white short-sleeved cotton shirt tucked into belted khakis. Betsy Harvey, in an ankle-length skirt, told the investigator that she couldn't speak to the children and that the children would not be answering her questions and that she knew all about what CPS tried to do and was putting CPS on notice right now—as well as the investigator as a private citizen—that if she tried to abridge their constitutional rights, both she and CPS ran the risk of a lawsuit. "Fine," said the investigator. "But the law says that in a case like this I'm required to discern that the children here are safe, and it also says that if I'm not allowed to do that I'm obligated to call for assistance from the sheriff, so I would suggest that you just cooperate with me and let me do my job."

Betsy Harvey opened the door to the house and called for the other children. Four more emerged: another boy, maybe ten or eleven, who wore a white short-sleeved shirt like all the other males, and three girls in calico dresses. The children formed a kind of tableau, one reminiscent, the investigator thought, of

Little House on the Prairie. She understood now what it was she was looking at—a family of fervently religious fundamentalists of a sort she'd encountered more than once, clans scattered up and down the county who on occasion had warranted visits from her for the same purpose as this one, and who, like the people before her now, had dark theories about CPS, including that it existed to kidnap children and hand them over to Satan. "I need to speak to the children in private," the investigator said, "because children aren't free, in front of their parents, to tell me if they feel safe or not."

Betsy Harvey said she would sue over that, because the Constitution didn't allow it, and anyway privacy wasn't necessary, because her children spoke the truth at all times. "So let's get through your little visit quickly," she sneered. "Children, line up."

The children lined up according to their age, from oldest to youngest, left to right, and Betsy Harvey put her right hand on the first one's head and said, "Ezekiel, do you feel safe?," to which he answered, "Of course."

They all said "Of course" as Betsy Harvey moved down the line, putting a hand on top of each head. Like little automatons, the investigator thought. Like the von Trapp children before Maria came along. The investigator, exasperated, repeated herself—that she needed to speak to the children privately to fulfill her professional obligation, and that if not allowed to conduct her investigation she would call the sheriff's department. "Call the sheriff's department, then," Betsy Harvey countered. "They're going to be on our side."

The investigator did what she knew was best from her years of experience in these matters—she left and opened a formal investigation. Soon, she'd obtained from a judge the court order she needed, called the sheriff's department to arrange for support, and then, with the judge's order in hand, a CPS colleague, three cars, and two deputies, returned to Stone Lane.

It was a Friday afternoon. Neither parent was home. One of the boys who'd defied her before came to the door and, taking in the two deputies, said that his mother was getting groceries and that his father was at work. The investigator told him that she and the others had come to take him and his siblings to the Children's Administration office in Mount Vernon. "It's lunchtime," he replied.

The investigator said they could bring lunch with them. Then she said that she was going to come inside but that her colleagues and the sheriff's deputies would wait where they stood.

She went in. The other six children were in the front room, frozen at first, staring at her, until she said that no one was going to hurt them and that they needed to get their coats and their toothbrushes, because all of them were leaving the house now and going where they would be taken care of and kept safe. Six went to do what she'd asked them to do, but the seventh, the oldest girl, hurried instead to the kitchen and began making peanut-butter-and-jelly sandwiches, pairing the bread slices and lining them up, spreading the peanut butter and jelly quickly, and sliding each sandwich into a plastic bag with the name of a child written on it.

The children soon assembled with their coats and toothbrushes. There were no tears, the investigator noted, and no signs of fear. They were all unusually and highly cooperative, polite in their responses, and prompt to act, including the three boys who'd bullied her on her first visit. "Here we go," she said, and led them all outside. The deputies watched without saying anything. Her colleague took the four boys in his car, and the investigator took the three girls in hers. When they were under way, a few minutes beyond Stone Lane, the oldest asked permission to open the youngest's sandwich bag. In a small voice, she said she was worried that her sister might get peanut butter and jelly on the upholstery. The investigator looked at her in the rearview mirror and said, "Of course you can open your sandwich bags and eat. I'm not a stickler on the condition of my car seats. It's an old car, kind of a beater. My own kids ate back there constantly. I'm not worried about anything like that. Just eat your sandwiches, go ahead."

She watched as she drove. The younger two ate, but the oldest one didn't open her sandwich bag. "Go ahead and eat," the investigator urged her. "We're going to feed you, don't worry about that, but for now, eat while you have the chance."

The girl opened her bag but left the sandwich untouched. "Excuse me," said the investigator after a while. "Your name is Rebecca?"

"Yes, ma'am," the girl answered.

"You're not hungry, Rebecca?"

"No, ma'am."

The investigator caught her eye in the rearview mirror—the eye of a girl who seemed not to want her eye caught and who looked ashamed and startled when it happened. As if they shouldn't be looking at each other. As if it was problematic. As if what they were doing was wrong. At the same time, the girl didn't look away, either because she felt she shouldn't or because, at some level, she didn't want to look away, and was at odds with herself about being eye to eye with a CPS investigator, even like this, with the buffer of a rearview mirror. "You're thirteen?" said the investigator.

"Twelve," said Rebecca. "But my birthday is next Tuesday."

"Happy early birthday, then. So let me ask you something. Not hungry at the moment or not hungry in general?"

"In general."

The investigator decided to leave it at that, turned her eyes to the road, and kept them there. She didn't ask more questions, she told the court, because Rebecca Harvey seemed frightened and fragile and could easily collapse in the face of another question.

REBECCA HARVEY TOOK the stand. She had a scarlet complexion and wore her hair in a sparse bun. She was thirteen now but appeared much younger, and her furtive, downward gaze never landed on her parents, whom she hadn't seen in nine months. Her refusal to look at them had a quality of tension; at the same time, it felt unassailable. For her day in court, she'd buttoned up a V necked sweater the approximate color of flax over a blouse with a Peter Pan collar, and cinched a long denim skirt tightly at the waist with a cloth knot. She had a scoliotic way of sitting and was canted so far leftward that an imaginary line from one of her shoulder blades to the other would have transected her chin. She also swiveled in her chair so much, and spoke so softly—in a reedy whisper—that the bailiff had to persist in reminding her to lean toward the microphone. Bangs hung over Rebecca's right eye. She suffered, on this morning, from an expectorating cough that welled up in her suddenly, and that caused her to duck her head low in the wake of coughing fits and bark into her fist, and then to hesitate, as if in anticipation of another fit, which would have to be quelled with the same fist. Each time, she apologized for the episode, which deepened her embarrassment.

Rebecca, for all her agony, was forthright. Since Abigail's death, she told the court, she'd engaged repeatedly in self-mutilation, spent two months in a mental hospital, abused painkillers and anxiety medications, and twice tried to kill herself—once, she said, by slitting her wrists, and once by swallowing a bottle of OxyContin. She was better now, she said, but fragile and recovering. She slept a lot, was trying to get her strength back, and lived—as did her sisters, Leah, eight, and Ada, five—with her uncle Bruce and aunt Ellen in Idaho.

When Abigail first arrived, Rebecca explained, it was "on an airplane in the middle of the night, so just my parents went to the airport and picked her up and brought her to our house. I heard them when they came down the driveway, so I got out of bed. I went into the living room and I met Abigail, and she was real pretty, and she was wearing this shirt they gave her at the orphanage that said 'Ethiopia' on it, a white shirt with that on it and a white skirt, both of them had like a trim that was red and green and yellow, because those are the colors on the Ethiopian flag, and white socks and white shoes, and her hair was in braids, not just two braids but lots of braids—they were pinned down to her head, and it was pretty. So she could talk in English, way more than I thought, and she had an accent, but you could understand what she said, and it was a really pretty accent. So then I asked her what she liked to do, what kinds of things she liked to do, and she said she liked to do whatever I liked to do, but also she liked to read and she liked to knit and she liked to play outside, but, still, she would do anything I wanted. So the boys had two bunk beds in their room and we had two bunk beds in our room, so we had a bed all ready, so I asked her which bed did she want, the top or the bottom, and she said that if I wanted the top I should have the top but if I wanted the bottom I should have the bottom, and I said, no, it's the other way around, you choose, so she chose the top. And we had these pajamas for her, some of my pajamas, so Abigail put on those pajamas and they fit her pretty good, and then she fell asleep, but I was too excited, so I couldn't fall asleep again. Then, like a couple of days later, Leah started feeling like this itching in her hair, so Mom got a flashlight and looked at her hair and found lice, and then she looked in Abigail's hair, and she found lice there, too. And then more people got it—I got it and Dad got it, all of my brothers got it, Ada got it. The only one who didn't get it was Mom, so Mom started looking up information on what to do, and she decided what we had to do is, we all had to use this medicine on our bodies that's supposed to take care of lice—like, you put it all over your body, this medicine, and then you have to wait, and while you're waiting you're not supposed to wash your hair or anything, because otherwise you could wash the medicine out. Plus, we had to take, like, all of our clothes and our bedsheets and our pillow covers and our blankets, we had to take everything and put it in the washing machine and let it soak for two hours to make the lice die. And then we had stuff you couldn't wash, like stuffed animals and stuff, and so Mom put all of that stuff in plastic bags and tied them shut and put those on the porch for, like, two weeks, because that would starve the lice. And we had to vacuum everything and check all the cushions and things for lice, and mop the floors and all, but there were still lice. So then Mom made Abigail take the braids out of her hair and untwist them, and she sat her down and got her flashlight again and looked into her scalp, and not only was there still lice, there was also this fungus that Mom thought was ringworm. So then she looked up ringworm, and she decided it was ringworm. So then she got some medicine for ringworm, and also she called the adoption agency, and I heard her on the phone, and she was mad at the adoption people, because she thought they should have told her about stuff and it was a lot of work. And then, when Dad came home, they took Abigail in the bathroom and they put a chair in the bathtub and they told her she had to sit on it, and then, while she was sitting there, Mom got these scissors and cut Abigail's braids off, and then Dad took a razor, his electric razor, and he cut Abigail's hair short, and he took her hair and put it in a paper bag and burned it with other stuff in the fire pit, and everything else, the smaller hair, it got washed down the drain, and then Mom, she cleaned the bathtub with bleach, and she put the stopper in the drain so the lice couldn't come back up. Then, that night, when we were in bed, I could tell Abigail was crying, so I asked her if she was okay, and she said in the orphanage all the kids had lice but they never cut their hair, and now her hair was cut and she looked terrible and she hated it. And I said, You don't look terrible, Abigail. And she said, yes, she did, so we stayed up talking and so did Leah and Ada, but they were just listening, because they were scared Mom and Dad would hear us talking, and they kept saying we were too loud. So I said, Abigail, you can come down here and get in bed with me so that way we can talk quieter, but she was, like, No, I'm okay, and we tried to sleep. Then, the next day, we were outside in the yard, and she had this hat on that was what Dad called a watchman's hat, and it was black and it had these letters on it, which were the initials of a church we used to go to, and Mom had put lice medicine in Abigail's hair and told her to wear the hat. And she was sitting there at the picnic table, and I asked her if she wanted to play hopscotch, but she was reading a book Mom gave her called *The Last Sin Eater*. She read that at the picnic table. Then we wanted to play capture-the-flag with her, like all of us kids did, and she said okay, so we did that.

"So then, one night, we were in bed and Ada said she was hungry. We talked about food, and Abigail said in Ethiopia they had this snack she really liked, and we wanted to know what the snack was, and it was sort of like pretzels but not shaped like pretzels, more like little balls, and then she told us about other food in Ethiopia, and also that it wasn't like here, with the four seasons, it was more like a long part of the year not much rain and then, for a few months, it rained so hard you wouldn't believe it. And also, people went inside at night, because of hyenas. And sometimes at night you could hear hyenas outside, and then, when they killed a goat or something, there was howling all over the city. Then Ada said again that she was hungry, and Abigail said, Why don't we go into the kitchen and get something to eat? But we didn't want to do that, because we knew what would happen, so we didn't. We went to sleep. But then, another night, Ada said she was hungry, and Leah said she was hungry, they both said it, it was just something they said all the time, and usually we just waited until breakfast, but Abigail said, no, they shouldn't be hungry at their age, that didn't seem right, and this one night when they said they were hungry, Abigail said, Guess what, I got some stuff from the kitchen and brought it with me into bed, it's saltine crackers. And everyone had to be careful, because the crackers are noisy, so we just chewed real slow on the saltine crackers, and I said, Abigail, don't get caught, on stuff like this we're supposed to tell on each other, but don't worry, none of us are going to tell on you about the crackers. So she understood she couldn't keep taking crackers every night, because then the crackers would all be gone and Mom would notice, so she took different things—like, every day, when Mom wasn't looking, she would get something and hide it so we could eat it at night, but then Mom found out, because there were crumbs, and Mom found the crumbs in our bedroom. Mom said, Who is responsible for this? Abigail said, I am, I ate crackers in my bed last night, and she got punished, she got spankings when Dad came home, he took her in their bedroom and gave her spankings, and that was the first time she got spankings. Abigail told me that in Ethiopia there were spankings, too, but not for anything like this, you would get a spanking if you did something people didn't like, like you were rude in your neighborhood, then people wouldn't like it, and they would talk about it, and then the parents could say, You're making trouble for us and not following the rules, but no one got a spanking for eating something. So we talked about spankings, and I told her that when we were little we got spanked all the time for a lot of stuff, but now we never did, because we followed the rules.

"This one time, we were out in the yard, me and Abigail, and she said it was hard getting used to how quiet it was where we lived; plus, there were no people around, just our family all the time, and she told me she thought then when she got adopted she would go to school. She said she thought everybody went to school in America, and she said she'd never heard of homeschooling, she didn't even know that could even be—in Ethiopia they didn't have it, anything like homeschooling. And I told her that not a lot of people in our country do it either, most kids go to school, but that our family didn't, because Mom and Dad didn't like what they taught you in school, like the universe is billions of years old and started with a bang and we came from monkeys and stuff like that, and at school they would brainwash you so you didn't believe in Jesus. So then we were homeschooling, and there were things we had to do, like work on our cursive handwriting and grammar and spelling, and Abigail, she was good at cursive, and she was good at math, in math she got all her problems right every time, it was easy for her, but since English was her second language, other stuff was harder, but, still, she wrote assignments—like, she wrote a book review on *Heidi* and another paper about the Pilgrims and she wrote a paper on the thirteen colonies during the Revolutionary War, but in all these papers there were mistakes, like capital letters and verbs and stuff, and Mom didn't like that, so she was always making Abigail do her papers over again until the papers were perfect, with everything spelled right and stuff. And Abigail got tired of that, because she had to keep doing the whole paper over again if there was just one mistake, and so she said to Mom that she wanted to go to school, and Mom said, No, that's not how we do things in our family, in our family we don't believe in school. And Abigail didn't like that.

"Something happened. Mom wanted Ada to sit up straight in her chair during dinner, and Ada would forget and start to have bad posture, so Mom would get her spanking tool out and use it on her. So this one time she gets out her spanking tool because Ada has bad posture, and she whips Ada on the back with it, and Abigail said, 'Don't do that, it isn't right to do that,' and Mom told Abigail to go outside because she was being disrespectful. So Abigail went outside, and then, later, Mom opened the door and said to Abigail that she could come in, but first she had to apologize, and Abigail said no to that, she wouldn't apologize, so Mom told her to come in and go sit in the corner with her face to the wall and take her notebook with her and write one hundred times, 'I am sorry for being disrespectful.' So Abigail goes to the corner, and when she gets done writing, she shows it to Mom, and she wrote 'I am sorry for being disrespectful' one hundred times, 'cept every time she got something wrong, like the period or the capital letter or spelling a word right or just bad cursive, not in the lines. So Mom said, 'Okay, I get it,' and she said Abigail had to go outside again and walk around the yard in a circle one hundred times and say the whole time, 'I am sorry for being disrespectful,' and Mom was going to stand there and watch and listen, and if Abigail didn't obey, then, when Dad got home, there would be spankings, and Mom told Abigail, 'You got spanked before, but not hard, because it was the first time, but this time it'll be different, so you better do what I say.' So Abigail went out there, and she walked around the yard one time, and then she sat down on the ground, and Mom said, 'Get up,' but Abigail ignored her, and Mom got mad, and she got my three older brothers and she said, 'Go out there and pick her up and bring her inside.' Next, the boys went out and got around her, and when they did she stood up and went inside, and Mom made Abigail sit in the corner until Dad got home. And that was late at night, and I was in bed, but I heard the spankings, and when Abigail came to bed she said it hurt, and she said she wished she'd never been adopted and was still in Ethiopia. I told her I felt bad about Mom and Dad, and mad all the time, really mad, and I told her my stomach was in knots all the time and that I held it in and was scared, and that I liked it best when I could sneak into the woods by myself. I told Abigail that when I was little I lived in a little fantasy world where there were fairies in the woods, and that I made these little houses for them out of moss and sticks and leaves, and I left them little notes about myself, but none of the fairies ever answered my notes, and then, this one time, one of my brothers followed me out there, and he saw one of my fairy houses and one of my notes, and he took the note to Mom, and I got in trouble, because fairies are pagan make believe creatures, and it starts with fairies and from there it goes to wizards and other stuff from Satan, so then I had to go out in the woods with Mom, and we were going to take apart my fairy houses, and I couldn't write notes. So we went out there, and I showed Mom all of my fairy houses except one, I tried to keep one, I kept that one a secret, but then, later, Mom found out about it and made me destroy it like the others, and then I got spanked by Dad with a paddle and put in time-out for a whole day.

"I remember that when things got real bad for Abigail—

like, she had to take showers under the hose outside, and had to use the port-a-potty, and Mom put her in the closet all the time—when it got like that, we weren't supposed to talk to Abigail. We were supposed to ignore her. The word Mom used was 'shun.' We were supposed to shun Abigail. But then, this one time, I went to the closet when Mom and Dad weren't home and I unlocked the door. And we sat there on the floor next to the closet door, and I told Abigail I was sorry about how things were. And she said, No matter how they treat me, I won't surrender. They can't break me no matter what they do. And she said, she said to me, she said, Stand with me. And I said I wanted to but that I was scared. And then Abigail said, You could make a new fairy house. You could make a new fairy house and hide it good this time, way out where nobody can see you. So I made a new fairy house in a secret place, and nobody found it, and I told Abigail, and she said, Did any fairies come and use it yet? And after she died, I felt guilty and tried to kill myself."

THERE WAS a recess. Rebecca needed one, Lincoln Stevens said, so the judge gave her fifteen minutes. Then Rebecca took the stand again and told the court, over the course of an hour, that she'd witnessed, with her own eyes, everything—the whippings, the beatings, the outdoor showers, the port-a-potty, the haircuts, the locked closet. She'd seen Abigail spanked both standing up and bent over, spanked on the soles of her feet while on the floor, spanked by hand, with a belt, and with "Mom and Dad's spanking tools." She'd heard Abigail plead "no" between spankings, and heard her father, whip in hand, yell, "Don't lie, obey!" "At first," she said, "they locked Abigail in the closet only at night, but then Mom started locking her in the closet for the whole day. And Abigail slept there and ate there, most of the time it was cold spaghetti, she loved spaghetti, but Mom would give it to her cold, and Mom would play the Bible on a cassette player she had outside the closet door, trying to get Abigail's brain to think differently, but that didn't work, and Mom got tired of it, and she said to us she didn't want to be around Abigail anymore, because she wouldn't cooperate and wouldn't obey, and she said she didn't like Abigail, she didn't like Abigail but she loved her, she loved her because she was a human being made by God, she said that to us, 'Abigail is a human being made by God,' but also she said it to the air sometimes."

"I know this is hard," Lincoln Stevens said, "but now I want to talk about the night Abigail passed away. Do you recall that?"

Rebecca: "Yes."

Stevens: "Start in the day. Start at the beginning. Start in the morning, the beginning of the day. What happened?"

Rebecca: "We were doing our schoolwork."

Stevens: "Where?"

Rebecca: "In the kitchen."

Stevens: "And was Abigail there?"

Rebecca: "Yes."

Stevens: "Was she doing schoolwork?"

Rebecca: "Yes."

Stevens: "And did she stop doing schoolwork at some point and go outside?"

Rebecca: "Yes."

Stevens: "Did she decide to go outside on her own?"

Rebecca: "No. Mom told her to."

Stevens: "Just Abigail? No one else?"

Rebecca: "She went by herself."

Stevens: "Why was that?"

Rebecca: "Because Mom punished her."

Stevens: "For what?"

Rebecca: "For not doing her homework right."

Stevens: "Did she make a mistake?"

Rebecca: "She gave Mom her math problems. And all of them were wrong. And Mom said, 'Abigail, you know how to do these problems. You got them wrong on purpose.' And then she gave Abigail the same math problems again, and Abigail got them wrong again, and Mom said, 'Abigail, this is rebellion, I want you to come over here and stand right in front of me.'"

Stevens: "Then what?"

Rebecca: "Abigail went to Mom. She stood in front of her. But then she took one foot and moved it over, and then she took the other and moved it, too, so then she wasn't standing in front of Mom."

Stevens: "And then?"

Rebecca: "Then Mom told Abigail to go outside and stay there, and that she could only come back if she apologized for her disobedience, and Mom said she would go out and check on her in an hour to see if she was ready to apologize."

Stevens: "Do you remember what the weather was like that day?"

Rebecca: "It was cold and it was raining."

Stevens: "Did Abigail have a coat on?"

Rebecca: "No."

Stevens: "And how long was she outside?"

Rebecca: "She was outside the whole time, until she died."

Stevens: "Did you or your siblings go outside and talk to her?"

Rebecca: "Mom told us not to. But, secretly, I did."

Steven: "You went outside."

Rebecca: "I went outside and I talked to Abigail. And I told her she should come inside, because it was raining and cold."

Stevens: "How did she answer?"

Rebecca: "She said she could take the rain and cold. And then she said, 'Rebecca, stay out here with me.'"

Stevens: "And what did you say?"

Rebecca: "I said I wanted to but that I couldn't, because I was scared."

Stevens: "So then what?"

Rebecca: "So then I went in. And it got dark. And she was still out there."

Stevens: "What do you remember happening?"

Rebecca: "Mom called all of us kids to the window. And we looked out there, and Abigail was stumbling around and falling. And then Mom turned on the patio light, the patio spotlight, and opened the window. And then she called out to Abigail, 'Okay, Abigail, go ahead, give us a big show!' And then she told us we should all laugh at Abigail because she was rebelling. So then we did that. We all laughed. And then Mom turned off the patio light and turned her back on the window and said that we should all turn our backs. So we did."

Stevens: "And then what?"

Rebecca: "I went back to the living room. But then one of

my brothers said, 'Look, Abigail just flopped onto the patio.' So then I came back and looked out the window and I saw her run into this big post we had. Then she got up and she walked a few more steps, and then she fell down again, right on the patio."

Stevens: "The light was on?"

Rebecca: "No. I turned it on. The patio spotlight. I turned on the light and looked out the window."

Stevens: "Then what?"

Rebecca: "I told Mom about it."

Stevens: "About what?"

Rebecca: "How Abigail had run into the post and fallen down."

Stevens: "And what did she say to that?"

Rebecca: "She said I should check on her every ten minutes. Look through the kitchen window every ten minutes to see what she's doing."

Stevens: "Did you do it?"

Rebecca: "Yes."

Stevens: "So you checked through the window every ten minutes."

Rebecca: "Yes."

Stevens: "And what did you see?"

Rebecca: "The third time I looked, she'd taken her clothes off."

Stevens: "In the cold and rain?"

Rebecca: "Yes. She had her clothes off."

Stevens: "What was she doing at that point? Do you remember?"

Rebecca: "She was lying on the ground. Not moving. With no clothes on."

Stevens: "Was she on her back, or facedown, or faceup, or on her side?"

Rebecca: "Facedown."

Stevens: "So what did you do at that point?"

Rebecca: "I told Mom."

Stevens: "What did your mom say?"

Rebecca: "To go out and check on her. 'Don't check on her through the window. Go outside and check this time.' That's what Mom said."

Stevens: "And what did you do then?"

Rebecca: "I went out and checked on her. And then I came back and told Mom she wasn't moving. I said I'd asked Abigail if she was okay, but Abigail didn't answer."

Stevens: "What next?"

Rebecca: "Me and Mom went outside together."

Stevens: "So you and your mother went outside to where Abigail was lying on the ground with no clothes on, facedown, and nonresponsive—not talking or moving. And what did you do?"

Rebecca: "Mom tried to talk to her."

Stevens: "What did she say?"

Rebecca: "She said, 'Abigail, come on, now, this is enough.' But Abigail didn't answer. And Mom got scared."

Stevens: "How could you tell that your mother was scared?"

Rebecca: "Because she got down on the ground and she rolled Abigail over, and we could see right then that Abigail wasn't breathing, and that she had mud in her mouth."

Stevens: "So then what?"

Rebecca: "We tried to take her inside."

Stevens: "How did you try to do that?"

Rebecca: "We tried to pick her up, but we couldn't lift her."

Stevens: "So what did you do—you and your mother?"

Rebecca: "We got the boys, and they carried her in. But first Mom got a sheet and put it over her."

Stevens: "Why?"

Rebecca: "So the boys wouldn't see her naked body."

IN THE COURSE of the proceedings, I'd acquired a friend, a woman named Georgette who was newly retired and, in sorting out what to do with her free time, had hit on this— attending a murder trial. Georgette had leaned in my direction on occasion to share her thoughts in whispered fashion ("That officer up there looks to be about sixteen years old, but, then, I can never tell these days") and during recesses had engaged me in conversation—to the effect, for example, that the Skagit County Fair had started, and that she'd gone to it and got- ten tired there; that pink salmon were currently running in the river; that pink salmon were also known as humpies; that her husband, every year, got excited about humpies and fished for them from a drift boat, and was fishing as we spoke; that tonight, at the Moose Club, she and her husband would attend a barbecue as part of an annual membership drive; and that all that work going on along the riverfront was phase two of a revitalization project that Mount Vernon's voters had approved by a narrow margin and that she had voted for, because she liked the idea of a boardwalk with flowers and hanging plants and evening lights, and it was about time the town did something like this, because the area along the river was in decline.

Once, at the end of a day of testimony, after Georgette and I had pushed through the courthouse door and were standing at a stoplight waiting to cross—both of us seeking to get our bearings in the white dazzle of late afternoon sun—a passing train, its endless coal cars heaped, made a grating cacophony. A teenager snaked past on a very short skateboard. From one of the cars held in check at the train crossing, a dog strained at an open window. "Out here, life goes on," observed Georgette, "like none of what goes on in there"—she pointed with her thumb at the courthouse behind us—"is real." Then she said I wouldn't see her the next day, because she and two friends were going on an excursion to the Glen Echo Botanical Garden in Bellingham, and had made a reservation for lunch at an Italian restaurant not far from the garden, with a view of the water.

Now, in the aftermath of Rebecca Harvey's testimony, Georgette turned to me and said, "Let me get this straight. This woman's daughter is facedown in the yard, naked. It's night. The girl's unconscious. It's an emergency. And what does this woman do? She goes inside and finds a sheet and spreads it over her daughter so her sons won't see her naked body. So her sons won't see her naked body!" Georgette touched my arm to emphasize her incredulity. "I'm sitting here," she said, "trying to put myself in this woman's shoes. I go out there and my daughter's face is in the dirt and it's midnight and rainy and she's got no clothes on. And the way I do this," Georgette explained, "is I imagine it's my own daughter, because I have a daughter. I have two daughters. I imagine it's my daughter, and I'm out there. I imagine that and I ask myself: Would I go inside and get a sheet? Get a sheet and put it over my daughter because my sons might see my daughter naked? What would be the thinking for me? Let's see. Do something for my daughter who's on the ground like that, or get a sheet so my sons won't see her naked? That's not a tough one," Georgette said. "I wouldn't even have to think about it. Probably, I couldn't even think about it. My mind would be going a million miles an hour on 'Is it CPR or mouth-to-mouth or chest compressions, or call 911, or should I sit down and put her head in my lap?' Or all of that, because I'd be going crazy with the fright she's dead. I'd be insane. This would be the worst thing that could happen. It's my daughter, my daughter, my daughter, my daughter. And there's these cuts from gravel on her legs, and her clothes are spread around and soaked, and she's been outside for hours and hours, and, me, this is a nightmare. This is the end of the world. This is the worst thing possible. No, no, no, no, no, no, no, please, please, please, please, please, please, please. This can't be. This can't be. I can't let my daughter be like this. There's nothing else on my mind at this point, nothing else to consider or think about. Just my daughter, nothing else. I don't stand there thinking, 'Okay, she's too heavy for me and Rebecca to get in the house, so I have to get my sons to do it because they're stronger than us, but the problem with that is, when my sons come out here, they're going to see Abigail naked, and that wouldn't be good for them, to see her that way, so the answer is, I'll leave Abigail on the ground here with Rebecca and go inside and get a sheet and bring it back and cover Abigail with it—that way, my sons won't see what they shouldn't.' I don't think that," said Georgette. "That never

occurs to me. And don't you think," she asked, "that everyone would be like me? Wouldn't that be the normal thing?
Wouldn't that be how a normal person felt? Sure, as a rule, I
guess I don't want boys to see a girl naked, I'm not going to sit
here and say I do. I'm not one who goes in for nudist beaches or
thinks it's okay for—you know—for people to see each other
naked. I'm not saying that. I'm saying it's mind-boggling. I'm
saying I'm trying to put myself in her shoes, but they don't fit."

WHEN REBECCA HARVEY WAS finished testifying, the sergeant in charge of night-service deputies for the Skagit County
Sheriff's Office took the stand. On the night of Abigail's death,
he said, a deputy had called him from Stone Lane to suggest he
come out there, which he did right away. At the Harvey residence, he found an ambulance, two patrol cars, and, "around
back of the house, a small female out there on a patio, where she
was getting CPR performed on her by paramedics." When
the ambulance pulled out with the girl inside, he followed it
to the Skagit Valley Hospital, and went inside to "keep tabs on
things and monitor and take notes and follow up." From the
foyer, he called the sheriff's office dispatch center for a copy
of the 911 call Betsy Harvey had made and asked a deputy to
deliver it to him on a compact disc. While he was doing that,
the coroner entered the emergency unit. He followed the coroner into the emergency room and took pictures of the corpse.
Then the disc arrived, and the sergeant took it down the hall to
an office and, using a computer there, listened to it. When that
was done, he went farther down the hall to the family waiting
room, which was off the lobby and behind secure doors, and

there he found Betsy and Delvin Harvey and a family-support officer. The sergeant explained that he would like to talk to Betsy Harvey privately, because she was the one who had made the 911 call, and then he and Betsy went down the hall to the room where he'd listened to the compact disc and, with Betsy's permission, he turned on his recorder and interviewed her.

Lincoln Stevens now entered into evidence the recording of the sergeant's interview with Betsy Harvey. We heard the sergeant ask Betsy for general information, such as the spelling of her name and her date of birth and address, the number of children she had, her husband's name and place of work, and the date on which they'd adopted Abigail. Then he asked, "What happened?"

"She stayed outside," Betsy answered.

"Why?"

"She wasn't happy."

"What wasn't she happy about?"

"We adopted her from Ethiopia. She had a terrible life there. No food and no house. Sick with diseases. Then she had to live in an orphanage. So she had all these *problems* from when she lived in Ethiopia. Mental-health problems and behavioral problems. Little did we know. We had no clue."

"Okay," said the sergeant.

"I really don't know what to say," said Betsy, "except that she was uncooperative and rebellious and had mental-health problems."

"Tonight," the sergeant said. "Tonight specifically. Tonight specifically, what happened?"

"Tonight specifically? Tonight specifically, she went outside and stayed there. Didn't matter how many times I said come in, she stayed out. She defied me. Wouldn't budge. I called my husband at work to tell him about it, and he said, 'Well, she'll get cold after a while and come in. Kids, they get cold, after a while they come in.'"

"Why wouldn't she come in? What was the issue?"

"The issue," said Betsy, "was nothing specific. It was just that things had built up with her mental problems, so she went outside and refused to come in. You know how some of these people do when they protest? You ever see these protestors that lay in the street? I kept telling her 'Come inside,' but she was so bent on her protest, and anyway I was the last person she was going to listen to. If I said A she was going to do B, and it didn't matter how cold or how dark it was. She had to follow through with her protest."

"I see."

"It's like people who stay on their hunger strike till they starve to death," said Betsy. "'Zactly the same. Only this was staying outside until she froze."

"Is that what you thought was happening, then? That your daughter was out there trying to kill herself?"

"I thought so," said Betsy. "She was so rebellious."

A Dr. Berg took the stand. She'd been the emergency physician on duty at the Skagit Valley Hospital on the night Abigail died. Around one-thirty, a member of a paramedic unit had called her to say that they were transporting in her direction a young female who was critical, unresponsive, and apparently not breathing, with no blood pressure or pulse, and that they'd performed CPR on her and had put her on a rhythm monitor to see if any heartbeat was detectable, but there was none, and that they'd shocked her seven times but she'd remained critical, at which point the ambulance arrived at the hospital and Dr. Berg took over, but to no avail, because the girl was dead.

"I went to speak to the family," Dr. Berg testified. "The mother and father. There's an office at the end of the hallway in the emergency department. It's the social worker's office. And someone had placed them in that room, and that's where I went to find them. And where I told them that their daughter had died."

"Okay," said Lincoln Stevens. "Starting with Betsy Harvey. What were her emotions like?"

"Very matter-of-fact," said Berg. "She was able to converse with me. She was very conversational. She was not distraught. She was not hysterical. It wasn't difficult to get information out of her. She was very verbal. Very verbal. And more than once she mentioned face planting, that the deceased had been out face planting on the lawn, which meant she was falling face-first, that her face was hitting the ground before any other part of her body, and Mrs. Harvey was matter-of-fact about it all."

"And what were the emotions of Mr. Harvey?"

"Mrs. Harvey did all of the talking. Mr. Harvey didn't have questions or anything to say. But I do remember that when I told them Abigail had died he dropped his head and shook his head, the way you do when you can't believe something is happening."

THE COURT ADMITTED into evidence the shirt, underwear, sweatpants, shoes, and socks Abigail—Abeba—wore on the night she died. Next we looked at slides, projected onto a screen, of the Harvey house and yard. These included mul-

tiple images of the closet where Abeba had regularly been confined, and photos of the room that included this closet, a room
that housed two bookcases. The closet door could only open
to ninety degrees because in its swing path stood one of these
bookcases, holding biographies of C. S. Lewis, John Smith,
and Laura Ingalls Wilder, volumes of *The American Girl Doll
Story Collection* and *The Complete Encyclopedia of Stitchery,* and
boxes of the Sonlight Science Curriculum. The other bookcase
held boxed audiocassettes, including *Building a Family That
Will Stand,* a hardback edition of *The Secret Garden,* and, on
its top shelf, a bridal photo of Betsy in a gold frame. Its background was gauzy, and she appeared to wear a nimbus.

One slide depicted, in diagram, the layout of the Harveys'
house—its rooms, hallways, and interior doors. It dawned on
me, looking at it, that when Abeba was forced into the closet,
she could have peered through a doorway into the Harveys'
bedroom and seen what we in the courtroom had seen in a
photograph: that mounted over the Harveys' headboard was
a painting of Washington crossing the Delaware, and that, on
one side of the bed, propped in a corner, were two stout sticks,
a sheathed knife, and a wooden sword.

I had to ask myself there in the courtroom: Who has a painting of Washington crossing the Delaware mounted over their
marital bed, and why do they have it there? Why this painting,
the familiar one, Washington aloof and heroic amid boatmen
at dawn on the ice-ridden river? Why this and not something
else above the headboard? But I couldn't think of a plausible
or reasonable answer. And I also understood that it wasn't an
important question. My wondering about the painting above
the headboard was just a response to strange information. I was

mining it for meanings because habit drove me. Because we work to understand things as an assessment of their dangers. The sticks, the sheath knife, and the wooden sword beside the bed—they were there in the shadow of danger, I thought, as weapons at hand for Delvin and Betsy Harvey should they be surprised, in bed, by enemies.

A FORENSIC PATHOLOGIST TOOK the stand and testified that he'd been called to the Skagit County Morgue twelve hours after Abigail died. He'd been briefed there by a sheriff's deputy, and had found the deceased to be five foot three and to weigh seventy-eight pounds, and, on visual assessment, potentially a victim of malnutrition, this latter hypothesis given credence by his observation of the contents of her stomach—some seeds and grains, but mostly fluid, suggesting that she'd eaten little on the last day of her life. Lincoln Stevens then projected an autopsy photo onto a screen (this is when the crying occurred that I mentioned earlier—the crying that provoked Judge Rasmussen's admonition) with the overhead lights turned off, and we listened to the forensic pathologist explain what we were looking at. "One thing I see initially in this photograph," he said, "and it will introduce us to what other photos will show in better detail later, is a bruise under an abrasion on the left forehead scalp. Here are smaller abrasions on the right forehead and on the nose. Here is one on the right pelvis, on both elbows, the right thigh, the left thigh, and the backs of the lower legs. You can also see the abnormal thinness of the body, with ribs showing. The cheeks are gaunt. The deceased's hair has been shaved to a length of no more than half an inch." The prosecutor displayed ten more photographs after this, all of them of the same grim and grisly nature, and then an eleventh, of Abigail's left thigh. "Here," said the pathologist, "I see a different sort of injury, a patterned injury. It's a long bruise that has two red margins and a blanched center. That can occur when the body is struck by any long, narrow object—a strap, a cord, a switch from a tree—something that hits the body and forces blood from the capillaries in that region to get pressed out toward the side of the object's impact point, causing these red lines where the blood vessels burst—the small blood vessels at the margin of the impact—and causing no bruised appearance in the center of the pattern, because there's no blood left in that site to discolor the skin. So it shows an outline of where an object struck, and there are four of these telltale injuries here, four of these impacts made by some object that was exerted in a striking fashion against the thigh."

Lincoln Stevens asked what kind of object. "As I said earlier," the pathologist replied, "any long, narrow object, such as a strap or cord, that is capable of a whiplike action can leave these sorts of impact marks."

"And you see four?"

"So far. But if we can put up the next slide, please." The next slide went up, and the pathologist continued. "This one shows the backs of the lower legs. Here are the ankles—the right ankle, the left ankle. The feet are beyond the picture. The knees are just up out of the picture on the right side of our screen. So we're looking at the backs of the calves. And this shows injuries that are sometimes as distinct as what we saw on the left thigh in the prior photograph, and sometimes less distinct. An impact such as I described, a patterned bruise such as I described, may be more distinct or less distinct, depending on the force and angle of impact. At any rate, I see ten similar-patterned bruises here, most of them horizontal, or nearly so. One is on the back of the right lower calf, where I'm pointing. Here is the second one. It slightly overlaps with a third one I'm pointing to. Probably the next one I can be clear about or certain of is the uppermost injury on the left calf. Here is another that I'm pointing to, down the leg here. And here are the two lower-most pattern bruises, the one I'm pointing to here, and this one, lower down on the left leg there. So these are all similar in appearance to the left thigh pattern bruises, and, taken in sum, I count fourteen of them, and I am confident that the deceased was struck at least fourteen times."

"Do you have an opinion, Doctor," Lincoln Stevens asked, "as to how old these injuries were when you examined the deceased?"

"Yes," answered the pathologist. "In my opinion, they occurred in the minutes or hours before her death."

A PHYSIOLOGIST TOOK the stand. She specialized in environmental medicine and had twelve years of experience as a medical technician attached to search-and-rescue units. She told the court that hypothermia sets in when body temperature drops below ninety-five degrees, and that its initial symptom is intense shivering, notably and steadily vigorous shivering, to the point where it constitutes a pulse or thrum, or a rhythmic shudder that can't be controlled. It has a life of its own, she said, an involuntary insistence that at first perturbs the nascent victim, who at onset retains a general coherence in the midst

of growing torpor, to the point of feeling frightened by circumstances. There is a consciousness of danger at this stage,
she told the court, but then, soon, confusion sets in, so that the
victim's sense of peril is undermined and things appear as if
imagined. The world takes on a dreamlike cast, and reality
unfolds in disjointed sequences. In this state, there are intermittent moments of struggle against conditions, during which
victims hug themselves, or bury their hands in their armpits,
or seek shelter beneath overhangs, or attempt to build snow
caves, or burrow under brush, or nestle amid leaves, but the
taking of such measures inevitably ends, and, thereafter, nothing the victims do appears logical. They stumble, fall, crawl
on their hands and knees, slur words, and sometimes—shed
their clothing. What is happening? What is happening is that
their blood vessels are squeezing shut, first in their feet and
hands, then in their forearms and calves, then in their thighs
and upper chests—and then their organs, one by one, go blood-
less. Eventually, their brains are all that's left, but soon, frozen,
their brains become useless. "And, look," said the physiologist, "don't think that all of this is peaceful. You don't just curl
up and go dreamily with hypothermia. Victims we've gotten
to in time say it's painful. I had a guy tell me—a climber we
saved—that he knew perfectly well that he was hypothermic,
but that he still believed he could get to the mountaintop. Not
soon after that, he understood he was no longer moving, and
that he couldn't move, and that he was never going to get to
the mountaintop. He felt as if his body was on fire, he said, and
wanted out of his clothes."

Stevens: "Tell me something. Let's take two people. One is
healthy and well fed and has normal body fat. The other is

abnormally thin and undernourished. Which is more likely to succumb to hypothermia?"

Witness: "The one who is thin and undernourished."

Stevens: "Why?"

Witness: "There's an obvious logic to it. If you're thin, you have substantial skin exposed to cold relative to interior body mass. You can't fight off cold weather as effectively as a result. Your limbs just don't have the fat or muscle. Your body is forced to vasoconstrict—to send the blood to vital organs and sacrifice the limbs."

Stevens: "The deceased in this case was five foot three inches tall and at the time of her death weighed seventy-eight pounds. The average weight for a female her height is between a hundred and four and a hundred and twenty-seven pounds. My question is, at seventy-eight pounds, was the deceased in this case more vulnerable to hypothermia than a female within the average range?"

Witness: "Yes. By all means. Absolutely."

◆ DAY SEVEN. The third-oldest of the Harvey sons, Reuben, took the stand, a relatively stout boy with the breaking voice of puberty. Reuben's nickname in the family was Boo, and his one-word answers more than hinted at defiance. Lincoln Stevens asked, "How would you describe Abigail's behavior?" Reuben answered, "Disobedient." Stevens asked, "Can you give an example?" Reuben answered, "No." After that, for a long time, Reuben's answer to everything was "I don't remember," but then Stevens produced a deposition from months before in which Reuben had been forthcoming, and he battered Reuben with it, as in "Do you remember stating that your father cut Abigail's hair almost all the way off because she'd mowed the grass too short? . . . Do you remember saying that on three occasions you observed Abigail moving a big pile of rocks from one location to another as a form of punishment? . . . Do you remember saying that on four occasions you saw Abigail walk for two hours repeatedly around the perimeter of your yard, also as a punishment? . . . Do you remember saying that you observed your father install a lock on the door to the closet Abigail was confined to? . . . Do you remember saying that you observed your father installing a post so that the garden hose could be draped over it for Abigail to shower under?" In the end, it didn't matter that Reuben, on the stand, couldn't remember anything. Stevens got around him with his deposition. "Do you remember saying that you saw your mother go outside that night? . . . Do you remember saying that you saw Abigail fall down four times, two of those on gravel? . . . Do you remember saying that you saw your mother spank Abigail out there? . . . Do you remember saying that she used what is now Exhibit Sixty-nine, a plumbing line? . . . Do you remember saying in your deposition that when your mother spanked Abigail out there, Abigail cried? . . . Do you recall saying that you saw your mother hit Abigail with the plumbing line on the back of her legs, specifically on her lower legs? . . . If you don't remember, Reuben, please turn to page fourteen of the transcript of your deposition and read, starting at line sixteen, to the bottom of the page. Out loud."

In this way—against his will—Reuben testified. His breaking pubescent voice, ranging across three octaves, soon became a croak.

Stevens: "So your mother went out with the sheet."

Reuben: "Yes."

Stevens: "And then she asked you and your two older brothers to go outside."

Reuben: "Yes."

Stevens: "And what's the next thing you remember happening?"

Reuben: "My two older brothers, my mom, and me brought Abigail inside."

Stevens: "Then what?"

Reuben: "My mom took Abigail's pulse."

Stevens: "How?"

Reuben: "With her fingers."

Stevens: "Then what?"

Reuben: "She said that she couldn't feel any pulse."

Stevens: "Then?"

Reuben: "She called Dad."

Stevens: "After that?"

Reuben: "She did what Dad said. She called 911."

MICAH HARVEY WAS gangly, had a long, wavering stride, and kept his glasses on a lanyard. These glasses, with their thick lenses, both magnified his pupils and made them appear cloudy. Now and then during his time on the stand, Micah checked on the knot of his tie, or tried to run it up against his prominent Adam's apple. Its pointed tip rode over his belt clasp. His dimpled chin receded, like his father's. His ears lay flat against his skull. He wore braces, which caused him to slur, and he often dropped his head when he spoke. Sometimes his lips moved but no words came out. Sometimes he pinched the bridge of his nose before answering a question, and sometimes he pressed on the stems of his glasses. His voice broke when he had to tell Lincoln Stevens that, on the night Abigail died, he'd gone outside on his mother's orders with the plumbing line in hand. "Okay," said Stevens. "And what was Abigail doing?"

Micah: "She was just standing there."

Stevens: "And what did you do?"

Micah: "I . . ."

Stevens: "Take all the time you need, Micah."

Micah: "I gave her spankings."

Stevens: "Where exactly? Where did you spank her?"

Micah: "On the lower . . . on the lower legs."

Stevens: "How many times did you spank her there?"

Micah: "Five."

Stevens: "Why five?"

Micah: "Because Mom told me to."

Stevens: "And after that?"

Micah: "I went inside and did homework."

THE OLDEST OF the Harvey children, Ezekiel, had joined the army on his eighteenth birthday, nine months before the trial began. He'd received a writ summoning him to testify, and been granted leave, and now here he was, wearing pressed blue jeans, a short-sleeved plaid shirt, white socks, and boat shoes. Ezekiel strode down the courtroom's center aisle with stiff poise and took his seat in the stand like a man of the world, and I recognized him as the anguished boy sitting between his grandparents on the day his parents were arraigned. Before long, he was asked if he'd ever seen his parents argue, to which he replied, "Naturally. Though they were very good about keeping their arguments behind closed doors."

Ezekiel swiveled in his chair. He touched his buzz cut. His eyes glistened. His face turned pink. "One could say that their arguments became more frequent with time," he said, "and that these arguments focused on acts of disobedience and on disciplinary measures that were potentially needed. One could say that the balance of authority, the framework of authority, broke down gradually after Abigail was adopted. I cannot say to what degree. I cannot say exactly how, but that is the impression that sticks in my mind—that something shifted."

Stevens: "What shifted?"

Ezekiel: "The balance of power."

Stevens: "In terms of your father being the overall boss of the family, you're indicating that that appeared to change, is that correct?"

Ezekiel: "Yes."

Stevens: "You're saying your mother became the boss of the family?"

Ezekiel: "No."

Stevens: "Can you clarify for me? What are you saying, then?"

Ezekiel: "I'm saying that a shift occurred, and that as the difficulties with Abigail became more severe, my mother became a more powerful figure in the decision making about discipline."

Stevens: "More powerful than your father?"

Ezekiel: "Yes."

Stevens: "Your father lost his decision-making power?"

Ezekiel: "No. But he became less powerful."

Stevens: "And your mother more powerful?"

Ezekiel: "Yes. More powerful. Not that she wasn't powerful already. She was always powerful. She'd always been powerful. But after Abigail came, even more so. She just seemed to gain a lot more power, and my father, he kind of shriveled."

FORTY MINUTES LATER, Ezekiel could barely speak through his hysterics. His stiff, formal diction had disintegrated, and he inhaled in gasps. Lincoln Stevens had led him to a kind of brink, where he reeled. He sobbed or held his face in his palms, but a strained insistence was working in him, too, and at intervals it shored him up enough that he could add to his narrative. He said, between convulsions, that on the night Abigail died he'd done exactly what his mother asked: he'd whipped Abigail a dozen times across the calves with the plumbing line. She'd cried, and he'd ordered her to come inside, just as his mother had told him to do. When Abigail refused, he'd whipped her another dozen times, but on the rear, as his mother specified. Again he ordered Abigail to come inside, again she refused, so he gave up, went inside, and, still holding the plumbing line, watched Abigail through a window.

She took ten or twenty steps, he told the court, and began throwing herself down. "And it wasn't just like a falling down, where you collapse on the spot. It was a lunging forward, like sliding on a water slide. She would throw herself down on her hands and knees, and get back up. She would walk a few feet or so and do it again. Sometimes she would get up on her knees and crawl, like one crawl or two crawls forward, and then get up. But most of the time she would throw herself down and get right back up. She did that on the gravel, on the slab that went along the back of our house, on the walkway, and on the back patio. She went on throwing herself down, and she hit her forehead, hard, on the concrete. And then my mother came to the window and watched, too, and then she said to me, 'This has gotten dangerous. Abigail needs to come in immediately,' and she went out on the patio, and I went, too, and she said, 'Abigail, apologize and come inside.' And Abigail just looked at her, and so my mother reached down and put her arms under Abigail's armpits and tried to lift her, and then Abigail went limp, completely limp, and my mother still tried to lift her, but she couldn't with Abigail being limp, and I remember my mother grabbed the back of Abigail's shirt, but that didn't work, either. So then she said, 'We'll go back in the house and get Micah,' and we did that, and she told us, me and Micah, to go out there and lift Abigail by the armpits, one on each side, but first, me, I was to go out there and take off Abigail's shoes and socks, because her knees were all scraped up and bloody, and because her clothes were wet from the rain, and water had dripped down and made blood drip all over her shoes, and so I was supposed to take off her shoes before she could come in. But first, my mother told me, I had to put on latex gloves. I had to do that. So I did that, and I went out there and knelt by Abigail and took off her shoes and socks, and she didn't fight about it or do anything, she just stood there. And I felt kind of funny then, like it was a nightmare, kneeling with her shoes like that, and getting her socks off until her feet were bare, and I knew something was wrong. But, finally, I got her socks and shoes off, and my mother yelled out the window to me to go around the side of the house and put them in the garbage can. So I did that, and then, when I came back around, Micah was there, waiting for me, and we went over there to where Abigail was, and she was down on the patio behind the picnic table now, on the ground, on her back, where there wasn't a lot of light, but I could see that she'd pulled her pants and underwear down below her knees, and she was looking up at me, and I could see her body, and Micah saw it, too, and then he turned around and bolted. And I yelled to my mother that Abigail was naked on the patio from the waist down, and she said, 'All right, that's it, I've had enough! If she wants to stay outside, she can stay outside! You come inside!' And I did—but first I looked at Abigail. It was raining and dark, and things were confused, so I just let my mother kind of fade into the background, and I looked at Abigail where I shouldn't have looked. And I said to Abigail, 'Abigail, come in. Come inside now. Come inside. Forget about everything and come inside. Please, come inside, you have to come inside.' And I was staring at her . . . at her . . . at where I shouldn't have been staring. And what I wanted to do, I wanted to kneel down there and pick her up in my arms, just take her in my arms, but I didn't do that, and maybe five seconds passed with me looking at her private parts, and my mother yelled, 'Come in now! If she wants to be outside, she can be outside!' So I went in. And my mother was by the kitchen window, looking up at the ceiling, whispering, 'I love Abigail because God made her, I love Abigail because God made her,' and when she saw me she stopped and said to me, 'Did you see her private parts?' And I said yes. And my mother said that it was wrong of me to have looked, and that it was supposed to happen for the first time on my wedding night, and then she gave me a lecture, or a sermon, maybe a three- or four-minute sermon, and meanwhile Abigail was still out there on the ground by the picnic table, naked from the waist down."

EZEKIEL'S TESTIMONY ENDED the day's proceedings. On my way out, I tapped my father on his shoulder and said that I'd wait for him on the third floor of the courthouse, where it was quiet, and would be sitting there on one of its hallway benches, ready, when he was, to drive home. Then I left and climbed the stairs to where the building felt hushed in an institutional way—a wide marble hall, dusted, mopped and polished, doors along it with frosted privacy windows underneath fluorescent lights that washed over portraits of retired judges—and sat down. It was after four-thirty. No one was around. The offices of the auditor and the county clerk had closed. The processes of county administration were on hold until tomorrow. The heat had been moving up all day, but three silent fans had pushed it around and were still at work steadily and evenly. I didn't know what to think, and felt bereft, and in the face of that did what I was prone to do at moments like this—that is, I called Alison. I called and told her, first, that I loved her, and then I told her what Ezekiel had said—that he'd wanted to kneel and take Abeba in his arms, that he'd known, in some place, that something was wrong, that he'd had to put on latex gloves and drop Abeba's shoes in a trash can, and that he'd looked at her the way he'd looked at her, as a boy his age in nightmarish circumstances, as a son who'd followed his mother's orders to go outside into the dark and rain and whip this girl, his adopted sister, first on her calves a dozen times, and then on her backside a dozen more, all of it under the guiding principle that in doing so he was assisting his parents' efforts to prevent her from going to hell. To which Alison said, "Are you okay?"

After I hung up, I went on sitting. A deputy came along with a pistol, handcuffs, and a baton on his belt, and said I had about fifteen minutes before the courthouse closed for the day. He went down the stairs, and my father came up with his briefcase in one hand and his cereal bag in the other. He was wearing what he always wore when it came to any professional matter—a polyester suit, a clip-on tie, and suspenders that always seemed loose. He sat next to me, sighed, and dropped his head, and for at least a full minute, neither of us spoke. We said nothing because it was possible for us to do that. We knew what our mutual silence meant—knew when the time was right for a joint understatement so full it came to zero. We sat there sharing the unspoken observation that everything about this case was sad, and that without much effort you could make the leap from the facts of this case to a very sad portrait of the human race. Which is not to say that my father and I were pessimists in that moment, or even realists, just that we were dumbfounded and appalled, and felt that the more we knew the less we understood; I knew he was thinking all of that while we both said nothing.

"I'm no psychiatrist," my father finally said. "I really don't know the first thing about psychiatry. But I'll tell you what I think about Delvin and Betsy Harvey. Now that we've heard from four of their children, the others being too young to testify. I think Delvin wanted to play the ocarina but that he was also a sadist. I think that, when Abeba refused to go along with the program in his house, he decided to pretend to himself that he was just following Betsy's lead. I think he was ashamed of the fact that he enjoyed meting out punishment to children. Then there's Betsy. She knows perfectly well that on the night Abeba died a part of her wanted that to happen. She knew that then and she knows it now. She thought that, if Abeba were to die, that would be bad, but only for a while. Time would go by, and then things would return to how they were before, with everything perfect and under her control. Now, Betsy would never admit this out loud. Not to me, her lawyer, and not to anybody. It's a secret she carries. A private thing. And it's a terrible thing to carry around. So terrible that, what a lot of people do, they talk themselves out of things like this—things like what Betsy felt on the night Abeba died. The fact that people do what they do, or think what they think, or say what they say—it can be so inconsistent with their view of themselves that they deny to themselves that it ever happened. They invent a story for themselves in which they didn't think or feel or do or say anything wrong, and that story becomes reality for them, so real that they'll defend it to the bitter end, even when the facts in the real world say otherwise. They play this trick on themselves because, if they don't, they'll have to accept that they're not the good person they thought they were. Or, in Betsy's case, not a perfect person. If they don't go back to the moment of their bad behavior and erase it forever and pretend it didn't happen, then they'll have to accept that they *are* what they *did*. They'll have to accept that they're flawed and human. Which you would think wouldn't be that hard for someone of the Christian faith.

"Think about this," my father said. "You remember that recording played in court? Betsy is talking to a deputy at the hospital a few hours after Abeba died, and she tells him she thought Abeba was trying to kill herself. That it was similar, in her mind, to a hunger strike. In other words, Betsy understood the danger. It was clear to her that Abeba might die. Yet, despite that, she went right on demanding that Abeba apologize before she could come inside and get warm. Which tells me something about Betsy's state of mind. She knows Abeba could die out there but isn't doing all she can to prevent it. Not at that juncture. But then it gets a little later, and her conscience starts to gnaw at her, so she sends her sons out to bring Abeba in. That should have been the end of it. Her conscience should have won at that point. But, unfortunately, it didn't win, because when her son reported to her that Abeba had removed her pants, Betsy's conscience lost the upper hand. She told her son to leave Abeba out there, half naked on the ground, when minutes before, she'd said to him that the situation was dangerous and that Abeba needed to be brought in immediately. For me, the linchpin moment in this case is the moment when Betsy tells her son to come inside without bringing Abeba in with him."

He paused, shook his head, and clenched his teeth. "So what is that?" he asked. "It's not Murder One, because there's no premeditation. Betsy didn't plan Abeba's death. Instead, she took advantage of circumstances—that's what the evidence seems to be telling us. Is it Murder Two? In Murder Two, there doesn't have to be premeditation, but there does have to be intent. Did Betsy intend for Abeba to die? You might be able to make that case—you might be able to make the case that when she told her son to come in and leave Abeba out there, she fully intended for Abeba to die. Maybe. But Stevens didn't try for that. He tried instead for homicide by abuse. He's trying to say there's a causal connection—that Abeba died because she'd been abused. And, the truth is, I think his case is made. For two reasons. One, the coroner pointed out that Abeba, on the night of her death, was abnormally thin. Food had been withheld, and she was underweight for her age. Two, the physiologist who testified about hypothermia pointed out that the undernourished are more susceptible to hypothermia than the well fed. They don't have the body mass to fight it off. You put those things together, one and two, and you have the ingredients for homicide by abuse. That's what Stevens is going to point out when he makes his final speech to the jury, and I don't think there's anything to be done about it. I think that, if justice takes its course, Betsy and Delvin Harvey will be found guilty, and you know what? That's as it should be."

He seemed distraught, though. He shook his head, and then he put his elbows on his knees and dropped his chin and said, "Let me rest for a minute. Just for one minute."

I figured he needed space. Another person—Alison, for instance—might have opted for more proximity, for putting a hand over his shoulder or against his back, and I wouldn't blame them, and in retrospect wish I'd done something in that vein, because you never know, but, anyway, I thought just then that all he needed was a little room, so I gave it to him by walking away ten yards and leaning over the broad, yawning stairwell with my phone in my hand so as to check the time, and then I lowered my head, too, like my father, and looked at the floor, and let a full minute pass.

When I returned to the bench, my father was poised in stillness. His briefcase and bag of bran flakes were on his lap. His head was up. His eyes were open. He looked meditative on first assessment, and then he looked dazed, and then he looked as if paralyzed by hypnosis. I thought to wave a hand in front of his face to see if he might blink, but quelled that urge, possessed as I was, for the moment, by the belief, or hope, that he was merely preoccupied, or that a case of vertigo was starting. On it went, though—my father at a remove, or as if suppressed beneath paralysis, for a duration that was overlong and progressively more troubling, until, at last, I did in fact wave a hand in front of his face, in a tentative way, eliciting nothing— not even a blink—and waved more, until I was forced to accept that my father was in the throes of a disaster, of what sort I couldn't yet say. At which point he jerked, slumped to his left, and would have hit the ground if I hadn't put my hands out as a stay against his fall. Which is what I'm still doing.

Post-Trial

After two hours at Skagit Valley Hospital, while still in the emergency ward, my father swam up out of unconsciousness long enough to say, "Can you bring me my shoes?" A little later, my mother, Alison, Danielle, and Danielle's husband, Leonard, arrived, but at that point, unfortunately, my father's eyes were closed, and they remained closed thereafter, and he never spoke again or moved beyond some twitching of his eyelids, fingers, and toes, and the rising and falling of his chest, and an intermittent pulsing in his gullet. And so his final words were "Can you bring me my shoes?," to which I'd answered, "Dad," before he sank again.

In the wee hours of the night—because, as slowly as things move in a hospital, they never stop—my father was transferred to an intensive-care unit, and there, confronted with the possibility of a mechanical ventilator, my mother produced from her handbag a folded copy of my father's Directive to Physicians, in which he'd declared, "being of sound mind," that he was willfully and voluntarily making known his desire that his life not be artificially prolonged and that he be permitted to die naturally. After my mother presented this document, my father was again transferred, this time to a room whose door opened onto the intersection of two corridors. It was a double room. Behind its bisecting curtain, someone else was dying. The window was on her side. Members of her family had to pass the foot of my father's bed in the course of their vigil. We got to know them a little from milling in the corridor together, and in a way that seemed inevitable. They were the Vargas family. Mrs. Vargas, who had been on dialysis for years, was dying from renal failure, and her two sons and their wives and children came and went while her daughter stayed entrenched, indomitably so, with a quiet insistence. There was something both delicate and intimate about our family interactions. We and the Vargases understood one another in a way not possible under other circumstances. We touched on small things amid the larger ones. It was as though we were traveling together on an oceangoing ship operated by medical personnel. As though we were leaning against its railings, side by side, while passing over depths. We were companionably miserable, though we also spoke, for example, about the contents of the hospital's vending machines. Then Mrs. Vargas died, and her corpse was wheeled from the room. It went past us slowly, pushed with stately respect. Mrs. Vargas's daughter quickly picked up the vestiges of her mother's habitation on the windowed side of the curtain, stuffed them into bags, and said, before exiting for good, that she wished us well and would pray for us. Minutes later, Danielle pulled back the mid-room curtain, and the room became larger and brighter both. The next evening, after all three of Danielle and Leonard's children had arrived—one from her Peace Corps post in Sierra Leone, and the others from their universities in Montana and Ohio—my father's breathing slowed, grew faint, then halted, and with astonishing immediacy he became, like Mrs. Vargas, a corpse to be wheeled toward a morgue.

I ended up doing what Mrs. Vargas's daughter had done— that is, picking up the vestiges of someone's last station in the world. Among them were my father's bag of bran flakes, stuffed inside his briefcase, where I also found documents pertinent to the Harvey trial—motions, rulings on motions, respondents' briefs, depositions, witness lists, incident reports, transcriptions of interviews, lists of redactions, investigative narratives, notices of intent, records requests, continuance orders, demands for disclosure, notes for calendar, warrants, summonses, notes for hearings. I sat there turning back the pages of these documents. And, of course, I wept.

Later, in bed, with the lights out and the windows open— and for me interrupting the interregnum between wakefulness and sleep wherein thoughts are like fireflies—Alison sang, very softly—

> *Alison, I know this world is killing you,*
> *Alison, your aim is true.*

—getting the lyrics wrong intentionally, as she had on numerous occasions in our marriage, although this time, in the wake of my father's death, there was no humor in it, only pathos. She was referring to an episode we'd come back to together repeatedly in a comic vein, an episode long past wherein my father—as he, my mother, Alison, and I were eating breakfast at the Pancake House in Snoqualmie Pass while on a journey over the mountains to visit his brother, Thorndike—exclaimed, out of nowhere, "Hey, I was fiddling with the radio on my way to work yesterday and I came across this singer who kept crooning your name, Alison, so I listened to what this guy was getting at, and what he was singing was 'Alison, I know this world is killing you, Alison, your aim is true,' and I thought that was true of you, that the world is killing you but your aim is true, if you know what I mean, in a loose way, sort of." These last qualifiers being my requisite rejoinder when the two of us engaged in this manner of remembering, so that now, in bed, sung into wakefulness, I said to Alison, "In a loose way, sort of," to which she replied, "I miss your dad. And everyone else. Everyone I've ever known who's died."

MY MOTHER ARRANGED for a cremation. The company that saw to it tried to sell her, beforehand, an urn made of bronze with a screw-top lid, and then something simpler with a pewter finish, and made sure she knew of its engraving service, and gave her phone numbers for nearby columbaria, but in the end, my mother asked the company to put my father's remains in a box Leonard built in his garage, because, as she told its salesperson, Leonard was her son-in-law.

Leonard's box was an object of staid beauty, dependent for its effect not on ornamentation but on its dimensions in relation to one another, on his choices while bringing grains into proximity, and on his keyed joinery. Its boards were of the deep color cedar attains under circumstances of unimpeded, steady growth over a considerable duration. Having frequented construction sites in his role as a concrete contractor over a long period of time, Leonard had collected, and stored, cast-off wood slabs of varying species, which his eye was drawn toward on the verges of clearings in heaps of refuse and slash, and which were on offer free of charge—the whorled boles of bifurcating maples, for example, but also bolts of tight-grained alder, lengths of yew, and twists of smooth orange madrone. Leonard had an ancient band saw in his garage, and a high-end planer, and of course a table saw with its associated span of surface, which meant, first, no room for a car there, but also that his garage was so tightly packed with woodworking equipment there was hardly room for him among it, and yet he generated, in his tight, dense, and disordered shop, cabinetry and furnishings of a high order, working in his spare time with a radio on that almost always delivered the play-by-play of sports events, which Leonard hardly listened to but liked in the background of his woodworking absorptions. At any rate, when it came to the box for my father's remains, Leonard was able to start with rough wood and, once he had it planed, follow the directions in a woodworking magazine for a keepsake container while modifying its bulk, and adding to it a tightly gasketed lid that dropped into its seating on brass quadrant hinges, and finish it with three coats of linseed oil. This reliquary of a sort ended up in my mother's living room on the fall-top of a secretaire my mother's parents had given my mother and father as a housewarming gift when they bought their first and only home, the year I was born. Leonard's box looked, to me, temporarily placed there, as if its siting was transitory, but my mother said that she intended to leave it where it was, at least for now, that maybe at some point in the future she would move it, but who knew when or where. Meanwhile, at the moment, she couldn't think about it, because the remains in Leonard's box were all that was left of her husband in the physical universe, so that to transfer them elsewhere would be a further loss—or "another grief," as she put it—which didn't have to be, she added, because about this she had agency and could prevent it from so being, although the day would come when Danielle and I would have to situate our father's remains, as well as her own, she understood that and hated to leave us with it, to pass on this obligation on top of the obligation to address the material effluvium of her life and my father's life, all of that on top of the financial and legal millstones that would inevitably attach to their estate, however simple it was, because, however simple it was, there would still be the headaches of probate and the many both mundane and esoteric tasks left behind in the shadow of parental death, which she knew about because, when her own parents had died, she'd taken care of these things—all of this got said as we stood in her living room, pondering the placement of the cedar box Leonard had made.

We rented a hall in Wallingford, three blocks from Cajovna, and invited 120 people to what we billed as a memorial and celebration, merging those terms because they made sense to us who'd loved my father intimately, and in the recognition that, although death is sad, he'd lived into his eighties and had died without pain and had done what he'd wanted to be doing right up to the end. We were mourning, like anyone would be, as it goes without saying—mourning because he wasn't among us anymore and we missed his proximity, his voice, his face, his opinions, all of it, of course and obviously—but, still, we were not going to carry on as if life was any different from what it was, or as if our circumstances—a death in the family—were anything other than an eternal human norm, or as if he'd died under circumstances someone might reasonably rail against, shaking a fist at the heavens because the death in question seemed unjust in some way. No, that wasn't what had happened, and so we decided that our memorial and celebration should take all of that kind of thinking into account, and we concluded that, though it would not be like a wake with its attendant festivities, neither would it be grim and solemn, and that a balance should be struck, as the dead person in question, we inferred from our knowledge of him, would probably have wanted. That said, he'd left no instructions.

We gathered on a Sunday afternoon, and my father's three grandchildren got up one at a time and went to the podium to illuminate him, each choked up while remembering small things—for example, that when they were little he sometimes walked them to a corner grocery and said they should pick out whatever they wanted there, and that he apparently didn't know how to swim other than by dog-paddling, and that they'd been surprised once at a playground to witness his facility when it came to bank shots with a basketball, always from the left and about twenty feet out; he could go nine for ten that way, and did it in a style that involved raising his right knee as his hands came up to release the ball from a low point but on a high trajectory. There stood my two nieces and my nephew, teary-eyed and reading what they had to say from notes, while I sat beside Alison holding her hand, which I squeezed a little now, so that the private message flowed between us that our mixed feelings about our childless condition were, for me, agitated at the moment by the beauty of what was unfolding before our eyes. Alison squeezed back.

Then Leonard got up and spoke, getting choked up, too, which was something I'd never seen before, telling us in hoarse fragments that when he was younger he'd felt like he wasn't good enough for Danielle and that she could have done better than to marry someone without prospects, and that back then he'd felt proud and defiant simultaneously in the presence of people who did better than he did, but that he'd never felt that way—proud and defiant—around Royal, nor did Royal treat him like he wasn't good enough for his daughter or, for that matter, not good enough in general. In fact, the opposite. And Leonard was grateful for that. Then he told a story wherein he's threatened with a lawsuit by a development company over a concrete retaining wall that, according to its lawyer, bulged because of shortcomings in Leonard's work, and wherein his father-in-law composes letters to this lawyer until the threat disappears, sending copies to Leonard so he'll know what's going on. Leonard's point being that he couldn't understand to this day how letters so nonconfrontational could achieve what they achieved, "but that was Royal."

When Leonard was done, it was Danielle's turn, and then Alison's and mine. Next came my aunt Cora—Uncle Thorndike's widow—my mother's sister Doris, a lawyer from my father's firm, and, unexpectedly, a man with a swirl of silver hair who raised his hand and said he wanted to speak. Which he did, softly, with what I took to be shame. He had a broken nose smashed flat and leftward, and a skein of broken blood vessels etched his weathered face, and, I thought, he'd put on his best flannel shirt for this occasion. "Here we go," he began,

in a muffled bass that made his words difficult to discern, so
that I had to lean toward him. "I got in some trouble a long
time ago, trouble with the law. I did time for what I'd done,
seven months and eleven days, and the deceased, who was my
lawyer, he didn't charge me, because he knew I didn't have it.
So there's that. Free work. Pro-bono labor. I got out and got
on my feet and started in commercial fishing. And whenever I
caught fish after that, I put one on ice for him. I chose a good
one, and I tried to pay him back that way. I put a fish in Styro-
foam and left it on his porch, because it so happened he didn't
live too far from where I keep my boat. Maybe seven or eight
times a year I did that, for twenty-two years. And every single year, the deceased wrote me around Christmastime to say
thanks for the fish, so there's that. Like clockwork. He mailed
his holiday cards like clockwork. Then, last month, I brought
a fish and found out he'd passed, and I was sorry to hear it.
And I'm still sorry to hear it, and that's why I came here. To
tell his family I'm sorry and that I tried to pay him back."

He disembarked from the podium, which my mother then
claimed. She pointed out how she was fully aware that at
memorials people focused on the exemplary and left out the
middling and the flawed, as it should be (muted laughter in
the hall, or maybe it's more accurate to say chuckles of affirma-
tion), and also of the tradition whereby widows didn't speak at
a time like this, but that she was going to do it anyway. She did,
and if anyone cried during our session of eulogies, it was likely
then, as my mother spoke, laying out not just her husband's
life but their sixty years together, how they'd met, the early
days of their marriage, their era as young parents, their later
years together, and how through it all her husband had been

the best sort of partner, one who understood what it meant to respect somebody and love them for who they are and not wish for them to be different, or need them to be different, that had been the key to their long and happy life together, but, also, her husband had been natively cheerful and essentially kind, and those things had helped a lot, too. "And now," she said, "my sister Doris, who has always had a beautiful singing voice and retains it to this day, is going to conclude by singing a song I know Royal would have liked at his memorial," at which point someone sat down at a piano, and Doris came to the podium and sang "My Cup Runneth Over," which is maudlin, yes, unmistakably and inarguably, and as such inescapably effective at eliciting tears. When that was done, Danielle got up again and thanked everyone for coming and told them to enjoy the cookies and punch, and to look at the displays of photographs if they wanted, and to sign the guest register if they would, and then her son, who'd driven fourteen hours from Bozeman, queued up a song list he'd put together that included "Over the Rainbow," "What a Wonderful World," "You Were Always on My Mind," and "Amazing Grace."

I was refilling the punch bowl, working from a cooler stashed under the table where our surplus was on hold, when a very old but determined-looking man approached and said to me that he hadn't seen my father in at least thirty years, and that he was exactly ninety, and that he'd retired from the law in 1975 on the heels of a payout that came his way when his firm won a major antitrust case, but that before that, in the late 1950s and the '60s and early '70s, he'd known my father relatively well; in fact, he said, they'd gone to trial together in 1960. I gave him a glass of punch, and took one myself, and came around the table and shook his gnarled hand, and then, without ceremony or preamble or presumptive apology, he told me in his croaking voice that he and my father had jointly been appointed to defend a rug cleaner named Ernie Bayer who'd been charged with murder. For seven years, he said, the case had gone unsolved; then a shipping clerk named Rodney Lindquist came under suspicion in the wake of new information, and in the course of a police interrogation asserted that he and Ernie Bayer had together robbed a grocer named Warren Jensen of eight hundred dollars.

I stopped this man to say that his memory was incredible, but he waved me off with a forefinger and said that, knowing he was going to be here, and intending to tell Royal's family about the matter, he'd reviewed old files and prepared himself. Then he pronounced the name "Rodney Lindquist," again, this time with a large hint of disdain. Rodney Lindquist, he said, told the police that the robbery of Jensen at first went as planned, but that Bayer, in the middle of their stickup, began to suspect that Jensen recognized him, and after that—according to Lindquist—Bayer kidnapped and killed Jensen, with Lindquist just along for the ride.

Big case, my informant told me. With stories in the newspapers and lurid interest in the details. In court, a sheriff's detective went over the ballistics: four shots from a .45-caliber pistol. A plumber and a carpenter described finding Jensen's body in the kitchen of a half-built house they were working on. Jensen's widow described her anxiety when he didn't come home that night. A butcher explained that only he and Jensen knew the combination to their safe. There was a householder who heard three shots fired, an insurance adjuster who saw

Lindquist in a tavern, a cab driver, a grocery checker, a hotel manager, an expert on signatures, and there was Lindquist's girlfriend, who testified that she was outside the market when Bayer emerged with Jensen in tow and stuffed him into Lindquist's car. But, mainly, there was Lindquist.

With his glass of punch quivering in his hand, this attorney told me that my father was having none of this, because Bayer was in Everett, twenty miles north, when Jensen was murdered, as five witnesses in succession testified, all of them rug cleaners who'd been working with Bayer on the night in question at a motel in the process of refurbishment. Lindquist's girlfriend, under cross-examination by my father, admitted she couldn't identify Bayer as the man who'd brought Jensen from the market at gunpoint; in fact, she couldn't remember much at all, and fell into a cascade of contradictory statements. Lindquist, too, fell apart under questioning. "So, look," the attorney said, while trying to calm his wavering punch, "I was busy, and I said to your father, Hey, why don't you do the closing, so he did the closing, and in his closing he made it clear that Bayer was being framed and that Lindquist, since he couldn't do away with evidence of his participation, was hoping to serve time as an accomplice and not a perpetrator by pretending that this guy he sort of knew but didn't like—Bayer—had done the deed. And then the jury went out and deliberated, but there was no verdict that day, and we had to wait."

At this point, he put his glass of punch down on the table and pulled from his inner jacket pocket a wad of folded paper. It took him a while, but he got it open. It was composed of two newspaper articles he'd copied and was giving to me. The first had run on page 2 of *The Seattle Times* on March 29,

1960, under the headline "Murder-Trial Jury Gives No Hints."
The second was from the front page of the next day's edition,
where the headline read "Eisenhower Sees Test-Ban Progress." Above that was a banner—"Bayer Found Innocent of
Grocer's Murder"—and under it was "Attorney Hugged by
Defendant." There was my father, age twenty-nine, clutched
by the rug cleaner Ernie Bayer.

"Take them," the attorney said, referring to the articles. "I
brought them for you and your family."

I took them. The attorney said, "We'd been appointed. By
a judge. Because Bayer couldn't pay. He'd mangled his arm
in an accident and lived on disability in a group home somewhere. What did we make—fifty bucks each? I asked your
father did he want to have a drink. I told him I'd stand him to
a couple of drinks. He turned me down. He said he couldn't
do it because he had this other case. Another appointed case.
Same thing. Fifty bucks. I don't think he was even thirty yet."

I said, "He was in the middle of a trial when the end came.
Maybe that was good."

My father's co-counsel in the case of *State of Washington v.
Ernie Bayer* reached, with a shaky hand, to pick up his glass of
punch again. "Good for him," he said, "but not for the State.
They're going to have to wipe everything out and start over
again with a new trial."

MY MOTHER STAYED in the house where she'd lived with
my father. About a month after he died, I went there to help her
get rid of things. Getting rid of things had been a staple of her
life starting at the age of about sixty-five, as it is for many older

people, at least where I live—namely, where a lot of them have
so much stuff that getting rid of it is a burden. So it was for my
mother, who was hyperaware—and ironic on the subject—of
the absurdity of these circumstances in which divestiture is
never-ending. She was sometimes self-abasing about it, but,
ultimately, she was serious in her concerted efforts, and felt,
too, that by getting rid of things she was beating down a bulg-
ing flaw in her DNA, or an instinct to hoard, or a debilitating
anxiety about material well-being, which, she said, had roots
part nature and part nurture, since she'd grown up during the
Depression and had seen her parents knot stray bits of string
together as opposed to buying string in length. We worked in
the basement, where she wore a sweater, because it was eter-
nally clammy there, a sweater she'd knitted while half watching television over the course of the last winter—it had a loose
warp and woof and was a pullover, roomy, but it gave her trouble, she said, because of her frozen shoulder; what she needed
was a button-up; that would be easier. At any rate, sheathed
in her sweater, my mother rummaged boxes and plastic tubs,
and vetted items with prolonged consideration, articulating, at
times, their associated pros and cons, pondering in or out,
yes or no, keep or toss, give, donate, sell, reconsider—she had
categories, one of which incorporated items she couldn't part
with because of sentimental feeling, and as she held, cupped,
and examined these, she spoke, sometimes, of their sources of
power. For her they were items not to be trifled with in the
name of their subtle but tangible resonances. Each was a talis-
man with magical properties. They were imbued with memory, story, and event, and in the course of time had gone from
mere phenomena to sacred vessels of personal history. They

were simultaneously a nuisance and completely necessary. My mother had grown old without losing the better part of innocence when it came to keepsakes. "Look," she said, after opening a box on the day I came to help her. "These are things I slated for repair. I had the idea that one day I'd come down here and fix all this." She unwrapped, then, a froth of light paper, revealing under it a porcelain swan figurine. The head and part of the neck had snapped off, and the loose piece had been taped across the closed left wing. "I thought I'd find the right brand of glue for this, but I never did," she said. "Your father gave it to me for my birthday before you were born. This is going to get me crying," she added. Which is something she'd been doing, off and on, since he'd died.

THE NEXT DAY, Danielle left Cajovna in the hands of her tea experts so that she and I could rent a van, park it at the loading dock beneath my father's office building, take the freight elevator to the twenty-seventh floor, and remove all traces of his existence from the premises. We came and went through a side door, wheeling rented dollies that squeaked as they progressed, hauling them up empty and then down again loaded with boxes held in place behind built-in straps. As discreet as we were about it, we were not unnoticeable, and as such received condolences and fielded inquiries, and were asked why we were doing this ourselves as opposed to hiring movers, a question Danielle fielded with the frank response that we had a hard time writing a check to someone for something we were capable of handling ourselves, elaborating that this was a way of thinking ingrained in us to the extent that it was hard to

turn it around, so here we were, and, really, it wasn't too bad of
a job because of the freight elevator, the dollies, and the loading
dock. Given that she was six foot four and had a tendency to
lurch about like a giant, and appeared, on top of that, generally
rugged, with thick, flat bones in her arms, there was no reason
for anyone not to believe her when she spoke this way. And as
for me, I stayed in the background and let Danielle take the
lead in addressing interlocutors, or, rather, she took it as she
always has, since she's older than me by four years and has a
tendency to lead anyway, in all of life's circumstances. (Though
she's not convinced that her style in this arena is conducive to
the best outcomes. Cajovna, she thought, would do better with
someone at the helm who wasn't quite so blunt.) At any rate,
on we went with our box packing and box moving well into
afternoon, until my father's office was stripped down to a bare
desk and a bare credenza, three chairs, empty file cabinets, and
picture hooks with no job to do, since we'd relieved them of
all the framed certificates and licenses my father had hung in
his office. We also left a small heap of keys in a drawer, since
we could associate them with no purpose. Then we were done
and had our last loads strapped to our dollies, and were about
to exit for good but hesitated, and at this juncture Danielle
said, "What do you think, should we pull the blinds?" And
so she pulled the blinds, darkening the emptied room, leaving
just a little afternoon light to bleed between the slats, and then
she led the way out, wheeling her dolly, and I switched off the
overhead lights.

———

THE THOUGHT OF incinerating my father's files, or of recycling them so that they ended up as molded pulp packaging—as egg filler flats, cushioning trays, take-out food tubs, or clamshell containers—was more than just unpalatable to me. I wasn't ready, and neither was Danielle, and so the boxes full of files ended up in the room where in past years I'd written novels, as I said at the outset of this book, and filled nearly all of it, but with enough left over for my desk and chair, and were stacked so high I feared they would topple and break a window. With that in mind, I opened the door to that room every now and then to see if they were canting or veering toward disaster; possibly, some effect of humidity, I thought, might have weakened the cardboard enough to undermine my precarious arrangement, or maybe the unfailing work of entropy, generalized, would be the ambiguous and inexorable root of their undoing. But no. They rested there the way totem objects rest in ancient crypts, inertly enduring and gathering dust—gathering it until, in the throes of one of my domestic fevers, I dusted that room, dusted right up to the ten reference books that had for years sat at the left back corner of my desk between bookends devised from beach stones, and while I was doing that, a bird glanced off the window in a sudden, rapping blur that caught me by so much surprise that I jumped. It wasn't the first visitation of this sort I'd absorbed in my garret. Over the years, my fictions, largely concocted in a welter of daydreaming, had now and then been interrupted by a sudden knock against glass, and by a flash of wings and feathers as a jarred bird canted off; anyway, this occurred now, while I was up there dusting books, and brought me to a halt, so that I stood for a moment collecting myself before determining to widen my domestic efforts by taking on the smear this bird had made. When I swung the window out to clean it, though, dulled black flies fell from their holds in the jambs onto my desk, so that I had to pick them up one at a time and cast them out. While doing this, I noticed that it was getting on toward evening, and that swallows were feeding in arcs behind our house, and that an owl waited on a tree branch as the light faded. I hung out by the open window, monitoring bird activity, and then shut it and read bits and pieces of things I'd made up, written down, left behind, and forgotten about. Naturally, my mind edited these variegated scribblings, pruning and grooming erratic dross that would never see the light of day.

The next morning, as I approached Cajovna—where I was headed to drink tea and read while in proximity to other people—I saw, seated in its coveted front window alcove, a man of my age, poised over tea, with his elbows wide and a book open in front of him, reading placidly through half-frame glasses. I knew who he was. I used to see him at the swimming pool where I go with Alison. After his laps, he would stand for long periods on his head outside the locker room, which, for no reason vulnerable to logic, I'd found irritating. In fact, his headstands were so maddening that toward him I'd cast spells. I'd wanted him to crash in a heap, or at least decide to do his headstands in private. Now, at Cajovna's door, something in my brain once again told my body to surge with irritation, and I became possessed by loathing of his slouch, by his self-serving appropriation of a window perch and street view, by the points of his elbows, by the close cropping of silver hair above his ears, and—most awful—by the way he looked up at me with a beckoning expression, an unbecoming half smile, as if to say I should acknowledge our familiarity as swimmers, as if to say I should recall with admiration his long, steady headstands, and, worst of all, as if to say that the two of us should converse on a regular basis because, his expression implied, we had things in common. When in fact, I insisted to myself, we had nothing in common and never could, that was impossible and infuriating both, the very idea that he and I could have something in common prompted in me a ridiculous anger, one that lingered past all reason. It was this aging tea tippler who was wasting his time, not me; it was this graying milquetoast who was wrong about everything, not me; it was this banal creep who was worthy of a shunning and deplorable to everyone he met, not me. Studiously, then, I refused to make eye contact with him, just as I had in the swimming-pool locker room, in tight quarters, where conversation about chlorine or water temperature would have been natural and polite, but, no, I'd consistently kept my head down instead and stayed mum—why? No legitimate reason. I went into Cajovna, passed him by, sat down, and opened my book, but I couldn't concentrate, nor could I enjoy my tea. Instead, I sat there thinking that certain Cajovna customers were dismissing me because I no longer exhibited vestiges of youth. I was beyond the pale. My existence was twilit. Then I remembered that, in John Updike's *Bech: A Book*, there's a vignette wherein Bech—a fictional novelist—sees "pulpy stalks of bundled nerves oddly pinched to a bud of concentration in the head" where there are people, the better to encourage detachment, for what difference did it make if "a hairy bone knob" was thinking this or that about him, it all came to nothing either way, those thoughts were just some "trillion circuits" generating "an excess of electricity" in "some pounds of jelly." So this was another way I passed my time in the wake of the Harvey trial. Milling at Cajovna, lost in human frailty, taking cues about life from Updike (who, just a few years expired, was already receding into a delegitimized canon), and, like the headstand man, looking out a window to where, since it was fall in Seattle, rain fell.

ALISON AND I HAD a lunch date with friends at a place called Bill's Diner. Our friends were a couple—Belinda, a poet, and Cal, who, guided by wanderlust, had passed a good part of her life as an itinerant English-language instructor; Singapore, for example, figured in her anecdotes, as did Okinawa. The four of us ate sandwiches and potato chips in a booth, where Cal explained that she now had "grandmother disease," meaning that she was addicted to her six-month-old grandson, to the impossibly pristine scent of his innocent cheeks, his cooing noises, his flailing hands and feet as she shook a rattle for him, his bottle time, his naps in her arms, and also—another category of symptoms—to taking profligate photographs and sharing them, and to detailing for the benefit of friends (Cal put "benefit" in air-quote marks) his latest developmental feats—for example, rolling over from back to tummy but not the other way yet, or eating sweet-potato mush for the first time.

So what else is new? Alison asked our friends. Cal said that she had relatives in Montenegro—a boatbuilder in Ulcinj and a nun in Podgorica—and that she now owned a condominium there, on the Adriatic, where she and Belinda had recently passed a sumptuous August ("Ridiculously sumptuous," Belinda put in) on a bluestone terrazzo beneath a deep awning, wisteria climbing a wall behind them, white sand stuck between their toes, a pitcher of lime-and-mint-infused water and a bottle of Polish vodka on ice close at hand, pickled herring and goat cheese in the refrigerator, rye crackers, almonds, and walnuts in the cupboard, grapes and satsumas on a wicker table in the shade, and sea salt encrusted on their arms while Belinda read poetry journals and Cal plowed her way, resolutely, through everything written by Virginia Woolf.

What else? Cal's father, who was ninety-three and lived in Carefree, Arizona, had gotten married for the third time. Belinda and Cal had gone to the wedding; in fact, they'd been the wedding planners and, as Belinda said, had met the couple's request for celebratory watermelon aspic with goose-liver terrine. What else? Belinda had a "grinding hip" and was seeing a physical therapist for it; meanwhile, Cal had "acquired a syndrome." "I go to sleep at night," she said, "and there's this noise like a bomb going off. I mean really, except no one hears it but me."

"Exploding-head syndrome," explained Belinda.

"Exploding-head syndrome," Cal said. "About twice a week."

"Sometimes they call it 'auditory sleep start,'" said Belinda.

"Our doctor had no idea," said Cal. "So I had to go to a sleep-disorders clinic."

"The same one I went to for apnea," said Belinda. "Which it turned out I didn't have."

"She just snores," explained Cal. "It's not apnea."

"But your thing . . ." said Belinda.

"Mine," said Cal. "One in a billion get it, and I got it."

"They ruled things out," said Belinda. "She doesn't have a tumor."

"Or epilepsy," added Cal. "Or any other real problem. Just exploding-head syndrome, which, let me tell you, is a rush."

"Honey," said Belinda.

"Sweetie," answered Cal. "Anyway, I thought you might like to know about it, in case it fits into a novel someday. A character with exploding-head syndrome."

"Why not?" said Belinda. "A character with exploding-head syndrome."

We ate. Cal said she and Belinda would be in Carefree soon to visit her remarried father. "We were worried at first," Belinda said, "because we didn't know the woman."

"I'm still worried," said Cal.

"We thought she might be one of those women who prey on men in nursing homes."

"She is one of those," said Cal.

"But then we got to know her," said Belinda. "She's eighty-six and in a wheelchair."

"What does that matter? I still don't trust her."

"And I would say she's cultivated," Belinda pressed on. "In the sense that she has a classical education."

"That doesn't mean she's financially solvent."

"Every Wednesday, she gets her hair done. Every Thursday, spa treatment. And a good sense of humor, which your father appreciates."

"He's lost his marbles."

"He's ninety-three."

"Anyway," said Cal, "you guys?"

We shrugged. Then Belinda asked me if I was writing anything. I said no. Cal said Belinda, who'd recently published,
had been assaulted in print by a fellow poet. Cal laughed about
that. She said that someone once broke into a bookstore overnight and not only riddled Billy Collins's *Nine Horses* with a
shotgun but defaced Collins's author portrait. She then regaled
us with a story about two poets who'd brawled at a convention
in front of hundreds of academics, and with a description of
the Stony Brook mêlée of 1960, during which Allen Ginsburg
sunk to his knees in an effort to promote nonviolence between
bards. There was, furthermore, the matter, said Cal, of major
poetry prizes judged by a rotating, incestuous cast of vengeful
backstabbers and the permanently pricked. Grants, awards,
endowed chairs, lectureships, all were bruised by insidious
envy. Hiring was marred by it, publication skewed by it. Poets,
said Belinda, were Machiavellian potentates, and their bodies
of work insecure city-states. "Be glad you're a fiction writer,"
she said.

THE NEXT MORNING, I went to a coffee shop to meet a
fiction writer I knew named Louden James who'd e-mailed
to say he'd like to reconnect. Arriving early, I bought coffee,
perched on a stool, and read a novel until he tapped me on
the shoulder. I actually didn't know Louden very well. We'd
met, we'd chatted at this or that event, drinks in hand maybe,
or standing in a corner, I suppose commiserating or name-
dropping or pretending to be busier and more important than
we were, two novelists. I liked him, though. He was droll in
a way I understood as a kindness. He appeared not to have

combed his hair, ever; there wasn't a lot of it, but what he had was like the snarled tendrils of a bird nest, gray, found where two walls still met after a tornado. That made him look, in his drab olive khakis and checked sport coat tightly bunched at its armpits, like Kurt Vonnegut—long face and drooping eyes suggesting whimsy, melancholy, eclecticism, and metaphysical propensities. He was, like me, in the middle of his life, steeped in his years but not brutalized by them. He did, though, exhibit compromised coordination; in his rumpled presence, you worried that he would knock over something fragile—a coffee cup, maybe—while sitting down or standing up.

He liked to talk. He was a profuse, disorganized, and hyperkinetic talker. He began by telling me that he was teaching a writing workshop that was in danger of dissolving under the pressure of health problems he'd come recently to suffer that lent a special duress to the act of reading manuscripts. His eyes, he explained, made of printed words a morass, and no corrective lenses, to date anyway, could resolve them into meanings. As if to prove this to me then and there in our coffee shop, he plucked off his glasses, folded their wings, held them at the bridge so as not to smudge their lenses, and unabashedly displayed for me the meandering of his pupils, their ticlike behavior and antic, eccentric paths, and the watery settings in which they wandered like amoebas; his eyes, he said, gave him eviscerating headaches, and prompted interludes he described as torture sessions; these, he explained, were periods of "viselike pressure from temple to temple and from brow to cerebellum," which he had no choice but to pass in a prone position with blinders strapped around his head—blinders he'd retained from a goodie bag provided gratis to business travelers on a flight to Frankfurt the spring before—all the while with "exploding quasars" behind his eyelids. He lay like this regularly on the floor of his campus office with the door locked and the lights off, during hours when he was meant to be available to students for tête-à-têtes about their fictions, suffused by guilt while they knocked for entrance fruitlessly, but also aware, he said, of "the comic absurdity of it all." Still, he was not without hope. There was a specialist in Dallas he was elated to see. He was only sixty-three; his life wasn't over yet, Louden assured me. Then, as if suddenly conscious of his extended self-absorption, he asked the question I knew was coming—"Working on something?"—to which I answered, "No."

We talked for another fifteen minutes, or he talked, and then he left, and I walked to the nearest bookstore. Its front shelves and tables displayed fresh titles under bright lights, but after that, beyond the points of purchase and the information desk—where a young man in wire-rimmed glasses sat swiping and clicking while looking formidably absorbed in screen gazing—a realm of used volumes in overflow began, reaching from there toward less well-lit recesses and toward stairs with worn but glossy banisters, allowing access to a cellar and a mezzanine. These stairs, too, were lined with books, or maybe banked by them, motley bulwarks of books stuffed in horizontally at regular intervals and so forming buttresses against their vertical neighbors, a feat of shelf engineering sorely compromised by irresponsible browsers; anyway, to find anything, it was necessary to check multiple sites in that bookstore, and to stoop beside floor stacks of akimbo hardbacks, which I did, gathering in the process three of Louden's titles. One was about as collapsed and antique as a book can get before it's no longer salable, the next was maniacally marked with a pink highlighter, and the third was heavily flailed, its spine barely holding up; in fact, it was possible, with even mild handling, to convert it to a three-dimensional parallelogram.

I sat down with Louden's books. His debut, according to its flap copy, recounted the travails of an accountant who finds himself with anterograde amnesia during a solo misadventure in a monohull sailboat meandering from Christchurch to Fiji. The second was a Kafkaesque fabulation about a court stenographer with restless-leg syndrome who devises a fantasy soccer league. The third featured a cast of five ecoterrorists bent on assailing the Democratic National Convention at the Moscone Center in 1984. The young man in wire-rimmed glasses at the information desk, with the dispatch of someone distracted from an important task by an unreasonable request (made by me), tapped with staccato aggression at his keyboard, then rotated his screen so I, too, could see that, though Louden had four novels to his name, he hadn't published anything in two decades. Actually, in twenty-three years. There was nothing from this millennium, literally. I leaned in. The novel not to be found in-house had been published between the fable of the stenographer and the tale of the terrorists. The next day, I found it in another bookstore—a tragicomedy, ribald, about a French mining engineer who wants to build a tunnel from Calais to Dover, complete with oil lamps and ventilation chimneys, big enough for horse-drawn carriages. By day, he courts Parisian support for his scheme; by night, he visits the red-light district of Pigalle under the banner of *plaisir à tout prix*. The tunnel is a no-go. Chastened, he licks his wounds in Taranto among

British expatriates who've formed an art colony replete with interlocking affairs. Soon the *ingénieur* is embroiled in heated cuckoldry and corralled into a project to build an artificial island off the coast of Puglia where a Bloomsbury-style utopia is meant to ensue, but simultaneously he incurs the wrath of a portrait painter with military bearing who, on uncovering his wife's proclivity for the Frenchman, peppers him with ad-hominem insults during a sailing venture in the Adriatic and sees to it that he drowns. The art utopia is never built.

But I'd better explain something before you go online to track down these novels. To begin with, "Louden James" threatened, with a cryptic laugh, to sue me if I didn't handle his appearance in these pages "with due consideration," which meant I had to let him read a draft. "You've screwed this up royally," he told me during a final meeting between us at the same small coffee shop, "because in your manuscript as it stands to date 'Louden James' is the author of books whose plot descriptions are descriptions of my books, which means that your readers, if you end up having any, can easily, if they want to, figure out the truth. What's the point of a pseudonym if you're just going to point readers toward the person behind it? Bottom line," said Louden, "if you want me in your book, you're going to have to"—here he turned my manuscript toward me—"put together plot descriptions in this section for books that don't exist."

AFTER TWO STRAIGHT DAYS of wallowing in bookstores, I returned to the domesticity that now sustained me through many hours of many days. There was a letter in the mailbox reminding me that my car tabs were expiring, even though I'd clicked on "e-mail only" regarding car tabs. The front door, I noticed, had swelled a little and was scraping against its jamb. The ink cartridge in the laser printer needed changing, and the dust needed to be vacuumed from the fins of the refrigerator condenser. It was unusually warm that day, in a way that used to seem like a gift but that now incites anxiety about the future of human life on earth, and so, in the evening, Alison and I sat in the backyard together, where our cat slinked into my lap and purred, and where the warmth of the day rose out of the flagstones, and where Alison said, "Tonight there's a meteor shower." Around ten, we lay down on a blanket and watched for meteors, but there weren't any for a long time, and then there was one trailing flicker, faint, and two more, less faint, and after that we didn't see any more, and talked, and eventually our conversation got to the point where Alison said, "The universe is so large and time is so long that no one has words for it, but still."

The next day, we swam laps for an hour—something we'd become more regular about since my father died. Maybe mortality had spurred in us the hope that by exercising vigorously we might stave off the Reaper longer than if we didn't. At any rate, in her swim garb, Alison looked hale. She also looked retro in round goggles and a rubber nose-clip. Frequently, from an adjacent lane, lolling at a wall, I spoke with her between laps. At these times, she propped her goggles against her latex swim cap and floated on her back, exuding effortless buoyancy, a talking head with chlorine-chafed cheeks and pink goggle-seal indentations. Frankly, everything about her in the water charmed me.

After our interlude of aquatic exercise, we went for lunch at an overheated café that was quiet, Lebanese in its cuisine, new to us, and empty of other diners. Soon our server stood before us, pencil poised. I seconded Alison's order, and he clipped up our double-down on shawarma before returning to muted televised soccer. He looked immaculate, unsullied by toting food, and had the trim profile of a disco king. "I visited your sister," Alison told me, "and she gave me this book." Which she then pulled from her bag. "*The Book of Tea*, by Kakuzo Okakura."

"How is it?"

"I'll open randomly and read."

She opened *The Book of Tea* and read, "'The East and West, like two dragons tossed in a sea of ferment, in vain strive to regain the jewel of life. We need a Niuka again to repair the great devastation; we await the great Avatar.'"

"What does that mean?"

"'Meanwhile, let us have a sip of tea,'" Alison read on. "'The afternoon glow is brightening the bamboos, the fountains are bubbling with delight, the soughing of the pines is heard in our kettle. Let us dream of evanescence, and linger in the beautiful foolishness of things.'"

Our shawarma arrived on the arm of our server. A young couple entered and took a corner table. Outside, a man in a T-shirt fed pigeons. We ate lunch and then, in our post-swim lassitude, ordered baklava and coffee. Ever the winsome cipher, our server cleared our table of crumbs with a handheld sweep, and repositioned our sugar jar. Soon our baklava and coffee arrived. The coffee steam, I thought, looked suspiciously alive—redolent, maybe, of excessive heat. I lifted my cup in exploratory fashion, and as I did so Alison said, "All baklava is not the same." She gouged at hers with the edge of her fork. "A lot of times," she observed, "when it goes wrong, the problem's honey. Too much honey makes baklava cloying. Want more trivia? If the many layered crusts of phyllo break immediately to bits the size of red-pepper flakes at dentation, the dough hasn't been handled right. Stuffing's spilling from the phyllo here," she added, raising a morsel of baklava toward her mouth. "That's a good sign."

She slid it between her lips then and chewed like a contest judge. "Very good," she pronounced. "Nicely done. So now, let us eat baklava."

"Let's."

"And let us dream of evanescence, too, and linger in the beautiful foolishness of things."

"Let's."

"Stress on 'linger,'" put in Alison. "We'll linger, like *The Book of Tea* advises, but then, in my opinion, enough of the beautiful foolishness of things. Let's linger, but then let's move on."

AT CAJOVNA—where my tea always came with a miniature hourglass, the better to know when a steep was optimal—I often hung around now, reading, late into afternoon. In that haven, amid quiet lovers and tea aficionados, I felt like that figure at the end of the local bar who has become an institution, so firmly ensconced that he appears to hold up an end of things or to be built in like a structural member. So what? Let others see what they see; it's of no account. Inside, I was a soul whose tea is a pause, a man who inhabits, for a while, his small eternity, and does so with the gratitude of a traveler redeemed by sanctuary; someone out of the rain and of all it portends, outside of time, too, practicing zilch. Which left me, I understood, ripe for caricature as the self-appointed titular teahouse king in his well-tapestried corner. Yes, I was a *New Yorker* cartoon, a nascent dodderer signifying absurdity, or at least the aimlessness of years.

One day, Danielle, seeing that I had time on my hands, urged on me a master's thesis one of her tea experts had dug up. Its pages were held together by three bronze-plated brads, and its exposed, frontal abstract was dimpled with appropriate tea stains. I sat for a languorous spell with it under Cajovna's moth-eaten tapestries, in a slant of commodious October light falling generously through a wavy, leaded window, scratching my head and refilling from a teapot kept at quaffable temperature by a small bowl of candle wax whose lit wick, as time wore on, angled and then fell into oleaginous dregs. The thesis argued, in the course of substantial pages, that certain Russian literary titans, while stringing together purportedly realistic narratives, had engaged in the imaginative pretense that pervasive tea drinking, and its associated culture, were older than the historical record bore out, and that, despite the many scenes in Russian novels and stories wherein tea and samovars are featured as normative features of nineteenth- and even eighteenth-century Russian social and domestic life, it was not until 1901 that annual tea consumption in Russia rose to one pound per person, or, to put it another way, to the point where, at one cup a day, "the average Russian" could enjoy tea on about 25 percent of a year's mornings. Why such widespread fabrica-

tion (beginning, said the thesis writer, with Alexander Pushkin)? What was in it for these lions of literature? But we could
not understand it without first understanding that, in the Russia of yore, writers were prophets who created past, present,
and future by uttering them narratively into existence, raising
mirrors wherein what at first glance looked to be reflected was
in actuality generative—that is, they pushed through in the
opposite direction, from the mirror world to ours, so that what
happened in the pages of their novels and stories had creative
power in a literal sense, meaning that Russian social life existed
as a manifestation of intentional fabrications, not propaganda
exactly but not far from it, or existed this way, at least, in impe-
rial Russia, where every writer held up for worship came, in
the end, from approximately the same class of people, while all
around them the necessary fields were harvested by illiterate
serfs with no tea to drink (though in the novels they indeed
drink tea, having returned from their scything to close-roofed
quarters made intimate by samovars, where they participated in
cozy domestic scenes marked by copious tea service). No matter the guilt of Tolstoy or the angst of Dostoevsky, it was one
and the same to them in the end, the virtue of tea drinking, tea
as a font of human affection, tea as nostalgia or consolation,
touchstone or counterpoint, hiatus or eroticism—"integrated
into the national idiom," as the thesis writer put it—tea everywhere, tea as a measure of passing time, of familial concern,
of life alterations, of love, death, birth, tragedy, all of it written before that historical moment, revealed to us by hard-won
and unprejudiced academic research, when the Trans-Siberian
Railroad, chugging under black smoke through the icy wastes
of reality, brought tea in volume to the Russian masses.

Admirably written, I thought on finishing, and retightened the brads my reading had loosened. My lamp had gone out, and my tea had gone cold. I felt creaky and mired, suddenly, sitting there. I got up with the thesis to return it to Danielle, and found her on a ladder poised before her chalkboard, finishing up the inscribing of a quote: "But to prefer teabags to real tea is to exalt the shadow over the substance," it read. "Anthony Burgess."

"And everybody thinks he's just *Clockwork Orange*," she advised me from her ladder.

Sometimes during my interludes at Cajovna, I saw Danielle loom over a table, gathering tea orders. Sometimes I saw her employ her ample basketball mitts as aids to elaboration, keeping their illustrating movements tight, though, confined to an imaginary box in front of her torso. Sometimes she closed in like a hulking presence, and sometimes like a towering bulwark. Sometimes she was a pop-eyed colossus; other times, a wild-haired Gargantua. Mostly, though, she kept her hands twined at the small of her back—a back crooked by years but charismatically. She had a way of jangling loosely at table side, and shuffled her feet as if to keep from toppling. She gave the impression of someone trying earnestly to back away from the waist down so that her head, like the hook block of a crane, could drop toward a position of engagement with seated customers. At times like these, if she was close by, I overheard her. "Good afternoon. My name's Danielle. As you can see, our menu is extensive. Fortunately, it's divided into sections. First, greens. Our Chinese greens have been pan-fired. Our Japanese greens are rapidly steamed. Next, whites, lightly oxidized in the traditional manner, the harvested leaves placed in the sun to wither on bamboo trays, the leaves then dried and hand sorted for impurities. We include in this section our three yellows, whose processing technology is a closely guarded secret, and we also offer a rare Huang Ya that is processed, believe it or not, only between March 27 and April 5, when the temperature and moisture of the air in Hunan Province are in balance. Oolongs. These are some of our most popular teas. Oxidation fifteen to eighty percent. Leaves roasted over open fires and tumble-dried to bring out floral qualities. A few are baked in bamboo baskets. Then blacks. In all of them, the freed polyphenols have been subjected to deep enzymatic oxidation. Result: caramel and tannic flavors are released. Very popular. Stimulating. Rich. Pu-erhs—these are an acquired taste. Earthy, even musty. Pile-fermented and aged, sometimes for years. Then, at the back, our tisanes, our special blends, our aromatized and flavored teas, our chilled teas, and, finally, our Argentine yerba mate, served in a calabash with a drinking straw, or bombilla. Yerba mate is a buzz drink, highly caffeinated; odds are, it ratchets up conversation."

Once, in a lull, Danielle sat at my table. I thought she looked tired. Or maybe just peaceful. Or maybe at the nexus of those two states. "Hey," she said, "did you notice my chalkboard? It's from Hemingway's 'A Clean, Well-Lighted Place.'"

I looked up at Danielle's blunt, powder-blue scrawlings. "Each night I am reluctant to close up because there may be someone who needs the café," they read.

MY MOTHER, who for many years had line-danced on Wednesday afternoons at the senior center not far from her home, and had taken Spanish there, and had joined with others at the center in Spanish-only conversation on a biweekly basis, began, after my father's death, to take a class at the center called Exercise with Eileen, an hourlong session every Tuesday and Thursday of cardio work, stretching, and light resistance training, aimed at better balance, decreased risk of falls, and improved well-being. Unfortunately, her back seized up during one of the course's stretching sessions, and thereafter remained intractably disabling, not to the point where inactivity became her lot, but nevertheless demanding long periods of rest. She stayed at home, situating herself for goodly spells on the half-sofa in the corner of her kitchen, a heating pad against the small of her back, her knitting and a book at hand, a stack of mail on her side table, an array of magazines, leaflets, circulars, and brochures on the cushion next to her, the television on but its sound muted—or sometimes my mother had her radio on, tuned to classical music punctuated by weather reports. She also kept her phone nearby, and pecked at it now and then with slow determination, primarily to manage her e-mail relationships, but also to investigate her lumbar condition, and to research possible treatments and interventions, and to consider questions raised but not answered on her television and radio. She had ibuprofen on hand, and boxed tissues, and a tumbler of drinking water. Water, she told me, was both bane and nemesis. Everyone everywhere agreed that drinking plenty of it was the right thing to do, but in her case it meant getting up off her sofa and into her bathroom with irritating frequency.

One day, I noticed, on my mother's side table, a manila envelope, nine by twelve, on which she'd written, in capitals, ROYAL. I'd already seen the folder where she collected notes and documents pertinent to her husband's death (letters testamentary, probate correspondence, tax returns, bank statements, health-insurance claims, etc.)—paperwork she and Danielle were attending to with a mutually voiced exasperation and a patience tinted with commentary on the administrative burdens of death in America—but I'd never seen this envelope before, which my mother explained was a repository for things forwarded by my father's firm. "I haven't gotten to it yet," she said. "My hands are full."

I opened the envelope. It included bills that had gone unpaid. One was from my father's dentist: X-rays and a crown. Another was from a periodical called *Judicature,* asking him to pay his annual subscription fee. A third was from the American Bar Association, reminding him to pay his dues, now late. A fourth and fifth were from a medical clinic requesting payment for lab work. Also in the envelope was a letter a prisoner had written from the Washington State Penitentiary in Walla Walla, inquiring as to the possibility of pursuing an appeal despite, as of his writing, 257 months of incarceration.

At home, I dug up the file attached to the person who'd written my father from prison. His name was Kalani Kaleikaumaka, and when he was nineteen and a student at the University of Washington, he'd killed the manager of his Seattle apartment building, Inge Billings, and bound, gagged, and beaten her daughter Sandra. After committing these crimes, Kaleikaumaka had flown to Los Angeles, where he bought three bottles of sleeping pills and took a room near the airport, at the Signal Motel. LAPD officers found him on his hands and knees, naked, in the yard of a private residence nearby, looking into the end of a garden hose. Later, he defecated on the rear seat of their patrol car. The officers dropped him at Los Angeles General Hospital, where Kaleikaumaka slashed his wrists. Before long, he was flown back to Seattle, driven to the county courthouse in handcuffs, and arraigned on assault and murder charges.

My father was appointed to defend Kaleikaumaka. His new client, tearful and subdued, told my father that he recalled nothing of his life during the eleven days prior to the murder—those eleven days had disappeared for him, he said. He only knew that at their end he woke up to find himself behind Inge Billings in the laundry room of their apartment building with his hands over her mouth. "The first thought I had was of my hands over her mouth," he said, "and my thought was 'Stab her.'"

Kaleikaumaka was then a sophomore, majoring in ocean-ography. He had never shown symptoms of mental illness or amnesia before. Now here he was, in the basement laundry room of his apartment building, attacking Inge Billings. He had with him a black valise, and inside the valise were a hunt-ing knife with a four-inch blade, a roll of adhesive tape, a roll of masking tape, two rolls of elastic bandage, and a pair of gloves. All of that was listed in an extensively detailed police report my father shared with his client. Kaleikaumaka told my father he didn't remember buying the valise on October 18 at the Bon Marché on Fourth Avenue downtown, or withdrawing $285 from his savings account that day, or missing his zoology class the following day or his chemistry class the day after that. He didn't remember anything until he had his hands over Inge Billings's mouth, when he awakened from his state of nonbe-ing to find himself pursuing a violent assault—an assault from which he hadn't recoiled, he said. In fact, in full awareness of what he was doing, he told my father, he stabbed Inge Billings in the chest. She ran then, but he chased her down in an adjacent storage room and put a T-shirt over her face. He lifted her skirt, detached her nylon stocking from her left leg, where it was attached to her garter belt, and, without tearing the stocking, rolled it down her leg and used it to strangle her, after which he covered her mouth with masking tape and stuffed her in a locker. Next, he went upstairs to the Billingses' apartment and, still fully aware of his actions, put tape over Sandra Billings's eyes and mouth, taped her hands behind her, placed her on a bed facedown, and tied her feet. If Sandra's father hadn't entered the apartment then, there would likely have been two murders in the building that day. Instead, Kaleikaumaka fled on foot.

My father asked his client background questions. Kaleikaumaka had grown up on Oahu, he said, where his father worked on a sugarcane plantation; he had two sisters and four brothers; he'd been christened at a Congregationalist church; he was a former Cub Scout; his hobbies included swimming and fishing. In high school, he'd been an honors student; summers, he'd worked from 5:00 a.m. to 2:00 p.m. in cane fields, saving his wages against the eventuality of college. Eighteen years old when he left Maui for the first time (he'd never even been to Honolulu), he flew to Seattle, enrolled at the UW, and found an evening job as a busboy in a restaurant, the Bistro, at 69th and Roosevelt.

My father soon arranged for a psychiatric evaluation. "The motive for the killing remains, as far as I am concerned, in the realm of speculation," a psychiatrist reported to him. "It is possible, too, that the motive for it may always remain obscure. Inge Billings had been indifferent to Mr. Kaleikaumaka's greetings, so the motivation for the crime might have stemmed from sexual fantasies which he oriented toward this woman who appeared to be a maternal figure source of hostility and an object of sexual inquisitiveness. The crime might have been motivated by some unconscious or even conscious sexual impulse but, as I say, this is in the realm of speculation. Currently Mr Kaleikaumaka is rational, coherent, cooperative, relevant, agreeable, and does not have delusions. His mood is in harmony with present events. He is not presently psychotic and there is no psychiatric bar to him standing trial."

My father began to formulate an insanity defense, but Kaleikaumaka, guilt-ridden, fended him off, pleaded guilty, and was sentenced to life in prison. Now here he was, a man in his forties, writing my father about an appeal. Not knowing what else to do, I tried to pass the matter on to my father's firm, where I learned that no appeal was possible in matters where the accused pleads guilty as charged. I had to write to Kaleikaumaka to tell him this, and to let him know that my father had died, and to suggest he try to find another attorney, because another attorney might see it differently from the one I'd talked to at my father's firm. This latter was probably self-serving on my part, as I didn't want to be a squasher of hope.

"I told him I wanted to take my punishment," Kaleikaumaka wrote back, "him" being my father. "He said I might change my mind someday so leave the door open but I was sure. Another time he said, 'This punishment you want to take, it's going to be life in prison. You're nineteen years old. You went nuts for a while.' I got sentenced and he didn't say a word. He just dropped his head and put his hand on my shoulder and left it there until they led me away."

THE YOUNG SOCIALIST tea expert I mentioned earlier in this book who couldn't sanction bliss on the backs of Russian footboys was named April Olsen, and looked, to me, like Little Orphan Annie as drawn in the original comic strip. That said, her hair was neither quite so orange nor quite so frumpy; it presented, rather, as a sprawling billow crowning an undaunted urchin. Closer to auburn than to red or orange, and profuse enough to pile up like cotton candy, it added 10 percent to April's height. Underneath it, her face looked secondary, even incidental, tucked in as it was between the billow above and the costuming below, which included multi-pocketed cargo pants and a Soviet army jacket. If I had to guess, I would have guessed she selected articles of clothing based on the primary consideration of self-defense, and in the hope that nobody would mess with her; for example, a Chairman Mao tunic and lubed-up waffle stompers. Once, while collecting tea things from a table near mine, she told me that she was thinking of entering a Buddhist nunnery. I asked her why she was thinking of that, and she answered, "Because I don't want any of the shit on offer in this country."

April's antagonist in the showdown over Russian footboys—also one of Cajovna's tea experts—was named Camille Porter. I remember noticing her once arriving for work on an olive-green moped and matching helmet, and looking sort of Italian in ambience as, across the street from my tea-shop window, she muscled her moped's center stand lever in a designated parking sliver, unstrapped and slid off her helmet, and removed her wraparound, tinted riding glasses. The sidewalk behind Camille was busy and crowded. As she stepped onto it, two young men, both with colorful scarves at their throats, maneuvered around her without breaking stride, flowing apart and then together again with no interruption of their conversational intensity. Behind them was a store where people could buy art supplies. A bus passed, and then I saw Camille again with a waterproof messenger bag over her shoulder and her helmet squeezed between her elbow and ribs. (By "waterproof messenger bag" I mean the kind of yellow-and-black bag made out of reinforced heavyweight vinyl that seals across the top with enough force to keep documents dry even were the bag to drop into the Colorado River at the east end of the Grand Canyon and ride all the way to Lake Powell.) There were three relatively young people sitting on the sidewalk in Camille's vicinity, hunched against the cold, not explicitly asking for spare change at the moment, as far as I could tell, one wearing a sweatshirt hood and a black leather coat full of rivets, the other two blurry for me, devoid of detail, though I might have noted more specific attributes and retained them in memory if another bus hadn't just then blocked my view, prompting me to transfer my attention to a bearded man passing closely by my window in a motorized wheelchair with a small dog on his lap, a man tilted so far back he might have been, in that position, sunbathing. On his face was an expression, I thought, of permanent surprise. His hand, gnarled as it was, clawlike, bloated, was nevertheless so subtle in its operation of his joystick that his movement along the thoroughfare was impressively seamless. I watched him, his chair, and his dog parting and passing pedestrians as he motored out of view, and then there was Camille again on the far side of the street, waiting for the light to change alongside other people, or, rather, looking at her phone.

One day, during a lull in tea traffic—in fact, it had ground to a total halt, so that no one was taking tea except me—Camille sat down not too far away, unrolled the top of her waterproof bag, and brought forth a mechanical pencil, a plastic vial full of leads, reading glasses in a hard-shell case, and a journal with a paisley cover pattern. This was long after her contretemps with April Olsen over footboys, yet a strong current of contentiousness still flowed invisibly between them—the sort of thing I inevitably noticed while spinning my wheels over oolong or matcha. On this day, with Danielle absent, and though I kept my nose in my book assiduously, I couldn't help bearing witness to a second eruption of fundamental disagreement between the two tea experts, which began when April took a seat at Camille's tea table—uninvited and unilaterally—and said, "Today's the day I quit, so I'm burning some bridges on my way out the door."

"Cool," said Camille.

I didn't look up. Instead, I kept my pretense of 100-percent reading absorption intact—absurdly so, as it had to be obvious to them that I was well within hearing range, a fact apparently of no concern to either, such was my significance in their eyes. I made myself a man whose book was like blinders, but listened like a man for whom listening meant survival, tuned in with raised antenna even as I sat there as if magnetized to *Home Life in Colonial Days,* by Alice Morse Earle, a text I'd picked up that morning while browsing in one of those Little Free Libraries that have popped up on certain residential streets and then brought with me to Cajovna without as much intending to read it as to treat it like a passing curiosity. However, *Home Life in Colonial Days* began, "When the first settlers landed on American shores, the difficulties in finding or making shelter must have seemed ironical as well as almost unbearable," and after that I was hooked by the mystery of what might have been ironical in such circumstances, and by the use at all of the word "ironical," and read on in the spirit of these sorts of pleasures. I even pulled out my phone to google "Alice Morse Earle," who turned out to have nearly drowned near Nantucket during an "abortive trip to Egypt."

"No," said April Olsen. "I mean—wait—no. You can't even think that. It's colonialist. It's imperialist. It's— I thought you were, like, Smash the Patriarchy. What are you thinking, Camille?"

"I'm thinking that if you're quitting today, great."

"Jesus, I can't do this anymore," said April. "You're not gonna think about it till I stuff it in your face. If you *think* about it"—this was sarcastic—"people like you were, like, 'Life is so hard, we have to do so much work, this sucks, let's attack these other people and take slaves to do our hard stuff.' But that meant putting energy and resources into mounting attacks, and making enemies you depleted resources to defend against, and other people making slaves out of you, so the system had holes in it."

"Could you get out of my space?" Camille asked.

"This isn't, quote, 'your space,'" answered April. "This is actually the people's space you're occupying at the moment."

"Get out of the people's space, then."

"Shut up," said April. "You're gonna listen to me. For your own good, dude. Because you're completely clueless. What happened was, people like you eventually figured out it was better to make slaves out of people in their own group than to waste energy taking them from other groups. That's called feudalism. Ten thousand people in your group live in poverty and work their asses off so one person can, you know, buy a moped and act all Italian."

"Touché," said Camille.

"But then it turns out you have to put a lot of resources into oppressing serfs, because serfs get tired and destroy all the mopeds, so you try a new idea. You say, 'No one in our group will be a serf anymore. We'll be free and vote on things, and the real serfs will live far away.'"

"April," said Camille, with mockery in her voice. "I'm feeling threatened."

"It's called colonialism," said April. "People like you get rich by stealing shit from other countries."

There was a pause. I looked up. April rose and walked rapidly to the loose teas behind the counter, which were arrayed in glass jars. She grabbed one of these, brought it back, and spilled about half of its contents out in front of Camille's paisley-covered journal. There sat the tea, a dark mound of dried leaves. "You see this?" April asked. "It's just like coffee or chocolate or sugar. Rich assholes in England got bored with meat and potatoes and made fetishes out of all that stuff. Just like they made fetishes out of beaver pelts and otter skins. Tea." She spread it around angrily; some fell on the floor. "Those complete assholes made serfs out of people so they could sit in tea shops in London and gossip. Like you with your motherfucking moped and sunglasses. That sort of thing hasn't come to a halt. You know why? Because of people like you who are too dumb to understand what's going on."

April rose. "Fuck you," she said, before spinning on her heel and heading out the door.

Camille looked at me. Then she started scooping up the loose tea April had spilled onto the table and putting it back in its jar. "Sorry," she said. "That was really weird."

"It's not your fault," I replied.

I CONVERGED one morning on Cajovna with a young writer named William Moore, author of a novel-in-progress with the working title *In a Warm Time* (first sentence: "Dane was on his way back from gathering wild onion roots that grew along the verge of the dunes when he saw her walking quietly in the arroyo"). William had found my e-mail address and, after engaging me in correspondence, sent me his novel, which I'd read (about a passionate and erotic romance between two beautiful people in a world weighed down by a global temperature rise of eight degrees), and now we were going to talk about it in person. Since this was our first meeting, I was greatly surprised by the atmosphere of personal dishevelment William Moore brought with him, as if he'd just completed a spate of dumpster diving or come directly from a crab-canning line. Matted—that was the word for his hair, brutish for his hands, blunt for his jaw, and then there were his bloodshot and amethyst eyes, especially the left, where the pupil, lodged as it was in the upper outside corner, was half concealed by an eyelid. A battered, sensitive Neanderthal, one whose deliberation over

Danielle's tea menu felt long. "Ancient Tree Dark pu-erh," he finally told her.

Cajovna was hopping. Danielle passed by with a samovar aloft. The tea tipplers beside us, a threesome—dressed for Arctic weather—spoke softly in Mandarin. Someone had ordered a pungent, smoky tea that, after the front door opened and shut, wafted its resinous odor toward our booth. At the front counter, an androgynous couple was unstoppering tea vials, sniffing, talking, and kissing casually. Behind them, two girls in hooded sweatshirts waited for their own chance at the tea vials, both with stony and resentful gazes, as if to say, "Come on, you guys, get a room if you need to do that." And farther back, behind them, another couple waited as well, turned in on each other and talking privately. Meanwhile, outside the big window at the front of Cajovna, a left-handed guy tried in vain to light a cigarette, contorting in a series of creative efforts to defy the power of the wind.

"So," said William, "as you can see from my manuscript, I'm having trouble."

I nodded ambiguously.

"Here's the problem," continued William. "The problem is that I don't have characters. Instead, I have puppets so I can write about global warming. And that's so dumb. Because, if what I care about is global warming, why don't I write about global warming? What I've been saying about that till now is that nonfiction is uninvolving, so if you want people to act, you have to tell a story. Now I'm starting to realize that there are three hundred million plus people in the United States, and best-selling novels sell, what, a million copies? One million, two million, three million, ten? Even if I wrote the greatest novel ever written and sold more copies than anyone ever sold, what about the ninety-five percent of people in this country who'll never read it? Not to mention most of the people in Europe even if it gets translated, and not to mention the billion people in China and the billion in India and the billion in Africa—that's three billion people. Facts are facts, and the fact is, almost no one'll read my novel no matter how great it is, so this idea that it's going to do something about global warming? Sorry—no—the climate crisis."

William's pot of pu-erh arrived. He poured, sipped loudly, and registered bitterness with a grimace. Then he produced, out of a battered paper bag on the seat beside him, *In a Warm Time*—rumpled, torn, bound by rubber bands—dropped it on our table with a dramatic thump, and sighed. "My anemic and pathetic magnum opus," he announced. "My piece of shit *de résistance*. My stirring adventure tale starring Dane, who comes off like Fabio, only sweatier, because of climate change."

"William," I said, "have faith in yourself."

"Faith in myself," William replied. "I'd say that, from the day I was born I had über, maxed-out faith in myself. When I was a kid, put me in any situation, no matter what athletic, academic, social, anything—me? I had faith in myself. Mr. Absolute Faith in Himself: that was W. Moore. But now W. Moore, with this complete piece of shit"—here he lifted his tattered manuscript—"with seeing clearly that, as a writer, he sucks, now W. Moore has lost all faith in himself, and not just because he blows at writing. There's another thing that's definitely related. The place I grew up was ninety-nine-point-nine percent white. There were Latinos around—whoops, Latinx—but all they did was keep their heads down, not talk, and mow our lawns. Then I came to campus, and little by little I've come to think not only that white people suck but that white males especially suck, and that the worst white males are the ones like me, whose parents have an annual income large enough to make playing golf regularly on a more-than-half-decent course no problem. Upper-class white guy—the villain in movies. I'm despicable doing nothing, just sitting on my ass. I take classes where I'm told, by everyone in the room, that I'm racist by definition, doesn't matter what I think—all I have to do is sit there inside my white skin to be racist, that's it—and if I don't respond to that, just sit there silently, that's racist, too, and at the same time, if I speak, doesn't matter what I say, it's racist, and it's about time I recognized it, because recognition is the first step, and after that, if I don't wear a sign around my neck saying I'm a racist, and if I don't become an activist working against racism, doing things that will lead to a day when white guys like me aren't in charge anymore, then that's racist, too. Shit," said William. "Put all of that on top of the fact that I suck as a writer and of course I want to run back home and be king of the white people again—wouldn't you? What am I supposed to be, happy about it? Every time I sit down to write, there's this voice in my head screaming, 'Hey, white guy, no one wants to hear from you! Both because you suck as a writer and because you're white!'"

William turned his manuscript over. "Right when I come along," he moaned, "it's like: Oh no, not another white guy. Oh no, wait, a white guy with a novel about global warming, great, just what we need, another white guy who thinks he has something important to say, another condescending and clueless white guy who should shut up instead of talk. What's that, white guy? Do I hear you complaining? Go ahead, bitch all you want—you still suck, by definition. You personally. And don't tell me your relatives only came here a hundred years ago from wherever, so you have nothing to do with slavery. It's still you personally, you, William Moore, who's a racist by virtue of being inside white skin; you, William Moore, who's wrong by definition; you, William Moore, who sucks, period. Hey, William, we read your novel and guess what? It's shit. It's shit even if we evaluate it on the basis of the dead, lame, warped critical and aesthetic theories white guys invented so they could define the terms and benefit in wealth and status, and it's shit, too, even worse shit, if we evaluate it according to the just, wise, and culturally broad criteria that are the right ones, as we now know, everybody except white guys, who keep clinging to their invalid, antiquated, racist ideas, because they're scared of losing their power and privilege, not to mention their jobs and affluence. How am I supposed to write a novel, can you tell me that? Me, William Moore, white guy?"

William pushed his battered manuscript toward me and leaned over it across the table. "Another problem," he said, "is that my main character is unlikable. I keep revising to make him likable. I gotta deal with the fact that he's a guy. All the books these days, the main character is not a"—here William made quote marks in the air—"'guy.' What I said about being white? It goes for being a guy. No one wants another story about a guy. If you wanna have a guy in your novel, you gotta hide his testosterone behind PTSD or something. He's gotta have problems. If he saves the world, it has to be against his will. People will give you a loner-type guy who doesn't chase women, but that's about it, that's the only formula left, and even that's dangerous, to the point where you'd better make him a secondary character. Just to be safe. 'Cause otherwise there's eye rolling: 'That idiot is so stuck in the past.'" William picked up his teacup and showed it to me. "This is better," he said. "Guys drinking tea. Guys who can sit in a tea shop drinking tea. Not guys like my character, who's running around with a Kentucky long rifle and springing traps on overheated rabbits. Lame. Maybe I should give up and become a tennis instructor. Or a dentist," he added.

William sipped his tea in a series of quick in-breaths. "Really lame," he said. "My novel is *so lame*. But I have an idea for a different one now. This one would be called *The Battles of Seattle*. *The Battles of Seattle* would be about an upper-middle-class white couple, the Battles, who are just trying to go about their normal lives—like, do their jobs, raise their kids, take their vacations, go out to good restaurants—but then what happens is the Battle in Seattle. Remember that? The WTO demonstrations?"

"I do."

"I was, like, eight or something. Weird time. Wow. And what a great setup. Because here are all of these demonstrators in the streets, trying to change the way the world works, and, meanwhile, here are these Battles, Mr. and Mrs. Battle, Joe and Sherry, or Bill and Kathy, just wanting life to go on the way it always has. Like, Mr. Battle is stuck downtown after his day as a financial analyst because the cops have cordoned off the streets. Or, better, Mr. and Mrs. Battle are staying at the Olympic Four Seasons downtown, like they do every year to go Christmas shopping, and eat a nice dinner, and have sex in a hotel room, and suddenly—all these anarchists."

William once again sipped pu-erh. "I'm not sure about this *Battles of Seattle* idea," he said, "because it seems like *In a Warm Time,* except with a different point to make."

I walked home carrying William's manuscript while hearing repeatedly this silent incantation: "So we beat on, boats against the current, borne back ceaselessly into the past." It's the line that ends *The Great Gatsby,* and a refrain that, on initial consideration, sounds, by all rights, wrong for my circumstances just then, but at the same time, and I suspect universally, the lyrics of mentation aren't necessarily voluntary or subject to the principle of cause and effect, the mind does what it does and only afterward makes connections (if it makes them at all), however tenuous, so, at the risk of forwarding a mistaken theory of personal psychology, I will venture that the last line of *The Great Gatsby* might have found its way to the surface of my homeward musings because at the end of my meeting with William Moore, after he left and as I gathered myself to leave—as I tidied up tea things—a man had leaned in and said, "Restroom back here?," and this man, it was impossible not to notice, wore significantly large owl-eyed glasses, fashionably prosthetic James Joycean spectacles, maybe of a sort I subconsciously, at first, associated with the owl-eyed man in *The Great Gatsby,* the one who ascertains that Gatsby's books are real and "have pages and everything." That could have been it, because I have a useless kind of radar for the world's owl-eyed men, and think of Fitzgerald's more often than he deserves, given that he hardly appears in *The Great Gatsby* at all. Anyway, from this character, the owl-eyed man, it's an understandable leap to "So we beat on, boats against the current, borne back ceaselessly into the past," which means what it means but—

putting aside meaning momentarily—is poignant as music, and as such infused with staying power.

When I got home, I looked for a copy of *The Great Gatsby* on our shelves, but only briefly, because I was distracted by other novels I came across, and ended up reading their endings with idle curiosity—for example, *Shamela,* by Henry Fielding: "P.S. Since I writ, I have a certain account, that Mr. Booby hath caught his wife in bed with Williams; hath turned her off, and is prosecuting him in the spiritual court." The last novel I opened was *Middlemarch,* by George Eliot: ". . . that things are not so ill with you and me as they might have been, is half owing to the number who lived faithfully a hidden life, and rest in unvisited tombs."

MY FATHER'S TOMB did not go unvisited. It was conveniently located in my writer's garret, and I visited it like a watchman at first, then like a voyeur, and, finally, like a researcher drawn restively to archives. I sat in my old Windsor chair with my elbowed reading lamp pulled close and turned pages, randomly at first—taking them from the nearest box—but then I cast a broader net and read chronologically, moving boxes in the style required for those handheld puzzles where you slide pieces around until a picture coheres. Spring came with me still doing this, and then summer, when, one night, around two, to the chorus of frogs in a detention pond near our home, I closed the last file.

The next day, I began hauling boxes to the transfer station. There I backed my car up to the paper bin, and one at a time pulled lids off and removed clips and brads from sheaves before tossing out files in ample armfuls, though I might have done my job more efficiently by just turning the boxes over and pouring out their contents. I didn't, though, because there was something calibrated to my feelings in these flings of mine. I kept at it that way through multiple trips—casting stacks of files long and high into the recycling bin and watching them twirl into their resting places, where they landed with a thump and nestled into a dense matrix, hurling files amid the busy din of the place with its odor of hot garbage and burning diesel, inhabited as I toiled by a bitterness aimed at life's basic facts, and by a self-conscious romanticizing of my circumstances, and by an urge to explain myself to whoever backed in next to me, which I quelled on every occasion except one, when a woman observed, "Somebody's files; I had to do that, too; it sucks," to which I'd replied, "My father's," before lofting more files, this time with my bitterness furthered by another human being's acknowledgment, which felt like permission and maybe even goading. And so it went until every file was gone and every brad and paper clip had been flung into the metal-recycling bin and every box had been dismantled, flattened, and dropped into the cardboard bin. But my ritual disposing didn't feel done yet, and so, after that last trip, I went to the nearest tavern and sat at the bar, publicly embodying a morose mood, and did nothing for a long time in relative darkness, with a can of beer in front of me, on a summer afternoon when it was eighty-five degrees outside under blue skies. And while there, I thought the kind of thoughts that are likely during an interlude of this sort—the bell tolls for thee; everything passes; today is a good day to die; buck up; why waste a single moment of life making yourself unhappy; someday the sun will overwhelm the earth;

it's all crazy and absurd; get out of here and do something useful. There was a jukebox nearby, and after standing over it for a while, I plugged in coins for "Dust in the Wind" as somehow a plausible antidote to my wallowing via speaking to it with comic force (I don't see irony as my forte but am subject to it in bleaker moments), and then, on the way back to my bar stool, I picked up darts and hurled them at a target and ran a set of quoits down the sanded course of a shuffleboard table, and while I was walking to its far end, a guy at the bar—the tavern's only other patron—swiveled in my direction and rasped, "'Dus' in a Win''?"

"Sorry," I answered.

He let it go. We didn't talk after that. I stayed for two hours, and it was just me and him. Me, him, and the bartender.

WITH THE LAST of the boxes gone, I vacuumed the floor of my garret—pine boards that, over the years, had contracted to the point where the gaps between them had become long wells best addressed with a crevice attachment. This meant that if I was going to service my zeal for domestic cleanliness I would need to be methodical and take myself up and down the row of boards one seam at a time in a crouch, which I did, while noting floor details—knots, flaws, pitch, grains—visible now that boxes were no longer stacked to the ceiling and light from the windows could fully play across the room. In doing this, I came across my father's briefcase, which I'd brought home after he died and tucked into the well beneath my desk, thinking it might rest there without being tripped over, and, furtive as it looked in that hidey-hole beside a footstool, blend

in nicely with the room's tomblike silence. It did blend that
way. It had a forlorn, battered, and antique ambience appropriate to my garret's stillness. I rummaged it with the glum
sense of betrayal people in the wake of a death are apt to feel,
since objects like the one I had my hands in and on retain, for
years, the proprietary residue of their onetime owners. Nevertheless, inside its flapped, front pouch I found three wadded
plastic bags—former carriers of bran flakes, no doubt—a bag
of lemon drops, and a plastic pocket protector that had desic-
cated and yellowed and developed nascent splits, and apparently been retired by my father but not discarded. Otherwise,
besides its considerable load of legal and professional paper,
my father's briefcase housed only a folded copy of *The Seattle
Times* made slim by the removal of its advertising circulars.

I laid the briefcase's contents out on my desk, which is long
and narrow, arraying documents from left to right as if they
constituted a display, and then I stacked all that paper up in
front of my chair, sat down, and pulled close my elbow lamp, the
better to examine these last vestiges of my father's working life,
the briefs, depositions, orders, warrants, and so forth from the
Harvey case, which I'd wept over the day he died. Among all
this, I came across the Abeba Temesgen adoption file, which I'd
printed out months before for my father—forty-seven pages
that make it hard not to ask why Delvin and Betsy Harvey
were allowed to adopt. At this point, I think I can say why. It's
because the constitutional rights of Americans take precedence
over the rights of children from other countries. Let me put
that differently. The Harveys could beat their children in the
name of religion, citing while so doing the First Amendment,
and the agency that approved them as adoptive parents, ham-

strung by the Fourteenth Amendment, couldn't ask about that in the process of vetting them. Wed the right to the free exercise of religion to the right to privacy, interpret it with blinders on at the place where it meets up with international adoption, and you get, eventually, what happened to Abeba Temesgen.

But this is an account of things that happened. My father, I found, had flagged with a sticky note the letter from the chief criminal deputy prosecutor of Skagit County—Lincoln Stevens—to the adoption agency's head office in Seattle, the one that read, in part, "Concerning the request for information regarding the circumstances of Abigail Harvey's death, please be advised, and please relay to the appropriate Ethiopian authorities, that an investigation is currently ongoing, and as is the case with any other law enforcement agency and prosecutor's office in this country, we will not reveal, or in any way discuss, facts, circumstances, suppositions, or anything else regarding the investigation until the investigation is complete."

I turned that page over. Behind it was a photocopy of a letter my father had written three weeks before he died, in longhand, to the minister-in-chief of the Ministry of Woman's and Children's Affairs in Ethiopia. "While it might seem odd for me to contact you," he wrote, "given that I represent a defendant in this case, I know of your interest in obtaining information pertinent to the death of Abeba Temesgen, and feel that it is appropriate for me to inform you that a substantial amount of information has now entered the public record and is therefore accessible to anyone in search of it, and furthermore, that as the weeks and months go by and more information becomes available, much of it will as well enter the public record, albeit, and inevitably, with redactions necessitated by privacy consideration involving minors.

"There are two ways I know of to access these records. The first is to request documents appearing on the case docket, which you can do by contacting the clerk's office in Skagit County, Washington. The second is to file a request under the Freedom of Information Act. While these sorts of requests are most often made by journalists, the law here does not limit access to information falling under the purview of the Freedom of Information Act only to them. It's available to anyone who makes a request—in this case, again, with Skagit County. In all of this I might well be saying what you already know but, erring on the side of caution, and just in case, I'm writing to you about it.

"I'm also writing because I want to say, and feel driven to say, that I'm bereft, maddened, and appalled by what happened to Abeba Temesgen. I feel it is wrong that the country of which I'm a citizen allowed Delvin and Betsy Harvey to adopt her. I wouldn't blame you for taking a dim view of us in light of what happened. We have regulatory work to do here with regard to international adoption and some of it can happen at the state level. We can make the adoption agencies licensed within our state borders do a better job. When this case is over, I plan to look into that."

I FILED a Freedom of Information Act request, and in this manner gained access to interviews, affidavits, investigation records, incident reports, lab results, witness statements, suspect statements, medical records, declarations of intent—in short, all manner of documents of relative interest, but none so much as a copy of one of Abeba Temesgen's homeschooling assignments. Its title was "Something I Remember from Ethiopia," and it read:

When I lived in Ethiopia, one time, I saw hyenas eat a cow. I thought Satan was present. In Ethiopia some children like me believe that at night certain people turn into hyenas and go around stealing chickens and things like that. And I was scared. I thought they ate children. That's what people said. They said there were hyenas who ran on two feet like people and eat children. They said hyena people go into the cemetery and take the graves apart at night if they can't find children. They said the hyena people say prayers to Satan. They said they knock down fences and open barns and eat the goats. At night I used to hear hyena people laughing. They barked like dogs do sometimes, but they also laughed. I remember that. The way they laughed. They sounded like people. Exactly like people outside the wall of my house. The same way people do right now in this country. But here, it's through a closet door.

WITH REGARD TO the Harveys, the State of Washington started over: it wasn't done with them just because my father had passed away. I had felt more than curious about what would become of Betsy and Delvin Harvey for a long time, and had kept myself apprised of developments, such as they were, by regularly referring to their online case dockets until, in the spring, a retrial date was set, and then I waited until the inevitable guilty verdicts had been announced and went up to Mount Vernon for the sentencings. It was windy in Skagit County, where, according to news reports, the annual tulip frenzy was winding down prematurely because the weather had been warmer than is optimum for their longevity; sure enough, the famous flowers had that flagging look and had begun to wither in the wide expanses of the delta. The stark, flat, and treeless qualities of the terrain yielded to a vast gray sky that blurred at the horizon. It was distressing and calming at the same time.

At the Skagit County Courthouse, I waited my turn at the apparatuses of security, and was put in mind of certain comical moments with my father there wherein he daily felt fated to be called out and frisked, since it was true that he often set off alarms, bells, whistles, and buzzers for inexplicable reasons, as if the walk-through metal detector had it in for him especially. The posted officer would tell my father that he didn't have to remove his shoes or belt but that he did need to empty his pockets into the bowl she pushed toward him, and, having done so, he would gather himself and try to bolt through as if speed might make a difference, and then a second officer would pull him over to one side and maneuver a wand in perfunctory fashion along his limbs, while my father stood with his arms horizontal and reminded him, "This all started after 9/11."

In the gallery, there was no Georgette, but there was, I noted, a sizable contingent of courtroom familiars, including the Ethiopian women in their white and gauzy garb, and including a man I ended up sitting beside, a man I'd often seen but never spoken with the previous summer, a man who attended regularly with his wife, a ruddy-looking man in his late sixties who, as we waited for the morning's proceedings to begin, introduced himself, and said that he was retired from a career as an architect during which he'd been inclined toward symmetry, that he had consistently sought to bring symmetry to his designs and had fought battles on its behalf with engineers and clients, and that during the trial last summer he'd taken notice, with pleasure, of this courtroom's many symmetries, its formal balance and order, all lending to the place, he said, a necessary dignity, without which the effort toward justice would be lesser, he felt, since he believed, strongly, in the psychological impact of symmetry. But one thing bothered him. The jury box sat on one side only, the side closest to the prosecutor's table; why not half the jurors on one side and half on the other? At this, his wife, sitting to his right, leaned in and changed the subject abruptly. She said that she'd been reading about Ethiopia, having become curious about the country after last summer's event, and that in the course of her reading she'd come across what she called "the mystery of the two calendars." On top of the fact that there were thirteen months in Ethiopia, she said, and that New Year's Day there came in our September, and that the year in Ethiopia was, at the moment, our year minus seven, on top of all of that, she explained, the day in Ethiopia began at dawn and not at midnight. The day began at what we would call 6:00 a.m., which made sense, she told us, because in Ethiopia, which is near the equator, the sun comes up at about the same time every day; Ethiopians had a regularity in that respect that they could count on, whereas

we, no. (This was her theory.) And so, she went on, con-
verting between the Ethiopian and Western clocks was a
matter, first, of using military time—meaning "zero one hundred hours" for one o'clock in the morning and "thirteen
hundred hours" for one o'clock in the afternoon—and then
of adding six hours. So, she explained, if you were in Ethiopia
and someone said to you, "It's eight," you would do your adding and mentally think, "For me, that's zero eight hundred
hours plus six, or fourteen hundred hours military time," and
from there you would do your conversion to civilian time, the
result being 2:00 p.m., which, she said, was the time when her
husband took siestas.

Lincoln Stevens entered, and then Pam Burris with her
client, Delvin Harvey, and then Betsy Harvey accompanied
by her new attorney, a woman named Angela Mullins who
was, I thought, in the vicinity of forty, and looked to me dour.
That said, I knew myself to have no objectivity about her; she
was, for me, primarily and conspicuously the person who had
replaced my father in this scene, and therefore she presented
to me as an astonishment and a sadness instead of as a person.
And as for Delvin and Betsy Harvey, they looked about the
same to my eyes, though both had lost a bit of weight, and both
had the jaundiced pallor of those who rarely see the light of
day.

By the time proceedings convened, at 9:00 a.m., there was a
full gallery—every bench tightly filled, and still more people
standing at the back, all of us poised to hear what Judge Mary
Ann Rasmussen had to say about this horrendously sorrowful
and infuriating case. And what she said, over the tops of her
glasses, was: "I think at some point in this trial each and every

one of us sat stunned and speechless without the slightest hope of making any sense of this whatsoever. I am at a complete loss when it comes to understanding it. This was not about mental illness or drug abuse or alcohol or any of those factors I more commonly see associated with homicide by abuse. This is something else. This is a form of evil, in my book—evil dressed up as a higher morality, as a superior or even supreme morality. Delvin and Betsy Harvey, you are not the victims here, you are the perpetrators. And yet I haven't seen a whit of remorse from you. Not one whit. Only more certainty. In your heads, you're still right. You remain right and will always be right. It doesn't matter what happened, you're forever right. I'm going to tell you something. I'm going to tell you what this sentencing isn't about. Number one, it isn't about deterrence. Not at all. No one is going to be deterred from your kind of evil by the sentences I'm about to hand down. Nope, there will still be people who think they're right in the way that both of you think you're right, and they will go right on doing evil things because of it. Number two, it's not about rehabilitation, because I don't believe that either of you can be rehabilitated. You're too sure of yourselves for that. You have one-hundred-percent confidence that you didn't commit a crime and that the legal system and the sheriff's office and CPS and everybody else is joined in a great conspiracy designed for the purpose of bringing you down. That's how you see it and will always see it. You will always look out onto a world that is misguided and in error because it doesn't agree with you, and that's no basis for rehabilitation. So, then, what is this sentencing about? This sentencing, Betsy and Delvin Harvey, is a *denunciation*. It is an expression of a common ethos that you, with your actions, have defied and denied. You are being denounced here. The society you live in is sending you a message, and also sending a message to itself, reminding itself of its rules of conduct, and confirming its vision. So you are being denounced here, and at the same time, equally important, I am acknowledging, with your sentences, that the life of your victim very much mattered and was equal to every life in value, and that it cannot be taken without society stepping in to say, 'Absolutely not, and if you do, you must pay.' And so you will pay. I sentence you, Del vin Harvey, to thirty-seven years to be served in a Washington State correctional facility before you can be released, and I sentence you, Betsy Harvey, also to thirty-seven years to be served in a Washington State correctional facility before you can be released. That is the maximum sentence available to me, and I have availed myself of it."

ONE OF THE THINGS I liked about fiction writing was that its harder emotions could be lived at a remove. I was making things up, none of it was happening, if someone suffered they didn't really suffer, if someone died they weren't really dead What happened, happened only in my head. What happened didn't matter in the end. If a character fell from a cliff while sitting for a portrait, lived twenty years with unrequited love, succumbed to a stroke on the third floor of a courthouse, or died in the cold after being starved and lashed, if any of these things happened on a page I'd invented, the consequences in painful emotion were felt only at a distance. I'm not saying that I never felt emotion while making things up and setting them on paper; I'm saying that what I felt lacked the force of things I didn't make up. "No tears in the writer, no tears in the reader," someone famous supposedly said, but that brand of tears, however integral to life, is foreign to it, too—tears of a different order, so to speak, that fall cathartically in the main, allowing us an out (or so it's been argued), and granting false cleansing. And as for my own tears, as I shed them over the years while fictionalizing, they were shed, it should be noted, obvious as it may be, in the midst of fabulation. How could it be otherwise? My tears fell amid world-conjuring machinations. There I mediated between considerations. There I arbitrated and ruled from the sidelines. I took what came and surrendered it again. I patched, scraped, glazed, and filled. No, it wasn't always volitional. Strains from within found their way to my pages. Largely, though, I was an engineer. I calculated stresses and analyzed spans. There was no Abeba Temesgen. Or if there was, it was only a character named Abeba Temesgen, whom, in the end, I kept to a script.

Sometimes now, when I think of my father—and after having written all of this—I think of King Lear, the character and the play both. "How does my royal lord?" his daughter asks him toward his end, to which he replies, "You do me wrong to take me out o' the grave: / thou art a soul in bliss; but I am bound / upon a wheel of fire, that mine own tears / do scald like moulten lead," before telling her, "You do not love me."

On the last page of his memoir *Patrimony*—subtitled *A True Story*—Philip Roth dreams that his recently deceased father, Herman, has returned from the grave to rebuke his son for having dressed him "for eternity in the wrong clothes." Roth's interpretation, on waking in the morning, is that clothes = *Patrimony*. He can't think of *Patrimony,* stuffed as it is with painful, naked incursions into Herman's mind, body, and—if you will—soul, without hearing, once again, the age-old paternal reprimand, and without a prick, even more, to his conscience. It's debatable whether the son has wronged the father by making a spectacle of his aging and death, but it's not debatable that Roth has articulated, for his readers, guilt about it. And yet his guilt is mitigated, he implies, because in *Patrimony,* Herman is sustained. Herman's light remains; it's not entirely extinguished. Even as a shade, the father goes on haunting the son—not just the son's dreams but his texts.

ONE NIGHT, shortly after we'd gotten into bed together—and while a steady wind beat against our house, rattling our framed wedding photo on its hook—Alison showed me a book she'd come across called *Japanese Death Poems* (subtitled *Written by Zen Monks and Haiku Poets on the Verge of Death*), and, cat-eye readers low on her nose, read a few aloud, finishing with, "'I long for people—then again I loathe them: end of autumn.'"

She plucked off her readers. "I long for people, then again I loathe them," she said. "That makes a kind of sense, I guess. But it surprises me as a death poem."

In the golden glow of the lamp beside our bed, she swooped her readers on once more and turned some pages. "Listen to this," she said. "'My whole life long I've sharpened my sword and now, face to face with death, I unsheathe it, and lo—the blade is broken—alas!'"

She turned out the lamp. "That's a good one," she observed. "So many of those death poems are about cherry blossoms or plum trees. And then there's *this* guy, who just decides to say, at the end, alas, I spent my whole life getting ready for this, and now my sword's broken."

We laughed. Then Alison said things of the sort that are sometimes said on the cusp of sleep. "Your dad kept his sword sharp right to the end," she said. Alison has a beautiful voice. "But now he's gone, and so are my parents, and your mother, I don't know, maybe she's wide awake right now in bed by herself with the wind blowing outside."

I turned toward her. We were close in the dark. "We can love people," whispered Alison. "What else is there?"

Acknowledgments

While working on this book, I was the recipient of so much goodwill, kindness, and support that, looking back, it astonishes me. Thanks especially to Eleni, Elsa, Sister Lutgarda, Sister Tsige Mariam, Eyo, Betty, Mulu, Metti, Membe, Elsabet, Hanna, the Barnts family, Cara, Jacob, Kristen, Joe, Leslie, Roseanne, Tizita, Zenebech, Yalew, Kassaye, Haimanot, Abel, Kassech, Kalkidan, William, Alex, Richard, Del, Gabriel, Thomas, Patrick, Raegen, Bob F., Bob M., Steven, Peter, Chris, Mary, Lisa, Sharon, Danielle, Melinda, Marianne, Kathryn, Molly, Julia, Melissa, Habtamu, Maureen, So-Can, Leanne, Cori, Tara, Monia, Yemisrach, Cliff, Eileen, Anke, Helga, Gay, Beza, Suzanna, Delilah, Stu, Joyce, Shelley, Dagnachew, Sasha, Lydia, Ezra, Addisu, Danielle, Jennifer, Derek, Nancy, Rita, Maxima, Jeanne, Endanchy, Jane, John, Mark, Adam, Diana, Georges, Anne, and Robin.

Finally, Audra Jo Yoder's highly illuminating essay "Myth and Memory in Russian Tea Culture" (*Studies in Slavic Culture,* Issue VIII, August 2009) provides the source material for the fictional thesis on tea and Russian literature paraphrased in this book.

A NOTE ON THE TYPE

This book was set in Granjon, a type named in compliment to Robert Granjon, a type cutter and printer active in Antwerp, Lyons, Rome, and Paris from 1523 to 1590. Granjon, the boldest and most original designer of his time, was one of the first to practice the trade of typefounder apart from that of printer.

Linotype Granjon was designed by George W. Jones, who based his drawings on a face used by Claude Garamond (ca. 1480–1561) in his beautiful French books. Granjon more closely resembles Garamond's own type than do any of the various modern faces that bear his name.

Typeset by Scribe, Philadelphia, Pennsylvania

Printed and bound by Sheridan Minnesota,
a CJK Group Company, Brainerd, Minnesota

Designed by Cassandra J. Pappas